Praise for
Rose House

"In *Rose House*, Tina Ann Forkner brings us back to the beauty of California wine country and draws us into a story fit for the misty gothic moors. Just as the Rose House itself sits within a mass of beautiful, entwined roses and vines, so is the story nestled in a masterful weaving of secrets, betrayals, hope, and healing."

> —ALLISON PITTMAN, author of *Stealing Home*
> and *Saturdays with Stella*

"Tina Ann Forkner pens a compelling tale of betrayal and grief, of hope and forgiveness in *Rose House*. The unique setting and her lyrical descriptions enticed me into the scene, where I was captivated by the appealing characters and the story's underlying mystery. I couldn't put it down."

> —ANE MULLIGAN, editor and weekly columnist,
> Novel Journey blog

"With *Rose House*, Tina Ann Forkner paints a breathtaking canvas of lush prose brushstrokes. Don't get lulled into a sense of calm; the story line casts suspenseful shadows on this masterpiece of women's fiction. Delightful!"

> —PATTI LACY, author of *An Irishwoman's Tale*
> and *What the Bayou Saw*

"Captivating... ...ically ... ...er's *Rose House* keeps the p...

> —...

Praise for
Ruby Among Us
by Tina Ann Forkner

"*Ruby Among Us* is a powerful story that will linger long after reading it. Forkner's writing transported me to California's vineyards and wove a fascinating saga of how secrets and decisions impact the lives of following generations—and how love can redeem."

—CINDY WOODSMALL, *New York Times* best-selling author
of *When the Morning Comes*

"Ms. Forkner has given us a gift that like fine music rises at an ever-spiraling pace. Neither rushed nor delayed, *Ruby Among Us* offers a satisfying journey I will long remember."

—JANE KIRKPATRICK, award-winning author
of *A Mending at the Edge*

"A multigenerational saga of hope, regret, and the grace that brings us home, *Ruby Among Us* evokes an invitational sense of place, a cache of characters you enjoy knowing, and a story that rips and mends your heart all at once."

—MARY E. DEMUTH, author of *Watching the Tree Limbs*
and *Wishing on Dandelions*

"Reading is a passion of mine, and when I find myself identifying with the characters, anxious to get to the next page to find answers to my questions, I know I'm into a good book! The daughter-mother-grandmother theme in *Ruby Among Us* pulled me in. Wonderful storytelling."

—JORDIN SPARKS, 2007 winner of *American Idol*

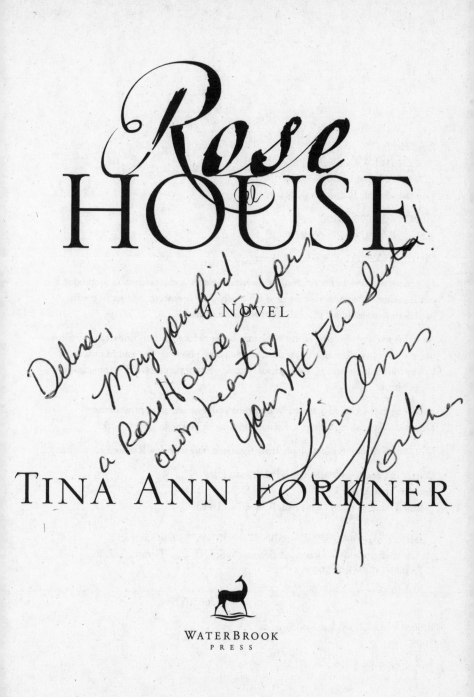

Rose HOUSE

A NOVEL

Debra,
May you find your
a Rose House in your
own heart ♡
Your ACFW Sister
Tina Ann
Forkner

TINA ANN FORKNER

WaterBrook
PRESS

Rose House
Published by WaterBrook Press
12265 Oracle Boulevard, Suite 200
Colorado Springs, Colorado 80921

ISBN 978-1-4000-7359-7
ISBN 978-0-307-45793-6 (electronic)

Published in the United States by WaterBrook Multnomah, an imprint of the Doubleday Publishing Group, a division of Random House Inc., New York.

WaterBrook and its deer colophon are registered trademarks of Random House Inc.

Library of Congress Cataloging-in-Publication Data
Forkner, Tina Ann.
    Rose House : a novel / Tina Ann Forkner. — 1st ed.
        p. cm.
    ISBN 978-1-4000-7359-7 — ISBN 978-0-307-45793-6 (electronic)
    1. Life change events—Fiction. 2. Sonoma Valley (Calif.)—Fiction. I. Title.
    PS3606.O7476R67 2009
    813'.6—dc22

                                                    2008052798

Printed in the United States of America
2009

10 9 8 7 6 5 4 3 2

For my parents,
Dennis and Barbara Ann Gray

*I*T SEEMED TO BE A COTTAGE that was alive, but it was only the vines twining in on themselves and clinging to the structure that were living, not unlike the memories and feelings people had attached to the house over time, making it mean more than mere sticks, pieces of wood, nails, and peeling paint could ever imply on their own.

The camera zoomed out to trace the rose brambles wrapping along the awning, curling over the banister and into the flowering borders along one side of the porch. The rest of the house gradually came into view, filling the scene with an abundance of roses in shades of scarlet draping the windows like curtains, then rambling across the roof, around the chimney and sweeping to the edges of the house, where they seemed to reach out their thorny branches toward passersby.

The lens didn't capture the woman's form at first as it swept away from the house down toward the yard and footpath with its border of snow white Shasta daisies and purple coneflowers. It leisurely zoomed in on a mass of daisies, capturing the breeze that sent an occasional ripple through the border, until the camera was forced to pause at the surprise interruption: a foot that intruded on the otherwise perfect scene.

To the artist behind the lens it was an exquisitely formed foot with a milky white ankle and pink-painted toenails. The lens suddenly tightened its view to capture the sandal decorated with pink and white pearlescent beads and a delicate pink ribbon that wound around the ankle and tied neatly above the heel.

The camera's focus rose to the hem of a white peasant skirt that billowed softly in the breeze. Traveling upward, the lens skimmed long sleeves of gauzy blue adorned with tiny silver beads that crisscrossed both shoulders, edging along the neckline where beads dangled from the ends of a pink ribbon tie. The camera paused on a silver cross pendant that sparkled with the morning sunrise, glinting off the red jewel nested in the center. Moving up her profile, the lens traced blond tendrils escaping from beaded combs that held back her amber-streaked hair threatening to tumble from a loosely arranged bun. The lens paused, studying the dampness of her flushed cheeks, the unsteady rhythm to which her shoulders rose and fell, how her slight body slumped forward just a little, as if she might throw herself at the mercy of the house.

She straightened, startled, when a succession of clicks broke the silence surrounding the Rose House. Rather abruptly, the lens zoomed out. She was looking directly into the camera. More clicks. Her reddened eyes grew wide as she turned unexpectedly and ran down the path toward the main house of the Frances-DiCamillo Vineyards.

The camera zoomed in on her departing figure, following her for a moment, capturing in its lens the way her glossy hair slipped from its bun and cascaded over her shoulders. After a few more clicks, the lens panned back to the house, zooming in on a flawless wine-colored blossom. It was a perfect rose, a work of art.

Click.

LILLIAN DROPPED HER CAMERA INTO her pocket. She had thought she was alone, but someone else was there, taking pictures of the Rose House—and of her. Ice encircled the nape of her neck as she recalled the words of the investigators.

"You probably shouldn't be alone until we have this figured out," they had said. But she'd gone against their advice, not even telling them she was taking a trip alone to La Rosaleda.

She paled as the man continued to photograph her. *Why is he taking pictures of me?* Then she noticed a second man. He was too far away to distinguish his features, but she could see that he held a cell phone to his ear and wore a hat and jacket, even though the morning wasn't cool.

Her hand flew to her mouth as he strode toward her. Her pulse raced and the chill on her arms seem to lift her skin away as she turned to run. *Who are these men?*

"There is more to this than you think, Mrs. Hastings, the investigator had told her. "Your family might have been murdered."

"Impossible!" she had cried, but the news footage of her precious babies and husband, covered with bloodstained sheets and lying dead beside Mosquito Road, had rolled through her mind, just as it had every day since she'd seen it on the local television station.

"Have you seen your sister since the accident, ma'am?"

Geena's face on the news had revealed shock and guilt, obviously distraught at the sight of her niece, nephew, and brother-in-law lying lifelessly nearby. What had her sister been doing there?

Lillian nearly tripped when the tie on one of her sandals came loose. She reached down and pulled off her sandal to keep running, fleeing thoughts of murderers and a traitorous sister. Not sure where she should go, she ran into the Frances-DiCamillo Vineyard tasting room, where tourists were gathering. She wanted to scream for help as she flew through the doorway, but she regained her composure when curious eyes turned to study her.

She turned to peer outside, careful not to lean so far out the door that she might be seen by her pursuers. She expelled a burst of air. The men she thought had been watching her were nowhere to be seen. She smoothed her hair and straightened her disheveled skirt, thinking of how paranoid she had become.

She was so distracted by her thoughts that she didn't notice the older woman when she spun away from the door. They crashed together. Lillian was horrified at seeing the woman wobbling on her cane and grabbed hold of her to steady her balance.

"Whatever is the matter?" said the woman. "What are you running from, dear?"

The woman peered at her through concerned eyes.

"I'm so sorry, ma'am." Lillian, still holding her sandal in one hand, patted the woman's arm. "I am so sorry."

"It's quite okay." The woman glanced down at Lillian's feet. "Whatever happened to your shoe? Come, sit down and put it back on. Catch your breath and tell Kitty what the matter is."

Lillian's eyes widened as she looked more closely at the woman. Everyone in the region knew who Kitty was, and Lillian recalled seeing her face recently on a television program. Assisted by her cane, the woman guided Lillian through the tasting room and into her office.

"You are Kitty? Mrs. DiCamillo?"

"Technically I'm Kitty Birkirt, but try telling that to anyone besides me and my husband. I think people will think of me as a DiCamillo until the day I die."

Lillian tried to hide her surprise. This was truly Kitty DiCamillo, the owner of the Frances-DiCamillo Vineyards. The Rose House had been her home decades ago, built for her by her husband, Blake. Lillian recalled the story. Blake and Kitty had had a falling out decades earlier. During their estrangement, Blake had cared for the vineyard. Kitty had been gone for so long that, during her absence, the roses Blake planted around their cottage had engulfed it, earning it its nickname, the Rose House.

Kitty, her caramel skin complemented by a red muumuu-style dress, smiled at Lillian. "Is everything okay, dear? It looked like you were afraid of something when you came barreling through the door."

"I'm sorry. It's just that I thought some men were—" She paused, shaking her head. "It's difficult to explain, but I thought someone was following me."

"Following you?" She looked alarmed. "One moment, dear." She leaned on her cane and walked toward a young man. Lillian watched through the open doorway as Kitty said something in Spanish to him. He nodded at Kitty and walked outside.

When Kitty returned, she sat down and patted Lillian's hand. "I've asked security to look around. Can I get you a cup of tea?"

Lillian risked a smile. "As nice as that sounds, Mrs.—"

"Just Kitty." She nodded.

"Thank you for the offer, Kitty, but I really need to get back home."

"Where is home?"

"Sacramento."

"Ah. A nice city. You are here with your husband? A little getaway?" She glanced at Lillian's wedding ring.

Lillian's smile faded and she looked away. Kitty began to apologize. Lillian shook her head again. "It's okay. Anyone would think I'm married since I'm still wearing this." She held up her hand to show her wedding ring. "I'm a widow."

Kitty nodded, admiring the ring. Lillian laughed in an effort keep tears at bay.

Understanding registered on Kitty's face as she reached for Lillian's hand. "It's recent, I can see. I'm so sorry to have pried, dear. And I didn't mean to gawk at your ring. It's just that it is stunningly beautiful." She patted Lillian's hand. "He must have loved you very much, dear." The words cut through Lillian, but she kept her face calm. Kitty continued her questions. "And your children—do you have children?"

"My children too. They aren't here, because—" Lillian glanced at her feet. "They are—" Kitty understood without needing to hear the rest of the sentence. She gave Lillian's hand a squeeze.

"I wish you would stay and have some tea, child."

Lillian would have liked to but couldn't explain her need to get back to Sacramento as soon as possible. She wanted to brighten up her family's resting place by planting flowers there.

She sat with Kitty for a few more minutes, talking about the vineyard's gardens and the Rose House, until a middle-aged man in black slacks and a white shirt walked in. He spotted Lillian through the open doorway and walked toward her.

"Mrs. Hastings, are you ready for the car?"

She nodded at her chauffeur, then turned toward Kitty. "I'm sorry for nearly knocking you over. I was just being silly. I'm sure nobody was following me." Her heart hammered at the memory of those men, but she didn't want to burden Kitty with her problems.

Lillian stood to leave but stopped all at once before a painting of the

Rose House. She stood in front of it, transfixed by how the painted images nearly came off the canvas at her. The way the roses rambled over the roof swept her into its warm colors. Unwittingly, she reached her fingertips toward the roses, their exquisite detail inviting her to touch them. Her hand hovered there but then drew back. She didn't want to harm the painting, but the roses looked so real, she felt transported. It was as if she stood, captivated, before the real Rose House.

"It is lovely, isn't it?" Kitty said.

"Yes, it's striking, almost as if the house is alive. It has a personality."

"Of sorts," said Kitty.

"Hopeful."

"I have noticed," Kitty said, "that people often describe the Rose House by whatever is in their hearts. Sad, cheerful, sentimental, and even hopeful, like you." She smiled knowingly. "I once asked the artist what he was feeling when he painted it, but he wouldn't tell me."

Lillian leaned in to read the artist's signature, but it was too small to identify. "Who is he?"

"Truman Clark, our little town's claim to fame. He is the painter of roses."

"I would love to see the rest of his work."

Kitty smiled. "You should be able to find it in Sacramento. I know for a fact that his paintings are on display at the private university's gallery. Do you know of it?"

"I do. I'll visit it," said Lillian.

"Let me know if you don't find his work, and I'll find out where he is exhibiting in your area." Kitty handed Lillian her number. "Call if you ever want to talk about painting or anything else. I'm a good listener. We could have tea." She squeezed Lillian's hand. "I doubt grief ever goes away, dear, but the good Lord willing, it will soften in time. It has for me."

Kitty's smile was so genuine, Lillian felt drawn, but the newness of grief residing so close to the surface kept her silent. Her eyes glistened at the kindness of Kitty's offer, but she did have her adoptive mother to talk to. Of course, Aunt Bren lived far away in Oklahoma, and her sister seemed to have disappeared, so really she was alone.

She returned Kitty's smile. "Maybe I will, sometime." Saying good-bye, she reached out to shake her hand, but Kitty gently brushed the hand aside as she leaned in and gave Lillian an affectionate hug.

-◠◡-

During the drive back to Sacramento, the familiar swell of the vineyards stirred memories of times she and Robert had visited wine country. They had both loved it, but truth be told, she and Geena had spent more time together in the Sonoma and Napa Valleys than Lillian had spent there with Robert. *Geena would have loved the Rose House,* mused Lillian, her heart growing heavy. Lillian had happened upon the well-known site once she arrived in La Rosaleda, trying to escape the emptiness of the quiet house she'd shared with her family only twelve days earlier.

Studying the trees as they passed through a heavily wooded area of the valley, she thought about the men she'd encountered at the Rose House. She regretted asking her driver to leave her at the vineyard alone, but the investigators' warning had seemed unfounded at the time. She considered mentioning the incident to Jake now but decided there was no need to worry him.

Jake had been her favorite driver for a long time, but she couldn't bother him with her problems. It was enough that he was kind to her, patient with her silence, and never asked personal questions. He had given up a personal day off just to take her on her much-needed drive away from Sacramento, where nothing waited but loneliness and grief.

She hadn't expected to find such beauty on this morning so soon after Sheyenne and Lee, with their curling ebony hair and liquid-blue eyes, were so violently ripped from her life. Like their cherub smiles, the lines of the cottage had etched themselves into her mind. Nestled within the thorny vines and softened by sloping vivid red arcs of rambling roses, the beauty of the cottage seemed to have spoken gentle words to her tired spirit. At least it had until those men showed up.

"Would you like to stop anywhere before we reach the interstate, Mrs. Hastings?" Jake's voice boomed into the backseat, surprising her. She smiled at him in the rearview mirror and shook her head.

"No, thank you."

Looking out the window at the vineyards, which stretched on for miles, she stroked the velvety petals she'd taken from the ground beside the Rose House and imagined her children weren't gone at all and that her husband was sitting beside her in the car. The twins would have loved the Rose House, and she could imagine them running around the house, dipping behind the brambles and through the gardens, playing hide-and-seek.

Warmth filled her chest as it had on the morning of the accident. It seemed such a short time ago, she'd kissed them both on their little faces before putting them into their daddy's car, kissing his cheek too, and sending them off to their lessons. Swirling grief welled and stretched into her throat.

Ignoring sad eyes that periodically glanced at her through the rearview mirror, she lifted the rose petals and brushed them in a circle against her cheek, a loving caress from what had passed from her life. She moved them to her mouth, feeling their softness graze her lips, and imagined she could hold Sheyenne and Lee one last time, their soft kisses warm against her face. Taking a ragged breath, she let the rose petals fall onto her lap. Her shoulders shook with the immensity of her grief as she tried to brush the petals away, until they lay crushed and bruised on the floor, like her dreams.

Jake's eyes in the mirror clouded, but he said nothing. He had driven her to the cemetery every day since the funeral and knew that she only wanted silence.

Two hours later, he pulled into the cemetery without being asked. He didn't make it around to open her door before she was out of the car and stumbling toward the gravestones.

GEENA SET HER GLASS ON THE coffee table. The tomato juice had soothed her stomach some, but the cheap candle's smoky scent only brought dark thoughts she wanted to forget. She pressed her palm against her temple, which was still pounding from last night's partying. She blew out the candle, fell back on the tattered couch, and lit a cigarette. Inhaling the smoke stung the back of her throat, dry now from her hung-over thirst. She exhaled slowly, trying to banish the sting of smoke from her memories.

She had tasted it first, the acrid dryness in her throat and the smoke that floated on the breeze, settling around the bed she shared that night with her sister, Lillian. No matter how many years had passed, Geena had never forgotten the smell.

The smoke had descended around Grandma's house, where they had stayed the night, mockingly seeping through the window screens, curling toward Geena and Lillian as they lay sweltering in their underwear and tank tops. The screams of the fire truck had come next, then the gravel crunching beneath tires that sped down the road past Grandma's house. The girls knew where the trucks were headed. There was only one house at the end of the road.

Their house was so close to Grandma's that Geena and Lillian could hear the shouts of the men as they worked to put out the fire. Next they heard Grandma's bare feet shuffle across the floor and heard her dial the phone. The pause grew heavy as Grandma waited for Daddy to pick up.

Nobody ever answered.

Geena folded her arms over her chest. It had been the most horrific time in her life until Mosquito Road. Memories of Sheyenne and Lee clouded her thoughts. She was responsible somehow. Not directly, but she was a part of it.

She couldn't stop thinking it was her fault. Even more than the guilt, she missed her niece and nephew. She craved their hugs, the way they had believed her when she told them fairies lived in their garden, and the way their eyes had grown wide when she told them that angels slept in their closet at night. She missed Lillian too. Sometimes it felt as if her sister had been lost in the accident, even though Lillian hadn't even been there.

Tossing a tattered pillow to the floor and settling herself deeper into the couch, Geena wished again that she had never convinced Lillian to move from Oklahoma to California. Had they stayed, maybe she and her sister would still be together, the Dynamic Duo, as Daddy had called them.

They'd both thought that by leaving Oklahoma they could escape the pain of everything in Wild Hollow that reminded them of their loss. They had wanted to forget the blaze that had taken their house in only an hour, and with it their parents and two older brothers. They never imagined that their shared dreams of adventure and escape in California would turn into the nightmare on Mosquito Road, an even bigger loss than the fire.

At least Sheyenne and Lee are in heaven, Geena thought, tracing a red polished toenail along the edge of the coffee table. It was possible that they didn't even miss their mommy and Auntie Geena as they played with the other angels. At least that's how she liked to imagine them, as little angels.

As for Robert, Geena didn't know how to feel. She wanted to imagine him with his children in heaven, maybe having a tea party on a golden quilt, but she knew he probably didn't deserve to be there with them any more than she did if she had died along with them in the accident. Robert hadn't believed in God, and Geena had always struggled with her own faith, even though she had been raised by Pastor and Aunt Bren.

The laughter of children playing somewhere outside her window intruded into her thoughts and she rose to slam the window shut.

"Bratty kids," she grumbled, her heart not able to block out the sounds that reminded her of Sheyenne and Lee.

She returned to the couch and buried her head in her hands. Hangovers always left her in despair. She wondered which nightmares were worse, the ones that visited in her sleep or the ones that haunted her during the day.

In her dreams, she worried about Lillian and saw her being chased by Robert's enemies. Lillian had told Aunt Bren she thought she was being watched, so the first thing Aunt Bren did was ask Geena to check on her sister.

Geena had asked Aunt Bren to promise not to tell Lillian they were in contact. Aunt Bren would only say: "Honey, I don't know what this is about, but she is your sister. You need to talk to her."

"I called her once, Aunt Bren. She hung up."

"Hmm. That's not what she told me. She said you called and never spoke a word. She finally hung up because she didn't think you were on the line."

"It's not good, Aunt Bren. If she knew the truth, she would hate me more than she already does."

"She doesn't hate you, honey."

"Are you sure, Aunt Bren?"

Aunt Bren had been quiet for several seconds. "Relatively sure, yes."

"Just let me know if anyone follows her again, Aunt Bren."

"Is someone following you, honey?"

Geena had not answered her. Aunt Bren had sighed and said, "Tell the truth, Geena. Do I need to call the police?"

"No, don't call the police. I just want to hear that she's okay every now and then. Will you let me know?"

⁓◯⁓

Geena wrinkled her nose at the candle's fading scent. She recalled how Robert had bought her candles of all different scents. They were the expensive kind, smokeless, and had lovely fragrances that had evoked memories of their time at the beach. She smiled at the memory.

Any time Robert had a medical conference in San Francisco, he and Geena had secretly met at the North Shore. Sometimes they would rendezvous at his fancy beach house; at other times they would meet at a little shack at the edge of the bay where they would toss bits of bread to the gulls that hovered over the shore.

Her ocean-scented candles had been used up long ago, their wicks burned too close to light anymore, but feelings she'd had for Robert had not waned since his death. Both love and bitterness were still as fresh as their last day together, when they whispered to each other so that Sheyenne and Lee couldn't hear.

Robert had swung by to pick her up during the children's lessons. They had driven to a secluded area of a park, but since they had lost track of time, she'd had to ride with him to pick up his children. They were still figuring out what to tell the children about Aunt Geena being with them when Robert had spotted a car following them in his rearview mirror.

The memory of Mosquito Road replayed constantly in Geena's mind. At times like this, it could pull her into a pit that spiraled downward. While she'd been plagued with guilt about her relationship with Robert when he was alive, she was tortured by it now.

It was impossible to think of Robert without conjuring up thoughts of Lillian. Though the relationship with her sister seemed to be broken beyond repair, she longed to feel her ten-year-old sister pull her close, comforting her from scary noises outside the window.

"What's happening?" Geena had whispered to Lillian on the night of the fire.

"I think our house is on fire," Lillian had answered.

"Grandma's?"

"No, not Grandma's. *Ours.*"

Their quick breaths had filled the quiet room, and Geena could feel Lillian's heart beating all the way through her back, pounding against her own.

"Mommy," Geena's voice had croaked.

"It's okay," Lillian had whispered.

"I want my mommy and daddy."

"Me too."

"It's so hot." Geena kicked the covers further away, as if their very touch would burn her. Lillian stood on the bed and switched on the ceiling fan. They lay side by side, wide-eyed in the semidarkness, staring up at the spinning blades.

"It's okay," said Lillian. Their fingers found each other's and entwined.

Geena shook herself back to the present. She stood and walked to the window where she observed the neighborhood kids playing in her yard.

One girl laughed at something her brother said, and Geena felt her grumpiness fade. She no longer wanted to chase them off her lawn and was actually disappointed when their daddy herded them back into their own yard.

"Lillian," she whispered into the window pane, "I'm so sorry for taking them away from you," she sighed, "and for taking him when you weren't looking."

"SIR, SURELY THE ARTIST WISHES to receive payment," the curator said. "And who would the artist be?"

She was sly, but he had worked nearly four years on this, his masterpiece, refining and improving the painting. His work was well known in the region, and he could get a pretty penny for it at a bigger gallery, but he hadn't painted this one for money. He wanted it to stay local. If Kitty had been working that day, donating the painting anonymously would have been less complicated. He wondered who this new woman was who seemed to think she was in charge.

"I like to know the story behind any painting I accept at the gallery, such as who painted it and why. What was the inspiration?"

Why? he thought. He wasn't sure why he had painted it, except that the subject was lovely and had engaged his mind for hours at a time. He had wondered what her story was. There had been something about her face and the way she held herself that had drawn him. Her grief—and he himself knew something about grief—had been apparent even in the way she stood.

"The artist wishes to remain anonymous, Mrs.—"

"*Ms.* Louise Roy."

He recognized the name. He had heard about a curator and critic named Louise Roy, but he thought she lived in Sacramento. He was surprised she would be working in a small-town gallery like La Rosaleda, but he didn't take time to ask her about it. It was to his advantage that she didn't yet know who he was. At some point they would be formally introduced, or she would figure out who he was from talking to Kitty, who owned the gallery. They would put two and two together, and of course Kitty would know. She would probably know as soon as she saw the painting, but by that time his wishes would already be known and agreed to. Kitty would make sure the painting stayed in her gallery and that it remained anonymous.

"Excuse me, Ms. Roy. This is an anonymous donation by an unnamed artist."

"Then at least let me give him—"

"Or her—" He was teasing her now.

She narrowed her eyes. "Or her," she echoed, "a receipt."

She pressed the slip of paper onto the mahogany countertop and searched for a pen.

"Kara?!"

A younger woman appeared from the storage room.

"Are we out of pens?" asked Louise, drumming her fingers on the countertop. The girl smiled at the artist standing before her. She knew exactly who he was but didn't let on when he winked at her. She walked to a file cabinet and produced a new box of pens, which she handed to the curator, and then returned to the storage room.

"Sign for it, please?"

He gently pulled the receipt from beneath her palm and shoved it into his jeans pocket, leaving the pen on the counter.

"Good day, *Ms.* Roy," he nodded and turned away.

"But sir!"

He stopped short. "Yes ma'am?"

"Why does the artist call it *Beauty and the Beast Within*?" Her eyebrows arched upward.

Truman gazed at the painting, remembering nearly every brush stroke of paint. He had spent many tedious hours on the house and the roses, trying to perfect the details. With each painting he had done of the Rose House, he had tried to make the petals softer, the thorns sharper, and the brambles seem to be crawling and climbing as if alive. For this painting, he had added the girl, or rather, the woman. He rarely painted people and only occasionally painted an animal or two, but this woman cried to be painted. Not out loud, of course, but it was her countenance that had captivated his thoughts and made him want to put her on canvas.

"Look deeper," Truman said. Louise peered closer at the painting.

In the painting, the woman's face was a mask of fragile beauty about to crumble. The thorny brambles reached out to her but were softened by the abundance of roses so that she didn't notice the thorns at all.

"It's not the woman who is a beast," he offered. "It's what she is trying to shed from her heart."

He turned to make a quick escape, but as he pushed open the door, he found himself face to face with beauty. The woman smiled, her eyes lighting up for a moment before glancing down to the polished wood floor. He struggled to catch his breath as he followed her gaze to where her sandaled feet met the hardwood. It was miraculous. He felt himself step back in slow motion, holding the door for her to walk through. She looked exactly like the woman in his painting.

"Thank you," she said and gave him a curious look. Suddenly, her embroidered satin purse slipped from her hands and fell to the floor between them. It landed with a *click* in the quiet gallery as the clasp hit the oak.

He reached down for the purse as her arm brushed his. If he hadn't felt the warmth of her hands weaving through his own, he wouldn't have believed she was real, but as they stood up together, his pulse responded to her accidental touch. Both their hands entwined around the purse: hers soft and manicured, his stained with flecks of paint. For a moment he was paralyzed, unable to move or breathe, but when her eyes met his and he saw her cheeks flush, he tried to disentangle himself.

He fumbled to unwind his hands from hers and propped the door open with his foot. He gestured as if to say, "Ladies first." Something tightened within him as he allowed his eyes to roam the profile of her face. The pink of her cheek provided a soft backdrop to the blond tendrils escaping the loose bun on the crown of her head. He was amazed. She seemed to be his muse, only in the flesh.

She paused in front of the counter where the painting was now propped on a brass easel. He watched her shoulders tense as she took an abrupt step toward the painting. The skirt of her dress draped forward, the hem still swirling around her calves from the abrupt halt of her steps. His eyes traced her profile and focused on the sparkle of her a necklace that dangled forward.

He saw her shoulders go slack. She released a soft gasp that he could hear from where he stood. She froze for a long moment, staring intently at the painting, and then slowly leaned away from it, as if the canvas might taint her. Truman held his breath as she turned slightly, paused, and let her gaze search the store. Truman stepped to the side, and her eyes swept past him. Turning back, she placed one hand over her mouth and leaned toward the canvas. Now he had a view of her face and could admire her more closely.

She suddenly straightened again, wrapping an arm around her waist and clasping her pendant with one hand. He watched, enthralled, as she raised it to her lips. The sparkling silver cross exactly mirrored the one his subject, Beauty, wore in the painting. His pulse raced as he tried to decide what to do.

She let go of the pendant and turned slightly toward him, a look of shock and alarm on her face. The red jewel in the center of the cross seemed to refract the light just enough to catch his eye, but the glint seemed to blind him as he began to feel like an intruder.

What had he been thinking? She looked thoroughly distressed, just as she had that day he had secretly observed her in her grief by the Rose House.

Truman moved to stand behind a shelf of pottery so he could peek through the colorful vessels without her detecting him. Her beauty was even more startling than it had been four years ago when he observed her standing before the Rose House. He ran his hand over his smooth head and massaged his neck.

He watched her rub her arms as if to ward off a chill. If he was in shock, what must she be feeling? A heaviness tugged at his chest, and he realized with a start it was regret. He no longer felt it was his masterpiece. Certainly no canvas could capture such beauty as was before him now. And was she pleased? Disappointed in what she saw? The way her eyes sparkled with unshed tears suggested the painting made her sad. Or worse: afraid. He was immediately sorry for the shock she must have felt but not for painting her. Now he only wished he could take the painting back and perfect it some more to show how beautiful she really was.

Truman glanced around for an explanation, as if it was a practical joke. He snuck another glance at the woman. She was studying the painting intently, her head tilted just a little bit. She had one finger over her lips, and the other hand was balled in the fabric of her skirt. This moment, he realized, was as private as the one he had inadvertently spied four years earlier. He shouldn't invade any more than he already had, he thought.

Truman turned to leave, but he felt rooted to the floor. He longed to see her reaction, every response of her body, the curious way in which she reached toward the canvas, and the rapid rise and fall of her breath.

He was sure she recognized herself in the painting now. His eyes stayed riveted on her profile as he struggled to keep still. He didn't even know her name, but he had painted her. Worry needled up his spine. He wished he knew what she thought of seeing herself depicted in what was obviously an intimate moment, when she had thought no one was watching.

Shaking away such thoughts, he reasoned with himself that artists did it all the time. There was nothing wrong with painting the likeness of people they observed. He was just being paranoid. Gazing intently from across the room, he studied the mirroring of her warm, soft image across the mix of oils on the canvas and was amazed at how nearly he'd actually caught her likeness, if it was indeed her.

As he watched her respond, he realized that he wanted her to like the painting. When he saw her eyes light up for a brief moment, like they had when she first came through the door, he couldn't help but wonder about her thoughts. His need to know, to reach out to her, even to apologize if he needed to, propelled him forward. He stepped from behind the shelving and started toward her, eager to talk to her, but when he saw her face pale, he froze, uncertain. He backed swiftly toward the door. He reached out slowly for the knob, hoping to ease out quietly, but when he pressed the door open, the bell jingled loudly above him.

She spun around. He found himself locked in her bewildered eyes, glimpsing yet another of her private moments. Nodding briefly, he hurried through the door, feeling as though he had lost something important. Irritated with himself, he hastened to his truck.

~⟡~

When he had painted *Beauty and the Beast Within,* he never imagined what it would be like for Beauty to see her own image in the painting. It hadn't even been a consideration. Why would it be? But when he saw the look in her eyes at the gallery, his only thought was to get away before he intruded further into her life.

Slapping his fedora on his head, he jammed the key into the ignition. The engine roared to life and he pulled out of the square, anxious to put as much space between him and the gallery as possible. He silently prayed she would doubt the painting was of her and simply go on with her life, but from observing her response, he guessed she was certain she had seen herself.

He had never before second-guessed himself for painting anything, but in a brief moment everything had changed. He wished at the very least that he had kept the painting to himself. Perhaps, he thought, he shouldn't have painted her at all, but he couldn't have stopped himself either... He'd been filled with inspiration the moment he saw her standing by the Rose House. The moment had lived in his mind since that day, and it wasn't simply her image, but the tempest of feelings that swirled around her. Perhaps he had just imagined it, but there had been something about the way she stood, the tears on her face, and a pain in her eyes that he recognized also in himself.

He had seen that she was grieving a terrible experience, maybe something even graver than what he had gone through. But he shoved aside memories of the family he'd almost had. Her pain, he was sure, was bigger. He wanted so much to know her story that he had painted her.

By doing so, he had revisited his own loss, and in a way it had helped him. But now, having seen her and witnessed her mixed reaction, he realized he should have at least kept the painting in his studio, for his eyes only.

The engine roared as Truman punched the gas harder. He drove away from La Rosaleda to his farmhouse in the country, driving every bit like the idiot he knew he was.

5

LILLIAN REMOVED THE SNAPSHOT OF the Rose House from the employee bulletin board and sank into the oversized couch to gaze at the picture. Her weekend getaway had been a strange one. During her short trip, she had never made it to the Rose House or had the chance to get in touch with Kitty, the kind woman who had reassured her when she had thought she was being followed at the vineyard. It had been four years since that first visit to the Rose House. She had never forgotten the seed of hope she'd felt there, and she'd gone back to recapture it. Unfortunately, she hadn't made it to the Rose House before an impromptu visit to the gallery in the La Rosaleda square. Now she was back at work with her only snapshot of the Rose House from four years earlier.

Lillian glanced at her wristwatch. She still had a few minutes to get Aunt Bren's thoughts before her shift started. Maybe the listening ear of her adoptive mom would help her sort her thoughts.

"Hello?" Aunt Bren's cheerful Oklahoma accent lilted over the cell phone.

"Hi, Aunt Bren, it's me."

"Lillian? Oh, honey. It's so good to hear from you!" She stretched it into *yoooou*, which made Lillian smile.

"But, honey, why haven't you been returning my calls? It's been weeks!"

"I know. I'm sorry."

"Oh, never mind. You just tell me what's happening, honey. How are things at the restaurant? Are you the head chef yet?"

Lillian smiled. "No."

"Well, you should be."

"Try telling that to Chef George, Aunt Bren."

"He sounds like a man who takes himself a little too seriously, honey. A married man who cooks for a living? That surely explains why he's so uptight."

Lillian giggled at Aunt Bren's joke, knowing that if she could sample George's food, she would probably change her mind.

"So, Lil, what is wrong?"

"I didn't say anything is wrong."

There was silence on the other end of the phone, then she heard water running, something clunk on the counter, and the click of a switch. Aunt Bren was making coffee. Lillian relished the thought of being there to drink it with her.

"Okay, I guess something is wrong. Do you remember when I went to La Rosaleda four years ago?"

"Yes. It was soon after the accident. Too soon, if you ask me, but of course you didn't. And then you ran into those crazy men you thought were following you."

"I know, Aunt Bren. I should have told you what I was doing, but that's not what I called for. I wanted to tell you about a strange thing that happened this past Saturday when I visited La Rosaleda again. Do you remember that beautiful rose-covered house I sent you the picture of?"

"Oh yes, honey. I remember. I still have the snapshot you took. I taped it to my fridge! It's so pretty."

"That one," Lillian said. "Well, before I could visit the Rose House, I went into this little gallery in La Rosaleda, and—well—you are going to think I'm crazy, Aunt Bren."

"Honey, I believe we are all a little bit crazy. Just spit it out."

"Well, there was a painting of the Rose House in this little gallery. It was stunning. So detailed and...almost alive. It made me think of that day four years ago when I visited the Rose House. Remember that?"

"You mean, it was *the* Rose House in the painting?"

"Well, yes, but that's not what was so amazing about it."

"Then what was it? What's got you all tongue-tied?"

"I was in it."

"Whaaaat?"

"Me! Or a woman who looked just like me! I don't know. Maybe I imagined it, Aunt Bren, but it looked just like me. I—the woman in the painting—was even wearing my pendant."

"With the red jewel?"

"Yeah," Lillian said. "The painting was called *Beauty and the Beast Within.*"

"Well, I'll be. Do you think you are the Beauty in the painting? How could that be?"

"That's exactly what I thought. It gave me a funny feeling to see it. I figured I was crazy to think it was me. And maybe I am. Maybe it wasn't me at all, but it sure looked like it." Lillian's heart quickened as she recalled how connected she had felt to it, but she had been confused too. She couldn't imagine who on earth could have painted her feelings so vividly, in such a private moment, without her knowing.

"I'll bet it did give you a strange feeling," Aunt Bren said. "Who painted it? Maybe you could ask them at the store?"

"That's the other strange thing, Aunt Bren." Lillian's voice grew softer. "It's anonymous. Both the artist and the person who donated it are being kept a secret. Even the curator doesn't know, although she said she might be able to find out."

"That is strange. If it's so pretty, then why keep it a secret?"

"I don't know," said Lillian. The painting was more than pretty. It was intimate and emotional. When she had seen it, she felt stripped bare. How had someone captured one of her most private moments?

"Maybe the artist is shy," Aunt Bren offered.

"You should see it, Aunt Bren. It made me feel so sad. All those miserable memories of Mosquito Road just came right back. It caught me so off guard, I nearly cried in front of the curator!"

"Oh, Lil," Aunt Bren clucked. "Honey, let it be. You shouldn't be dragging these old feelings up."

Lillian wanted to say that the feelings weren't old to her. She had tried to keep them just beyond reach so she could function, but it only took something minor to pull them close again. That's what seeing the painting had done.

"Aunt Bren, it's not just that it made me sad. I'm intrigued and—" Lillian sat forward in the chair and gestured with her arm, even though Aunt Bren couldn't see her frustration. "How dare somebody paint me without permission!"

"You're a beautiful woman. Why wouldn't someone want to paint you? And maybe it isn't even you in the painting."

"I've thought of that. You might be right, but what if it *is* me? What if someone painted me without my knowing? Do you think they could have been there that day all those years ago, watching me?" She tried to recall the men she had thought were following her that day four years ago, but neither of them had struck her as artists. One had hidden behind a camera, the other had been talking on a cell phone. Maybe the camera man was the artist.

"Maybe the artist just thought you were pretty and decided to paint you. You are Miss Wild Hollow, you know."

Lillian's worry dissipated for a moment as she stifled a chuckle. She had been Miss Wild Hollow in her hometown pageant. Aunt Bren still acted as if that made her royalty, even though only four girls had competed in the pageant and each of the other girls had won the title of runner-up. The next year, Geena had won the pageant, and Lillian had been required to crown her own sister. Things certainly had changed, mused Lillian, but there were no more tiaras in her life.

"Even if that were true, Aunt Bren, who has the right to do that? Paint somebody—at their most…most private, maybe saddest moment? It's—invasive. Horrifying, in a way."

Lillian heard her aunt sigh. "So that's what it's really about, honey. Someone secretly watched you and then splattered your grief on canvas. And it's making you all dramatic."

"Well, it wasn't really splattered," Lillian said, "but isn't that enough to be upset about? In some ways, it reminds me of how I felt when the news kept displaying the accident on television."

"Why don't you just buy the painting? That way you can get it out of the public eye. If I know you, that's what you are worried about. Your loss of privacy."

Lillian knew Aunt Bren understood her feelings about the sensational publicity the accident had caused in the Sacramento area. It was as if the reporters had been hungry for news, so they'd nearly become stalkers, plastering not only the accident but her private pain on the TV screen for everyone to see.

"I tried, but the gallery said it's not up for sale."

"I don't think you should worry, honey, but if you're concerned because of what happened after Robert died, call the investigators." Aunt Bren's light tone faded, and Lillian heard worry creep into her voice. "Do you want me to call them for you?"

Lillian considered it. "No," she finally answered. "Let me think about it a bit."

"Try not to worry, honey."

"You too," Lillian reminded her.

The line grew silent before either of them spoke again. "Lillian, you can always come back home, okay? It might do you good to get back into church and be around your friends. Everyone loves you here in Wild Hollow."

Lillian smiled. She would have loved to do that, but going so far away from where her babies were buried was something she wasn't ready for.

"I know, Aunt Bren. I better get off the phone. They're waiting for me in the kitchen."

"Oh, hey, Lillian?"

"Yeah, Aunt Bren, what is it?"

"Do you ever talk to Geena?"

Angry comments about her sister stuck in her throat. "No, I'm sorry. We still haven't spoken."

"Okay, honey. I just wondered. Good-bye."

Lillian tacked the photograph back onto the bulletin board and shook off her frustration. There were more important things to worry about than her manipulative, deceitful sister. She wished Aunt Bren would just keep certain comments to herself, but Lillian knew she couldn't. She was Aunt Bren. She just wanted everyone to get along.

Lillian grabbed her apron from a nearby peg, her mind returning to the strange events that had occurred right after the accident.

She had listened to the investigators arguing about whether they were some freak occurrences or if they were related to Robert's supposed murder. "But what about the strange letters that were shoved under her door?" they had speculated. "How do you explain someone letting the air out of her tires? A random act? Not when it happened four times. Her sister? She hasn't been seen in years, but she's not really wanted for anything at this point."

Lillian had shivered at their mention of Geena. As much as she disliked her sister, she didn't believe Geena would try to scare her.

"She has information about her sister that nobody else does."

"No! It isn't her," Lillian had interjected. "Maybe there is no stalker. Maybe it was just all a terrible accident!"

There had never been any real evidence of a stalker, never anything plausible.

Something about the painting at the gallery wasn't plausible either, but like Aunt Bren, she doubted the appearance was related to her being followed, if indeed she ever had been.

She thought again of the painting, and her curiosity was piqued. She couldn't deny it was a beautiful scene, breathtaking. Whoever painted it had seen her hurting as nobody else ever had. But why had the artist put it on display for anyone who walked into the gallery to see?

6

*"W*HY DON'T YOU JUST CALL your sister?"

Geena downed the rest of her drink and slid the glass across the bar toward the head waitress, Edna, then blew a perfect smoke ring and waved it away.

"Stop that." Edna shook her head and swatted at the lingering smoke. "Put it out. You aren't allowed to smoke in here."

Geena snuffed out her cigarette and mumbled, "Stupid law. This is a bar."

"Stupid or not, I think it's ingenious. My teenagers don't need a mom with lung cancer." Edna wiped the counter between them. "Now, tell me, Geena, why is it you sit here every Friday night before work, and while everyone else is telling me about their sad love affairs, you're telling me the woeful story of a sister whom you refuse to call?"

"It *is* a sad love affair. My sister doesn't want to hear from me." Geena pulled another cigarette from her purse, but Edna shook her head. Geena rolled her eyes in response and leaned in toward Edna, trying not to wrinkle her nose at the older woman's flowery perfume.

"There's a love affair in that story," Geena continued. "A sordid affair, to be exact."

She shook her long auburn hair and swiveled her lanky legs away from the man who had parked himself on the bar stool beside her. She had been telling Edna the story for weeks now. She knew Edna wouldn't want to miss this new twist that promised more drama than her afternoon soaps.

"Hmm. So what about your sister? The chef? What did you do...her husband?" She smirked, amused at her own bad joke.

Geena shot a dirty look at Edna. "Must you be so crude? This is my sister we're talking about."

"You did, didn't you?"

Geena frowned, shrugging off the question. "Don't look at me that way. You already figured it out anyway."

Edna raised her hands in surrender. "I'm not your judge, honey."

"Well," mumbled Geena, "the affair didn't happen the way you think it did."

"Oh?" Edna leaned her elbows on the bar, ignoring the man who hollered for a waitress.

Geena shook her head, pushing a strand of hair from her face. "It was drug induced. Actually, drugs and alcohol."

"You're saying it was an accident? That's what people always say, Geena. I see it happen every Friday night. The thing is, they always know it's going to happen. That's why they get intoxicated before they do it."

"We didn't plan it."

"So it only happened once?"

"Well, no. It was an accident the first time."

"Wow, honey. You are in quite a mess with your sister, aren't you?"

Geena ducked her head. It had happened and she couldn't change it.

Edna fell silent, but her face showed compassion. Geena pressed her fingertips against the bridge of her nose, fighting back tears that threatened to fall. Edna reached across the bar and rested her hand on Geena's shoulder.

"I'm sorry, honey. I don't know the circumstances. I say you should call your sister. Not now, of course. The boss is due in any time now."

Geena swigged from the bottle of water Edna had placed in front of her, wishing it were something stronger. *Time to go to work,* she thought.

"Lady!" a man called from the corner of the room.

Geena turned toward the voice. "Don't be so bossy, boys!" She grinned, picked up a tray, and sauntered toward the group of greasy men who'd been sitting in that corner table for a decade. She sighed, reminding herself that sometimes nicer guys came in. She would try to make eye contact with them, but they always looked right through her. She was just a waitress.

She smiled at the more upscale-looking man in the group. He ordered a beer and turned away to watch the game on television, immune to her charms, aloof toward her.

She wondered, as she set his drink down, what he would think if he knew she'd gone to college for a while. She'd even tried cooking school with Lillian and had been good at it but had decided cooking wasn't in her future and studied cosmetology instead. Geena knew that she wasn't stupid, but she imagined these men thought so. Even though she'd let her beauty license expire, she told herself it was only a matter of time before she got it reinstated and could get out of this dead-end job.

She carried the tray back to the bar to be refilled, sauntering and smiling at her customers as she walked by. She still looked good, which translated into good tips. Sometimes a drunk customer would ask her if she was a model.

She always retorted: "You bet, honey. That's my day job."

It was a joke, but she actually had done some modeling in San Francisco. The jobs were nothing like the runway jobs in New York, but they were legit and helped pay the bills. She lied to herself about her prospects, though. At almost thirty, it would get harder and harder to find modeling jobs, so it was good that she could fall back on serving drinks.

As she leaned over one of the men to set his drink on the table, she felt his hand rest on a place on her body that she was so tired of being touched. The smile left her face.

"Here's your drink, honey." She used her sweetest waitress voice.

The man looked shocked when the whole tray of beers landed in his lap. Glass shattered on the floor around him. Geena emptied the beer in her hand over his head and slammed it down on the table in front of him. He bounced to his feet, glaring at Geena.

She trembled at the sight of him, his eyes filled with malice. In the movies men never retaliated against the waitress who made them wear their drink. Luckily, there were others in the bar who weren't jerks. Several of them stood and stared down the angry man.

"What the—" said one of them.

"Are you crazy, man?" said another one.

The beer-drenched one gave the other a warning glare as he walked out the door.

Suddenly, Edna was standing in front of her. Geena did not feel sorry about dumping the beer on the creep, but she worried that her actions might cause trouble for Edna. She glanced around to see if the boss was there yet.

"He ain't here yet, honey, but you'd better go before he shows up."

"Okay," Geena said. "I'm sorry."

Edna's face softened and she placed a hand on her shoulder. "Don't come back here. You can do better."

Geena grinned at the chorus of agreement from the men in the bar.

"Bye-bye, boys," she retorted. They rewarded her by placing their hands over their hearts, like they were truly crushed about her departure.

She hugged Edna. "I will be back."

"I wish you wouldn't."

"You'll still let me work, right?"

"Of course, honey, but you don't want to end up like me."

"You aren't so bad, Edna." Geena patted her back, then she grabbed her purse and hurried out the door.

Outside, in the dimly lit parking lot, Geena searched in her purse for her keys. She heard their jingle at the bottom, buried beneath lipstick cases, wadded-up tissue, a jeweled flask, and an assortment of napkins with phone numbers written on them.

"Stupid keys," she muttered, heading toward her green Pinto. A curse escaped her lips. "Finally!" she exclaimed as she freed the keys from her bag. She looked up and froze in her tracks. The man she had drenched in beer stood leaning against her car.

Her heartbeat quickened. Chills crept across the back of her neck as he grabbed the front of her shirt and ripped it open. He spun her around, and her face slammed into the hood of the car. She gasped as her keys scraped across the parking lot. She opened her mouth to scream, but the pain settling in her lower back silenced her. The car hood pressed against her cheek. Her eyes rolled back as heat shot up her spine. Her assailant grabbed and twisted her hair, wrenching her head back. Again he slammed her face against the hood. She tasted blood.

Geena attempted to raise herself off the car, but he clasped the back of her neck and pinned her down. A scream stuck in her throat.

Her mind searched for a way out. Aunt Bren's voice rang in her ears. *"Pray."*

"Pray!"

Geena would have laughed at the irony, but the man bashed her face into the hood again. It was then that she felt the door of her heart creak open and a wordless plea drifted toward heaven.

Geena felt a sudden lightness as the weight of her assailant lifted away. She heard a *thunk* against the car, but this time it wasn't her body. Grunts and cursing echoed from somewhere behind her. She raised herself to a standing position and prepared to run, but when she turned around, she saw a man in a flannel shirt pummeling her attacker with his fists.

Edna appeared beside her. She called to one of the men who were gathered in the parking lot, and Geena felt herself being whisked back into the bar. "Thank you," Geena whispered.

"The ambulance and the police are on their way," Edna assured her.

"I'm fine," Geena stammered, but her body trembled violently.

Edna cupped Geena's face in her hands as tears flowed freely down Geena's cheeks. "Don't be afraid now, honey. The boys will take care of him until the police come."

Even as her body screamed out in pain, Geena smirked at how "the boys" were taking care of him. She silently wondered what Aunt Bren would think of her answered prayer. *"God can use anyone,"* the words reverberated through her. Lillian had said those words too. She had been in her garden with Sheyenne and Lee, who were peering at an ugly insect that was crawling up Lillian's leg. Lillian had batted it away.

"Aunt Bren says that God can use anyone and anything," she'd said to Lee. "Even scary-looking bugs." She'd glanced up to the porch then where Geena sat. "Isn't that right, Aunt Geena?"

"That's what Aunt Bren would say," Geena had mocked as she raised her glass in a toast. "God can use anybody."

"Even an insect?" asked Sheyenne, smiling.

"Even an insect," she had said, her demeanor softening for the children.

Geena ached at the memory. She wasn't sure if Lillian was right. She had found God only during times of crises, and then it wasn't in a profound manifestation of the Spirit, as Pastor and Aunt Bren would say. Their religious sensibilities were often expressed in annoying clichés, such as *God bless* or *God can use anyone,* but whether she wanted to admit it or not, their spiritual beliefs were deeply ingrained in her too.

"Shh now. You'll be fine." Edna's voice brought her back to the present as she felt the coolness of a cloth against her cheek.

7

LILLIAN TIGHTENED HER APRON. The photos of other families on the bulletin board made her sad, but seeing her snapshot of the Rose House reminded her that hope might be waiting when she decided to climb out of the deepest part of her grief and grab hold. The fact that somebody had painted her in front of the Rose House was as miraculous as anything to her. If she hadn't been so bewildered by the painting's appearance, she might have even seen it as a sign.

Lillian pushed through the swinging doors to the kitchen and walked past the whir of a blender. Hurrying to her work counter, she hoped Chef George wouldn't notice she was a few minutes late.

"Lillian! There you are. Would you please run down to the grocery store and buy eleven dozen eggs? Our new intern dropped the whole batch this morning." He glared across the room at a girl whose face turned crimson despite her bronze skin.

Lillian smiled apologetically at the intern and turned toward George. "Sure, but in case you forgot, they will deliver."

An icy smile met hers. "But I want *you* to go for them." She glanced away, hiding the angry flush that crept up her neck.

After returning from the market, Lillian chopped vegetables for chicken soup with a hint of rosemary. It was a customer favorite.

Lillian liked being busy and didn't complain anymore about the more menial tasks her boss often assigned her to do, but when he hollered for her to stop what she was doing and answer the phone that was ringing in the office, she didn't try to hide the sigh that escaped from her lips.

As she passed the break room, Lillian glanced at the Rose House photograph on the bulletin board. She wondered again about the painting that now haunted her. Where had it come from? Was it truly her image on the canvas? She felt a swirling in her chest every time she thought about it and felt drawn to see it again, to see the roses that seemed to reach for her image in the painting.

She should go back, she thought. Maybe take a vacation, return to La Rosaleda, and convince the gallery to sell her the painting. She paused, seriously considering the idea as she ignored the ringing phone. Why hadn't she thought of it before?

She spotted Chef George in the kitchen, barking orders, and decided she definitely needed a vacation. She stared, satisfied, at the phone as it stopped ringing and transferred over to voice mail.

"Lillian!" barked George. He eyed her suspiciously as she shuffled back into the kitchen. "Who was that?"

"I don't know." She looked down at her hands. "I didn't answer it."

George stared through the slits of his dark eyes. In his fifties, he was a handsome man, and Lillian could see why his wife had fallen for him. It was his grumpiness in the kitchen she didn't like. He intimidated people, and he seemed to like doing so.

"I'm sorry," she mumbled, fiddling with the ties on her apron. "I'm just—burnt out right now. I'm getting bored answering the phone and chopping carrots, I guess."

The grin on his face was unexpected. She took a step back as she waited for sarcastic words that would no doubt come next.

"Why didn't you say so?" he asked. "I'll move you to something you like better."

"What?" she blinked, wondering if he was mocking her.

"I just didn't think you were ready, Lil, because you've been going through so much the past few years." He turned back to the counter, dipping his hand in a container of wheat flour. "I would love to have you do more."

Her face flushed, but she still did not trust him. His mood often changed without warning. "Well," she said, "I will take you up on that, but really, I think I just need some time off. A vacation." She hesitated. "I think two weeks would help."

The noises in the kitchen stopped as the other cooks listened. She glanced down at her hands and her mouth went dry.

The smell of yeast filled the air. George turned his attention to kneading the lump of dough in his hands, smoothing it into a satiny loaf. His hands didn't stop when he looked up. "Okay, Lil. You seem a little ragged lately. But only one week."

She began to protest but stopped herself when she saw the sincere expression on his face.

"I can't spare you for two weeks with the gala coming up, so don't even think about asking for more than a week."

She wondered what the gala had to do with her. Would he actually give her more responsibility, or did he just need another waitress? Maybe she could get him to give her more time later.

"Thanks."

He nodded.

She returned to her counter and started dicing celery. The phone rang again. Ignoring it, she focused on slicing perfectly uniform moons. After a few more rings, George ordered the intern to answer the call.

When her shift ended, Lillian paused to look again at the Rose House photo. She wondered if she should actually take it down, if it looked silly among the family photos. The happy faces stared back at her, laughing and smiling. She sighed as she reached out and smoothed the photo, its corners now curling from being pinned at only one edge.

Stepping back, she imagined the Rose House as a focal point for all the faces around it. Every picture on that board represented someone's dream: a marriage, a newborn baby, a celebration, hopes and plans. She decided to leave the photo in its place.

Maybe, she thought, as she turned to walk out the door, *the Rose House photo does fit in with those other hopes and dreams.*

8

THE BLACK SEDAN TRAVELED THROUGH the Sonoma Valley along Highway 12. Lillian could easily imagine she was in another country. The rolling hills, gnarled trees reaching to one another across the road, and lines of grapevines and roses soothed her cluttered mind. But with the calm came a familiar bittersweet ache.

Jake was his usual quiet self as he focused on the road. She hadn't called him to drive her in a long time, but since she wouldn't really need a car during her stay in La Rosaleda, she had thought it was a good idea to have him drop her off and return for her when her vacation ended.

Upon arriving in La Rosaleda, she asked Jake to take a turn around the town square. She loved the roses that surrounded the fountain, the ducks, the blossoming trees, and the renovated buildings from the 1800s that had now been called into service as quaint shops and restaurants. Lillian wanted to stop and buy olives and farm-fresh cheese, but a glance at the clock on the dashboard reminded her that she needed to first check in to the bed-and-breakfast.

Her primary goal for the trip was to visit the Rose House. On her last visit to La Rosaleda, she had been so alarmed by the painting of *Beauty and the Beast Within* that she immediately returned to Sacramento without visiting the Rose House. She wanted so much to again capture the glimpse of hope she'd felt there four years earlier.

Her spirit lifted when they pulled up to the bed-and-breakfast. It was a beautifully restored Victorian mansion that sat a few blocks from the plaza, towering between two mature magnolia trees. Intricate gingerbread, gableboard, and scalloped cresting gave it a storybook personality, reminding Lillian of the dollhouse she'd been building for Sheyenne and Lee before the accident.

A gentleman stood on the wraparound porch and waved as Jake opened Lillian's door. Lillian stepped out of the car and waved back. She scanned the landscape. Weeping willows graced the outer edges of the yard, their branches swaying in the welcoming breeze. A secretive path wound between them, inviting visitors to venture into a wonderland of budding trees and lush greenery.

Jake retrieved her luggage from the trunk while she admired the vibrant reds, purples, and pinks of impatiens that crept along the edge of the porch. She could imagine herself sitting on the porch with a glass of cold lemonade, a book in her hand. The man approaching them walked past petunias, ranunculus blooms, and nasturtiums that spilled over wine barrels and other containers.

"Ms. Diamon?"

She nodded, wincing at his use of her maiden name. She'd chosen to use her maiden name after some details of Robert's death became public, but she didn't know when she would get used to it again.

"Yes." Lillian smiled and extended her hand to shake his. "I'm Lillian Diamon."

"Like *diamond*?"

"No, just Diamon, without the *d*."

He nodded. "Good, then I haven't misspelled it. I'm Mark Tenney. It's nice to meet you."

"I'll call you when I'm ready, Jake," Lillian said. "Thank you so much."

"Of course, ma'am." He smiled back. For a moment she was surprised to see some gray strands of hair peeking out of his cap. Ten years of driving for her, and he had aged without her noticing, but so had she. On some days she felt as if more than a decade had passed.

Waving as the car pulled away, she let Mark lead her along a pebble path at the side of the house toward three small cottages. She'd chosen a cottage behind the house, hoping it would allow for more privacy.

The grounds were as beautiful as the plaza itself, with birdbaths and even more flowers and blossoming trees. The cottages were cozy with jasmine vines climbing on trellises that sheltered the front porches. There was a swing on each porch, and each cottage had a large overturned barrel overflowing with pink and white petunias and nasturtiums. Her cottage boasted a hydrangea bush in full bloom.

"Oh, how lovely!" She was delighted to see that it was as charming as it had appeared on the Web site.

Lillian walked up the steps and smiled at a hanging basket of trailing fuchsias that were suspended from the porch roof. She loved the oversized wicker chair that sat in front of the large window and overlooked the yard. The English cottage garden motif reminded her of the way she'd cultivated her own backyard in the house she had shared with her husband and children.

Painted mint green and yellow, the interior of the cottage was as pleasant as the outside and smelled of lemon verbena. A kitchen and a living room were furnished with a café table and cushioned wicker chairs.

A green door led to a bedroom decorated in earth tones and an assortment of framed drawings of herbs and plants.

Mark set down her bags next to an iron bed that was covered by a cozy quilt. Lillian noted a white painted desk in the corner decorated with framed photographs of the lush Rose House and other La Rosaleda scenery.

"Will this work?" he asked as she followed him back to the kitchen.

"Yes! It's adorable. Thank you."

He walked toward the door. His khaki pants and white silk T-shirt made him appear more casual than his sharp features, olive skin, and neat black hair suggested. His smiling brown eyes caught her off guard. Memories of Robert enveloped her, and she found herself looking for a ring. A wedding band blinked back at her, causing her cheeks to warm.

He paused at the door. "My wife, Paige, will have breakfast ready between 7:00 and 9:00 in the morning. Her specialty is omelets. She's an amazing cook," he bragged.

Lillian was relieved to finally close the door behind him. Glad to be alone again, she went into the bathroom and looked in the mirror. Her blue eyes seemed too large for her face, and a sprinkling of freckles across her nose took away any hint of glamour her blond hair might have hinted at.

"I'm not much to look at these days, am I?" she said.

She blushed, feeling foolish for having admired a married man, for having noticed another man at all. Her relationship with Robert had turned out differently than she'd expected, but the truth remained that she had been deeply in love with him. It felt like cheating to look at another man now, even though she was almost sure he had been unfaithful to her. Robert's death had left her with unanswered questions and a deep emptiness.

She unpacked her suitcases, hanging her clothes in the closet and organizing her toiletries on the wicker shelf in the bathroom. Doing so reminded her of the trips she'd taken with Robert. The beach house had been so small they'd had to cram their belongings together on the only small shelf available, her face cream and lotions nestled beside his aftershave and razor. Her belongings didn't look right without Robert's beside them.

Fragrance from the fruit trees wafted on the breeze that flowed in through the open windows. She went into the kitchen, shaking far from her thoughts the idea of being attracted to another man, and reminded herself that, despite the beauty of this place, she was not a character in a romantic novel. Robert had not been Prince Charming, and he wouldn't ever be coming back riding a white horse.

Lillian rummaged through the cabinets looking for some fruit tea, but found only a box of mint and one almost empty of Earl Grey. Shoving aside the mint, she grabbed the Earl Grey and made a note to ask for some fruity herbal teas from the Tenneys.

She glanced out the window and considered going to the main house to meet Paige Tenney. When she asked about the tea, she could also inquire about the gallery. Since La Rosaleda was such a small town, the locals would know almost everything that went on there. Maybe Paige could provide inside information about the gallery that would help Lillian know how to approach Louise Roy about purchasing *Beauty and the Beast Within*. Or maybe Paige would know something about the mysterious artist.

She toyed with the idea that the artist's identity might be purchased. The teakettle whistled and she shook the thought away. Now she sounded like Robert, as if money could buy anything, even a secret.

THE TOWER ROOM AT THE Tenneys' bed-and-breakfast was a place of inspiration for many artists. It was the perfect vantage point for capturing exquisite shots of the valley, many of which were on display downstairs and in the local gallery.

He aimed his lens through the panoramic windows toward the square below, panned across the vineyards to the historical structures of downtown La Rosaleda, then back to the gardens around the B&B. The gardens were spectacular at this time of year, the roses being his favorite subject because their beauty begged to be photographed.

Sometimes the people were irresistible too. Their faces, so full of hope for a relaxing vacation, made the best photographs. The Tenneys had given explicit instructions about not photographing the guests without their permission, but when Mark Tenney had walked the woman to her cottage, he could not resist zooming in for a closer look.

"What is *she* doing here?" he whispered to himself. How strange it seemed. The B&B was the last place he expected to see her.

The photographer had stared through the lens as she stood on the stoop, waiting for Mark to open the door. The lens zoomed in on her face. Her smile was halfhearted until she noticed the flowers on the porch. At that point a series of clicks filled the room. It was a perfect face, at least from an artist's eye, a face worthy of being photographed or painted.

Rules forgotten, the camera continued to click until she was out of sight.

It was late morning when Lillian left the cottage and walked to the Rose House. It sat on the west side of the Frances-DiCamillo estate, tucked into a corner where two fences converged, joining the rolling landscape of vineyards.

A few people worked nearby but paid no attention to her. Gravel crunched under her feet as she walked up the driveway and onto the cobbled path that led to the tasting rooms on one side and to the Rose House on the other. She paused for a moment to study the tasting rooms, which had just opened for the day.

They were connected to the main house, a formidable building of stucco mission-style architecture with a rambling front porch and a bell tower from which the bell signaled the top of the hour. The tasting rooms had been designed to match the house perfectly, with old vines climbing the walls, just like they did the main house.

Lillian started along the path that led to the Rose House. The emerald grass tempted her to remove her sandals and venture off the path.

Nearing the Rose House, her breath caught in her throat. She instinctively glanced around, thinking about *Beauty and the Beast Within*, but she was alone. A nervous laugh escaped her lips.

The house was as she remembered, but the roses had grown more lush. The buds were in full bloom, dripping from the roof and spilling over the wraparound porch, ambling down the sides and framing each window and door as if the house itself was part of the roses. Lace curtains peeked through the windows, and a border of pink and purple petunias danced in the morning breeze.

She walked along the chain boundary to peek through the brambles into the porch. Beside two rocking chairs was a child-size rocker with peeling white paint and faded red and blue roses across the back and along the arms. Perhaps it had belonged to the couple's little girl, Ruby. In all the tales Lillian had read about the Rose House, Ruby was the central focus.

Lillian recalled the stories, amazed that she'd actually met the matriarch, Kitty, the last time she had been there. The Rose House had come to represent the miracles in Kitty's life and had become famous among tourists. Like Lillian, others had come to see the house as representing hope for the future. Something wonderful had happened to the DiCamillo family who owned the Rose House, so maybe something as equally amazing could happen to them too.

Lillian was lost in her thoughts of the Rose House until a man's cough startled her out of her reverie. She spun around and spotted a man rushing away. She shivered. Where had he come from?

He had something in his hand, but she couldn't see what it was. It could have been a hat or even a camera. Her heart raced as hazy memories of her last visit came to mind. It had been so long ago, she couldn't remember it clearly.

She drew in a deep breath as she watched him jog to the parking lot and disappear. She thought of the painting, and goose bumps sprang up on her arms. She rubbed them vigorously and told herself she was just being paranoid.

She shook off thoughts of being watched and turned to study the house. She had waited four years to come back and didn't want anything to tarnish the moment. She stared into the Rose House as she might have observed a painting in a museum. She willed herself to fall into the moment, trying to capture again the promise she had once felt there. In her mind, she glimpsed happier thoughts, but they were suddenly erased by another face in her memories.

An unexpected longing to talk to her sister surprised her. She closed her eyes to ward off the thoughts, but Geena's image filled her mind. She toyed with the idea of pushing anger aside and calling her. She knew her sister would love to hear the story of the Rose House. Throwing caution away, she pulled out her cell phone and found Geena's number. She stood with her finger poised over the send button. What would it be like to talk to her again, to share her fears, to get her advice like old times?

Lillian snapped the phone shut and shoved it into her pocket. She was accustomed to having these fleeting thoughts of Geena and had grown to realize they were simply longings for the past. Geena was the past. Now it was just Lillian.

She gazed at the child's rocking chair and imagined she could hear laughter echoing from the Rose House. What had the little girl, Ruby, been like? Thoughts of Sheyenne and Lee swept through her mind. She let them settle over her in a heaviness of loss, as she was forced to meet grief among the roses.

A sudden gust of wind swept across the path, rustled the leaves of the rose vines, and found the dampness of her cheeks. She pulled a tissue from her purse and dabbed at her face.

A bell from behind her signaled an approaching cyclist. It was Kitty, the woman who had been so kind to her during her last visit to the Rose House.

Kitty was dressed in a turquoise sari embroidered with white flowers. She wore lime green garden clogs and a big straw hat that didn't match and was perched on a red cruiser. The basket attached to her handlebars was filled with freshly cut flowers.

"Hello, dear!" she called, pedaling toward Lillian.

"Hello," Lillian said, as Kitty climbed off her bike and grasped the fence post to balance herself.

"Whoo! I lose my balance when I get off this thing! It's my arthritis. I have to use a cane most of the time, but I can't carry it on the bike, now can I?" she laughed.

"Miss DiCamillo." Lillian reached out her hands. "It is a delight to see you again! Do you remember me?"

"Now, it's simply Kitty, remember? And you are Lillian, right?"

Lillian smiled. "It has been a while, hasn't it?"

"Five years, isn't it, dear?"

"Four."

Kitty poked brown and silver curls into her hat and straightened it on her head. "I think you are right, dear. My memory doesn't serve me as well as it used to." She motioned toward her basket, which was filled with red and purple zinnias, lavender cosmos, pink carnations, and a variety of other long-stemmed flowers. "I was just collecting flowers to make some bouquets for folks at the retirement home."

"Those will be quite the bouquet," Lillian said. "You're lucky to have such a beautiful garden at your fingertips."

Kitty chuckled. "Well, I wouldn't say it is at my fingertips. Blake and I work hard, and we do have employees who help us. Also, volunteers from the Sunshine House school help out."

"Sunshine House?"

"Yes, dear. The volunteers from Sunshine House are adults who need a little extra loving care. We give them that here! And then there are several folks from the retirement home who volunteer. I'm not sure what they enjoy the most, working with the people from Sunshine House or working with the flowers."

"If I lived here, I would love to volunteer," said Lillian.

"With all us old people?"

"Sure!" said Lillian. "You don't seem that old to me. You certainly don't look old."

"You are a dear!" Kitty cried. "Thank you!" She set her hand on Lillian's shoulder. "How are you, dear? Better than last time I saw you, I hope."

"I'm getting there."

"That's good. Now help me cut some of these roses." She didn't seem to notice Lillian's surprise as she stepped with her over the low chain boundary. Kitty took Lillian's arm and walked toward the Rose House with a slight limp. Before she could have protested, she had been recruited to help trim the Rose House. She could hardly believe her luck.

Lillian accepted a pair of clippers and helped Kitty snip the prettiest roses and prune the withered blooms. They worked silently for a while as Lillian breathed in the scent of the hundreds of roses around her. Lillian thought Kitty had to be one of the luckiest people in the world. What would it be like to live at Frances-DiCamillo and tend the Rose House every day? By the time they were finished, Lillian realized she was having more fun than she'd had in years.

"Kitty, do a lot of artists come here?"

"Oh yes, dear. Several." She straddled her bicycle. "Both painters and photographers, amateurs and professionals. I just let them roam the grounds at will, but there are some who tend to be more drawn to this house."

Lillian thought of the painting in the gallery.

"Why do you think they are drawn to the Rose House?"

"Different people have different reasons. Not just artists, either. People like you. Some of their yarns have become so tangled up with fable that they aren't even plausible. People love drama and make up all kinds of stories about this house."

"Like what?"

"Well," Kitty said, looking beyond the house toward the vineyards, "for instance, some people think this place is haunted. Can you believe that? And some think that miracles will happen if they go inside and pray. Someone even claimed to have communicated with the spirit of my deceased daughter, Ruby, when they stood on the porch."

Lillian shivered. She could see why they'd added the chain boundary.

Kitty shook her head sadly. "The one about Ruby made me angry, but I like the other stories about people who visit the Rose House because they've heard its story about the love, grief, and hope my husband put into it."

"You are so blessed, Kitty."

"I am. If only you knew the whole story, dear. Hope does dwell here. It's what the house represents to me. This is where I lost hope, and where I found it again. Isn't it neat how God let it happen that way?"

"It does remind me of hope," said Lillian. "That's why I came here. Well, that's partly why. It reminds me of that day four years ago after I lost my family. Did I tell you I lost my husband and children just two weeks before I met you?"

"Only in very vague terms, dear."

"I was so sad back then, but when I stood here, I felt the promise of hope. It sounds silly. It's just a house. But it was the only beautiful thing I could see that day. Everything else around me seemed ugly and dark. I felt like I was being pulled under." She sighed, her voice just a whisper. "When I came here, I let myself experience beauty and remember my babies as they were, when they were alive, if only for a little while."

"It sounds like you are still sad, Lillian." She gazed at Lillian the way a mother might. "And rightly so. You can come here as often as you want, okay? I can even arrange it so you can be here after hours for more privacy."

Lillian's spirit brightened at the thought of such privacy to view the Rose House. "Thank you, Kitty. You are too kind."

"I like to share the Rose House. I'm not responsible for what some people see as the house's healing powers. I am of the opinion that God uses it to touch others the way He chooses, but I do feel obligated to make it available to the public."

"Is it hard to keep it available to the public when it's your private home?"

"Well, I don't live in it anymore. In some ways, it is only a house now. Special, yes, but I have a new home."

Lillian looked toward the main house. In size, it was more spectacular than the Rose House. She could see why Kitty might prefer it over the smaller house.

"I learned that a home is more than walls or even beautiful gardens. Without people who love us going in and out, walking down the halls, sitting at the kitchen table for a meal, a house is just an empty shell."

"You mean a family?" asked Lillian.

"Not just a family, but friends who come to visit. I need people who love me in my house."

Lillian thought of the home she had shared with her family before the accident. It had become a shell. Her new apartment was empty too, void of the squeals and laughter of her babies, the touch of Robert's hand on her back when he walked through the front door.

To Lillian, a home was not permanent. People in homes died. Her childhood family had died, and then her own family had died. Geena might as well be dead too.

No, Lillian thought. *My house is worse than an empty shell. It is full and overflowing with what is missing.*

LILLIAN KNOCKED AT THE OFFICE door of the B&B. The woman who greeted her was tall and dark with short-cropped hair that stood up in gelled spikes.

"I'm Lillian Diamon."

"Lillian! I was hoping to meet you today. Come in!" She led her through the side office and into a large living area.

The inside of the B&B was a mini art gallery that included paintings of vineyards, fruits and herbs, and people working the land. Some of them had been painted in the 1800s, others were modern. They hung in the open stairwell and throughout the living area. While Paige Tenney collected pamphlets for her, Lillian walked from frame to frame, wondering how the Tenneys had come to acquire such beautiful works of art.

"These paintings are really beautiful," she said.

"Thank you! Mark and I are collectors of sorts. We're mainly interested in art that depicts the local history and traditions. We aren't all that concerned about the worth of the paintings, although we have been offered a lot of money for some of them. I couldn't say exactly why."

"The photos are beautiful too! I bet this valley is a photographer's dream."

"Oh, it is. Look at these black and whites over here." She led Lillian to a wall next to a staircase with a worn oak banister. "These are roses photographed by three different artists in our area: Steiner, Smith, and Stillwagon. Aren't they amazing?"

Lillian studied the pictures. They were all closeups of various types of roses and were exquisite, even in black and white.

"And look at these," Paige invited. "These were all taken around the B&B by various artists. We often get photographers wanting to take photos from our tower room, and our requirement is that we get a photograph from them to hang here. Would you like to see the tower?"

"I'd love to." Lillian followed Paige up a spiral staircase that scaled three floors and spilled them out into a circular room with panoramic windows. As soon as they entered, a young man with a camera jumped up, startled by their sudden appearance.

Paige patted his arm. "I'm sorry, Charles! I didn't mean to scare you!"

He smiled and collected his equipment, saying he was finished for the day. On the way out, he paused to introduce himself to Lillian and then was gone.

Paige rattled off the history of the house and the tower. In 1870, the lady of the house had used the tower room for reading. Another occupant had been a writer who had crafted a number of poems that were available in the La Rosaleda historical archives. The children of the house had studied their lessons in the tower and practiced the fine arts of painting and music.

"So," Paige finished, "it's an inspiring room with a long tradition of artistic occupants."

Lillian turned in a full circle, taking in the view of the grounds, the town square, and the valley beyond. "What a great view."

They exited by way of a different staircase that led into the kitchen.

"This is the old servants' quarters," Paige explained. "Usually only our family uses it, but occasionally patrons get lost and find themselves in the kitchen."

As they entered the living room, Lillian stopped before an oil painting titled *The Rose House in Winter.* Just looking at its stark angles and colors chilled her. A coolness seemed to sweep through the room as she unconsciously rubbed her hands in front of her. Its subject was the Rose House, but the roses were trimmed back, and the house's brown siding looked tired through the twisting brambles. Shriveled black roses on naked branches with treacherous thorns seemed to tell intruders to stay away from the house until it leafed out again and the blooms unfolded to soften their branches.

"I've never seen this house without blooms on it," Lillian commented.

"Most people don't because tourism dies down during the winter season. That's why we bought the painting. Truman Clark really captured something in that painting, don't you think?"

"Truman Clark?" Lillian tried to remember where she had heard his name before.

"He's a local artist who paints mostly landscapes, but in the past four or five years he's been fascinated with painting the Rose House at Frances-DiCamillo. His paintings are quite distinct from the pop art you find in the gift shops."

"Why the Rose House?"

"I don't know. He doesn't give interviews, so people just speculate. Some people think it's because he's heartbroken about a lost love and the house's history soothes his spirit."

Lillian nodded. She understood having a broken heart. She wondered what had broken Truman Clark's heart. Lillian stared deeper into the painting. He certainly had shown a side of the house nobody else had captured. The house was still lovely in its unique way, but sad, maybe even a little angry, a feeling she could relate to.

Lillian peered closer and noticed that the ground looked wet, as if a rainstorm had just passed through. Worn paint showed through the bare brambles. The windows were dark and the house looked empty, no pretty lace curtains in the windows, no rocking chairs on the front porch. "It's an evocative painting." Lillian said. "Do you think having a broken heart makes an artist a better painter?"

Paige shrugged. "I suppose it can't hurt. I don't understand all the intellectual discussions by critics, but I know what I like, and I like Truman's paintings."

"Do you have any of his other works?" Lillian asked.

"There are several scattered about the house. Most of them aren't so dark. Feel free to browse. The last time he was here, he said he had been working on his masterpiece."

Lillian straightened. "So you know him personally?"

"Sure, I know several local artists. His paintings are also displayed in several studios in the Bay Area and beyond. He occasionally drops by the B&B and brings something he's been working on."

"Interesting. Has he finished his masterpiece?"

"Oh, I don't know. Last time I asked him, he blew me off, like he'd changed his mind or done something else with it. Who knows? He's pretty shy." Paige walked back toward the kitchen. "Would you like a cup of tea?"

"I can't stay," said Lillian. "But I would take a box of fruit tea for my cottage if you have one. I also wanted to see if I could rent a bike."

"Of course!" Paige exclaimed. "Let me show you where the bikes are. And there's no need to rent it. They're for guests to borrow." Paige led her outside and down a cobblestone path to a storage shed. She pointed out a red mountain bike, saying that the gears helped on the hills in the area.

"Oh, I don't want to ride far. Just a mile or two. I'm looking for a cruiser. I don't need gears."

Paige looked doubtful and reached for another bike. "Then try this." She rolled a bright red cruiser onto the lawn.

"That's perfect." Lillian smiled at the cushioned seat and slid her hands along the handlebars. It was just like Kitty's bike. "The basket is a plus. I can use it to carry a picnic lunch."

"That would be my department," said Paige. "My daughter, Gracie, and I will pack it up for you."

"I would appreciate that." Lillian turned to go and then hesitated. "You said you know quite a few artists in the area. Would you mind asking them something for me?"

Paige raised an eyebrow.

"Don't go out of your way." Lillian waived her hand in the air. "If you happen to see any of them, would you mind asking them about a painting?"

"Sure. Are you looking for someone to paint one?"

"Well, no. It's a painting of a woman and the Rose House by an anonymous artist. I want to purchase it, and I'm trying to find out who the artist is."

If Paige had heard of the painting, she didn't let on. "Sure, but I have to warn you. When a painting is anonymous, they usually protect the artist's identity."

"Well," said Lillian, "this particular painting is special to me, and I want to buy it, but the gallery curator won't sell."

"Louise Roy?"

"Yes. She was apologetic but adamant that it wasn't for sale, so I'm trying to find out who painted it."

"That must be some painting," Paige mused.

Lillian nodded but didn't explain that it was a portrait of herself, of her very private grief.

"Thanks for the bike," she said.

Lillian rolled the bike to her cottage and folded down the kickstand.

She stopped to sit on the porch swing for a few minutes and admired the beauty of the grounds and the magnificence of the main house. Her gaze scanned the lush vegetation of the yard and traveled to the lace curtains that peeked from the windows. She let her eyes scale the walls of the house to the tower until they came to rest on the windows, where a camera lens met her gaze.

She stopped swinging and stared. Could it be Charles, the man she'd met earlier in the tower? But she had seen him leave. She sprang from the swing and darted into the cottage, slamming the door behind her.

12

LILLIAN PEERED THROUGH THE lace-covered window to see if she was still being watched. The camera was now aimed away from her cottage. Her shoulders relaxed. "Get ahold of yourself, Lillian," she said out loud. It had probably just been one of Paige's artists at work.

As she made her way into the kitchen, a large spray of flowers greeted her from the café table. She leaned in to inspect the bouquet and found a card tucked between the blossoms. It read: *Lillian, Have a nice vacation. Love, Aunt Bren.*

A smile of delight spread across her face. She hadn't received flowers since Robert had died. He'd been so good at sending her flowers for special occasions and sometimes for no reason at all. It was one of the things she missed about him, one of the little ways she had known he thought of her.

She was so surprised Aunt Bren had sent them. She really was on vacation, she reminded herself. She should be relaxing instead of worrying and constantly dredging up sad memories.

She walked aimlessly through the cottage, mentally planning her week. In the bedroom, she ran her hands across the wedding ring quilt. She couldn't resist sitting down on the edge of it for just a moment.

Robert wouldn't have liked this room. The one time she'd tried to put one of her own quilts on their bed, he had hated it. Tracing a design along the quilt, she vaguely wondered if Geena still had the other quilt their mother had made.

Soft curtains billowed into the room, and with them, the giggles of a little child. Lillian's heart caught in her throat. So much like Sheyenne and Lee.

How much she missed her children and husband at times like this, when there was nothing in the quiet to distract her mind from rambling. Leaning her head on a pillow, she ran her hand over the other embroidered pillowcase.

Pink fruit blossoms were visible from where she lay. It was the same variety of fruit tree that had been visible from Robert's office window.

She watched through the bleary eyes of her memory as gauzy curtains stretched toward her. The faint fragrance of the cherry blossoms tickled her nose as she clutched the edge of her pillow. In Robert's sleep, he had sometimes clutched at the edges of her nightgown, as if he were in a nightmare.

She never knew what he had dreamed, but after his death, she had continued to wonder what had haunted his sleep. She often contemplated whether he had also known the sensation of being watched, whether he was the reason she had been watched after his death. Had his addiction to drugs, to a different way of life, caused him to endanger his own life and their children's?

Even if she still didn't understand how it had happened, she knew his addiction ran deep in their marriage and was what united him with her sister. The two had grown closer and closer as the years passed. She had noticed but chose not to see it as anything but innocent. Even now, she chose not to fully accept it without Geena's confirmation.

The mere thought of Robert's unfaithfulness to their marriage and family curled around her heart, squeezing at the emptiness, as if trying to get a new grasp.

When she heard a light tap at the door, she tried to rouse herself to answer it but decided the knock was only part of her imaginings. She closed her eyes against the light pouring through the window, welcoming the elusive sleep that had so often been stolen by her worry and grief.

The knock grew louder, followed by the rattle of the doorknob, but the next breeze that blew past swept her into old dreams of when she still had a family, of when she still had her husband and a sister to share her hopes with.

The knocking on the door ceased, and from her sleepy state, the retreating footsteps that faded down the pebbled path were only part of her dream.

13

"WHAT DO YOU WANT from her, Geena?" Chef George asked.

"None of your business," Geena said. "She's my sister."

George gestured toward the bulletin board on the wall of family snapshots. "Do you see that?"

"Yeah, it's a bulletin board."

"Yes. All these pictures are of our employees' family and friends. Lillian doesn't have any family, so she put up a photo of a place. Don't you think that's sad?"

Geena sighed, "Look, George, can you just tell me where she went on vacation?"

He shook his head. "No."

George's voice grew angry. "Do you have any idea what you did to her?"

Geena held both hands up. "Look, not that it's any of your business, but I am sorry for that. Just tell me where she is."

He raised one eyebrow. "No! I'm not going to help you. Lillian doesn't talk to me about her personal matters, but I know enough not to trust you. Please leave." He turned and left the room.

Geena brushed away a tear, picked up her purse, and grabbed the picture of the house draped with roses from the bulletin board. She realized that she'd seen that house before, either in a painting or on a postcard. Yes, it had been on a picture that Lillian sent to Aunt Brenda. She'd seen it once on Aunt Bren's refrigerator during a visit.

Looking at the Rose House photo made Geena's stomach ache. It really was sad, and the photo seemed so out of place. She felt responsible for Lillian's pain. That's why she had left in the first place, but now that she'd received the phone call, she simply had to talk to her sister.

She shivered, remembering the phone call, the horrible words he had said to her. She had just returned to her apartment from a counseling session at Safe Circle, feeling uncommonly happy for the first time in months, when the phone rang. She answered it without checking her caller ID, assuming it was Aunt Bren. His menacing words had assailed her ears, causing her legs to buckle as she dropped to the cold ceramic floor in her kitchen. She hadn't known if it was a prank call or real, but it forced her from self-imposed exile and inspired her to make up with Lillian.

Shrugging away the memory, Geena removed the photo from the bulletin board. It was a beautiful image. The entire house was engulfed with rose bushes. She thought it was quite beautiful. She didn't know the story of the house, but she knew it must have meant something to Lillian. She shoved the photo into her purse and slipped quietly out the back door.

She slid into her Pinto, the caller's voice invading her thoughts, describing the things he would do to her and to her sister. She wanted to call the police, but he had warned her not to. She had tried to convince herself that he was just a random scumbag who was trying to scare her, but she couldn't stop worrying. The bodies of Robert, Sheyenne, and Lee lying dead on Mosquito Road were still branded on her mind. She just couldn't dismiss the call as random. Even though the case had never been solved and was finally ruled an accident, she knew it hadn't been an accident at all.

His words kept running through her mind. "Have you seen your sister lately? She's so pretty."

14

THE CHURCH BELLS FROM THE mission rang out.

Church bells on a Saturday afternoon? Lillian wondered.

Birds sang in the trees outside her window, and the little girl's voice she had heard earlier called, "Mommy! Mommy! Look at this!"

She took in a deep breath and tried to clear her senses. Did she smell bacon and coffee? Lillian rushed to the window and saw people strolling in and out of the B&B with steaming coffee mugs and morning newspapers. Had she slept all night? She ran into the kitchen and retrieved a newspaper that had been pushed through the mail slot. It was the Sunday edition. There was also a menu, announcing that breakfast would be served in the dining room between 7:30 and 9:00 on Sunday morning.

She laughed, realizing her nap had lasted all afternoon and night. It was the first time in years that she had slept through the night. Dashing into the bathroom, she washed her face. A pink glow tinged her cheeks when she looked in the mirror. Her laughter bounced off the walls.

Lillian mentally planned her day while rushing to get ready. She glanced longingly at the claw-foot tub and an assortment of soaps and bathing potions but decided that a bubble bath would have to wait. Instead, she chose a lavender shower gel and reveled in the warmth of the water that rained down on her body from the old-fashioned showerhead.

On the cottage porch, her toe hit rubber. She raised her arms to keep her balance, remembering that she had left the bike in the yard the previous afternoon. She appreciated that somebody had brought it up to the porch.

The aroma of breakfast and a growling stomach pulled her down the path toward the kitchen. A half dozen people were sitting at wrought-iron café tables on the lawn, eating and chatting or reading the paper. In the dining room she found the bacon and coffee that had called her out of sleep, along with an array of scones, eggs, muffins, and fresh blueberries, strawberries, and melon wedges.

Paige was dressed in loose linen pants, a white T-shirt, and a red and white checkered apron. She ran from table to table, pouring coffee and making sure the diners had what they needed. Mark was flipping pancakes at the buffet table. Lillian started to take a seat, but before she could, a pixie-faced girl of about four ran over and stopped abruptly in front of her. The girl's smile tugged at the mothering part of Lillian's heart.

"Gracie!" called Paige. "Let Miss Diamon get her breakfast."

"You are Miss Diamond?" the girl asked. "Are you a diamond girl?"

"No, but you are!" Lillian chuckled.

"She loves to talk to the customers," Paige said, walking over to Lillian. "She's delightful!"

"And so are you today!" said Paige with a welcoming smile. "I wasn't sure you would make it to breakfast this morning. You were so tired yesterday. You got some sleep, I take it?"

"I did. I feel so rested, I might ride out to one of the vineyards and have a picnic."

"Ambitious! Would you like us to pack you a lunch?"

"I'd love that," Lillian laughed as Gracie tugged at her sleeve.

"Gracie, let Miss Diamon eat. Go ahead, Lillian. I'll get you a cup of coffee. Breakfast is buffet style, and Mark is serving up pancakes and omelets made to order."

"I'm tempted."

"Give in," Paige said. "The omelets are dreamy. Fluffy as clouds, huh, Gracie?"

Gracie nodded her head. "Yes, just like clouds!"

"Then I have to try them, if Gracie says so."

Gracie was right. By the time Lillian had finished her spinach-and-mushroom omelet, she wondered if she would be able to pedal the bicycle.

~◎~

While Lillian waited for her picnic basket, she took her mug of coffee and walked through the gardens. Her own garden had at one time been admired by friends and colleagues during dinner parties she had hosted with Robert. She felt at home among the flowers and greenery and realized how much she missed gardening. She vowed to make more of an effort to bring plants and flowers into her apartment.

Pausing in the shade under one of the magnolia trees, Lillian listened as Gracie's giggles reached her. It sounded so much like the laughter of Sheyenne and Lee in her own garden. She recalled how Sheyenne would often peek around a bush at Lee, stick out her tongue, and run away. Inevitably, Lee would chase after her, laughing heartily. Lillian wanted to embrace memories of them instead of keeping them at bay, but the memories also brought bittersweet feelings that were difficult to accept.

A giggle erupted from behind her, and Lillian spun around to see Gracie holding a basket that was nearly as large as she was. Her mom approached a few feet behind her. Lillian recognized the basket as the one that belonged to her cruiser.

"Hi!" Gracie said. "I brought you something, and it has a surprise in it!"

"A surprise?" Lillian said. "I can't wait! Thank you, Gracie!"

Paige helped Gracie set the basket on the ground and pulled from the basket a cooler, two bottles of water, and a picnic blanket.

"Can I go with you?" Gracie begged.

"Gracie," Paige chided, "Ms. Diamon wants some quiet time today."

"Is she in trouble?" Gracie asked, looking perplexed.

Lillian stifled a chuckle. "Your mom means that I need time to relax," she tried to explain. "Sometimes it's easier to relax when you're alone." She winked at Gracie.

"Oh." Gracie said, flapping her hands at her side.

"But maybe we can sit together one morning."

"Okay!" she cried.

"Let's go now, Gracie." Paige grabbed her daughter's hand as they turned to leave. "Have a nice day, Lillian."

"Paige!" a voice came from the house. They all turned to see Mark leaning out the kitchen window.

"Tru is here," he said.

Paige turned back to Lillian and sighed, "Must be Truman Clark. It never ends. Stuff to do."

"Truman? Do you mean the artist of those paintings in the house?"

"That's him." Paige turned to walk away.

What if Truman was the artist of *Beauty and the Beast Within*? Hadn't Paige said he was the local expert on painting roses? Lillian tried to remember where she had heard that name before Paige mentioned it to her.

"Paige, wait!"

Paige turned back. "What is it, Lillian? You look like you've just seen a ghost."

Lillian waived her hand like she was swatting at a fly. "Oh, it's really nothing. I just wondered if you would introduce us, so I can tell him how much I like his paintings."

Paige laughed. "Sure! He's not that famous yet, but Louise Roy at the gallery thinks he will be someday. Come on. He's probably heading upstairs to meet his student in the tower room."

Lillian's face drained of color as she remembered being watched from the tower room the day before. "You know, actually, I don't have to meet him right now. I need to go."

Paige looked at her quizzically.

"Could you, uh—," Lillian stuttered. "Could you just ask him if he has heard of a painting called *Beauty and the Beast Within*?"

"The one you want to purchase?"

Lillian nodded.

"I've seen that painting," Paige said. "I visit the gallery almost every week, and sometimes I trade my paintings for theirs. They wouldn't let me trade for that one."

Lillian tried not to look overly interested. "That's strange."

"Yes, it is. You want me to ask Truman about it?"

"Would you mind asking him if he knows who painted it?"

"Sure," she answered, "I don't mind at all."

"Thanks," Lillian said, turning quickly and walking toward her cottage, where the shiny red bike waited. She glanced over her shoulder toward the house, hoping to catch a glimpse of Truman Clark. She was rewarded as he walked out onto the front porch to meet Paige. She couldn't see his face clearly, but she watched him place a somewhat battered-looking fedora on his head.

When she rode her bike past the front porch a few minutes later, he tipped his hat. As she waved back, she drove straight into the mailbox. The next thing she knew she was sitting on the driveway, picking gravel out of her palms. The picnic lunch was scattered on the ground. Tears pooled in her eyes, more from embarrassment than from pain, as Truman and Paige ran toward her.

"Oh my goodness, Lillian! Are you okay?" Paige asked.

"What a klutz I am."

Truman took her hand and helped her to her feet.

"Thank you," she said, as she found herself looking into blue eyes set in a tanned face and a smoothly shaven head. She studied his face. *Where have I seen him before?* Something about the intensity of his gaze made her feel uneasy.

Trying to laugh at herself, she brushed debris from her clothes. "I guess I lost my equilibrium." She swayed, but Truman steadied her with his hand, which sent shivers up her arm. His eyes seemed to drink her in as she stiffened, backing away from his touch.

"Are you okay?" His voice was gentle and kind.

She nodded without looking at him and turned toward Paige, who offered her arm. They walked toward the house together.

Inside, Paige gave her alcohol swabs and showed her to the bathroom. By the time she returned, the room was empty. Outside she found her bicycle sitting beside the porch, its picnic basket reassembled.

"Rats!" she whispered to herself, half relieved and partly disappointed. Asking Truman about the painting would have to wait. She gingerly walked the bicycle out to the end of the driveway, still smarting from the humiliation of such a clumsy accident.

Lillian climbed carefully onto the bike and peddled toward town. She wanted to visit the gallery, hoping to speak to Louise Roy and make her understand why she wanted the painting so badly. If Louise recognized her image in the painting, maybe she would change her mind and sell it to her. At the very least, she hoped Louise would tell her who the artist was.

After a few turns around the square, she parked her bike in a rack near the fountain and strolled past the shop windows, peering in. She realized that since it was Sunday, many people were in church, so most of the stores wouldn't open until 11:00. It had been years since she'd been to church. She hardly thought about it anymore on Sunday mornings, so it hadn't dawned on her that the town would be closed down.

Cutting back across the square, she walked to the gallery and tried the door, not surprised when it didn't open. Leaning close to the window, Lillian shaded her eyes and peered through the glass. She stood on tiptoes but couldn't see *Beauty and the Beast Within* anywhere among the displays.

Her cell phone rang, and she found herself staring in shock at the number. It was Geena, after all this time. Over her brief longing for her sister, she pressed the End button, programmed the phone to vibrate, and shoved it back in her pocket.

Instead of waiting for the gallery to open, she would take a ride in the countryside. She would pretend that Geena had not called, but the phone vibrated in her pocket. She pressed the silence button and walked away from the gallery.

⁂

As Lillian stepped off the sidewalk to cross the road, she walked past a battered blue pickup that was parked in front of the gallery. The window rolled down, and her heart skipped when she recognized the driver as Truman Clark.

She shrugged off the funny feeling of excitement in her chest and decided that she had horrible luck. Maybe if she continued walking, as if she hadn't seen him…

"Excuse me, Miss—," he said.

Acid rushed into her stomach as his blue eyes locked with hers in a way that made her feel as if all her secrets were revealed. She inched closer to the window but didn't answer.

His gaze faltered. "Miss Diamon—" He cleared his throat. "This is going to sound really strange, but would you have lunch with me?"

Her eyes widened. How long had it been since she had been to lunch with a man? "I don't know you, Mr. Clark, and I already have plans today. Thanks anyway."

He looked down at the steering wheel, and then twisted his mouth as though choosing his next words carefully. For a moment, she felt sorry for him, but he was being rather forward, considering they had only just been introduced.

His gaze met hers. She felt dizzy. *The bike wreck must have short-circuited my common sense or I wouldn't still be standing here,* she thought.

"I understand. It's just that when we met this morning, I remembered you from somewhere. Then I saw you just now and thought—" His voice trailed off.

"Me too," she said, keeping her voice noncommittal. "I recognized you too, but I don't recall from where."

"So you will have lunch with me?" His eyes sparkled.

She smiled. "Actually, I do have plans, but maybe another time. That is, if I can ask you a question."

"Sure," he said.

"Since you are an artist, you must be familiar with the gallery. Do you know anything about the painting of the Rose House called *Beauty and the Beast Within*?"

He cocked his head as if he were trying to remember.

"This is going to sound silly," she said, "but I want to buy that painting, and the gallery is reluctant to sell it to me. Would you happen to know who painted it?"

"Well, it could be any artist," he said matter-of-factly. "A lot of us have painted the Rose House, but I can't tell you who painted it."

She frowned. "That's too bad."

"Why do you ask?"

When he tried to meet her eyes, she concentrated on toying with the cross around her neck. "I'm just drawn to it," she said. "It's so beautiful that I would love to own it. I thought maybe the artist could help me out, maybe convince the gallery to sell it to me."

He looked at her as if she had said something amusing.

"Had you heard of it?" she asked.

He drummed his fingers on the steering wheel. "*Beauty and the Beast Within?*"

"Yes."

"A very nice painting, no?"

"Flawless," she replied. "The way the artist painted the house is amazing." She wished she knew more about art to describe what she felt. "I mean, the Rose House and the landscape around it is stunning."

"What about Beauty? The image of the woman?"

"Very nice," she said, careful not to let her emotions show.

"I think the image of the woman is quite flawless," he said. "In fact, my favorite part of the painting is how the woman's beauty is more radiant than the Rose House itself. The only thing is, the woman looks so sad. When I look at the painting, it makes me wonder what she has suffered."

His eyes pinned her, and she wasn't sure what to say. Was he asking her a question? "I guess painters can do that," she said.

"Sometimes they don't have to, if their subjects wear their hearts on their sleeves."

"Hmm, then maybe it's all in the eyes of the artist."

He nodded. "Probably, but maybe the artist sees Beauty as she truly is. Maybe that's why she's so stunning."

She looked toward the gallery, wondering if anyone could see her as beautiful. But what did the artist mean by the Beast within? Her sadness? Or was it something more?

"Maybe," continued Truman, "the artist sees her as a full person, and not just her shell of beauty."

"Then why did he name her Beauty?" She drew in a deep breath, suddenly unnerved by the direction of the conversation. The artist had captured something she hadn't meant to show, which was exactly what made her curious about the painting.

Again the intensity of his eyes made her feel dizzy. Instinctively she reached out for the truck door to balance herself. His hand slid over hers; its warmth traveled through her fingertips. She felt her face flush.

The palm of his hand felt slightly uneven, like fine sandpaper. His hands weren't rough like her father's had been from working outside every day. Nor was it soft like Robert's doctor hands had been. Obviously, he didn't spend all day indoors with his paint brushes, nor did he work the land all day for a living.

"Are you okay?" he asked. "You look sort of wobbly. Maybe your fall earlier rattled you more than you know."

She stared at his hand, still resting on hers. "I'm fine," she said, realizing that she didn't want him to remove it. And he didn't.

Suddenly uncomfortable, she pulled her hand from beneath his. She reached in her pocket for her phone, pretending to be interested in her missed calls. She saw that Geena hadn't called back again, and then she glanced up at Truman. "Just checking to make sure I didn't miss a call."

He nodded. "So lunch is out of the question, huh?"

"I—I don't even know you," she laughed.

He sighed. "Technically, we've met."

"You mean this morning at the B&B? Do we have to count that?"

"Let's not," he said. "How about we count this as our first meeting."

She nodded. "I like that much better."

He placed his hat on his head and tipped it slightly forward. "Nice to meet you, Lillian Diamon."

"Likewise, Truman Clark." She stepped back from the truck and said good-bye. The engine rumbled to life. "It's too bad, though," he said over the sound of the motor.

"What is?"

"That we don't already know each other. If we did, I could get you to have lunch with me." He winked. "Maybe I'll see you around."

"I'm only here for a week," she said.

"I know where you're staying." He tipped his hat and shifted into reverse.

"Maybe we could have breakfast at the B&B." The words tumbled out without warning.

A grin broke across his face. "I'll see you in the morning!" he said and pulled away. As he turned the corner, he gave her a salute.

She waved back, staring after the truck. "I said *maybe*!" she called after him halfheartedly, but he was too far away to hear her mock protest.

15

A CHING-CHING CHIMED FROM behind her once, then a second time. Lillian spun around to see Kitty riding her bike on the sidewalk.

"Good morning!" Kitty called as she braked to a stop and climbed off.

Lillian noticed she had tied together the hem of her dress, apparently to keep it from tangling in her bike chain. It looked ridiculous, but Lillian had to admit it was practical if nothing else.

"I see you've met Truman. Nice boy."

"Yes, nice guy. He looks so familiar though, like I've seen him before. And his name seems familiar too."

"You admired his painting when you and I first met, remember? We were in my office at the tasting room, and you said you would look for his paintings in Sacramento."

Lillian nodded, suddenly remembering the way the painting in Kitty's office had affected her. "Yes! You know, I didn't even think of him again after leaving La Rosaleda. I was so caught up with everything else going on in my life at the time."

"I see," said Kitty. "But it looks like now you will have opportunities to actually talk to him about his work."

"Maybe so," said Lillian, not wanting to give Kitty the wrong impression.

"So we're both going to be late to church today?" asked Kitty.

Lillian cocked her head. "Late for church?"

"You are going, aren't you?"

"Well, it's not that I wouldn't love to, but I wouldn't know where to go." She smiled, recalling the church she grew up attending. If only she could find the same joy it brought to Pastor and Aunt Bren. "If I did go," she said, "I think I would just walk down Main Street and find the church with the loudest singing. That's what church was like when I was growing up."

Kitty chuckled. "Oh Lillian, I am so glad to see you are in good spirits! I hope you are enjoying your vacation."

Lillian enjoyed talking to Kitty. "Did you deliver the flowers yesterday?"

"I sure did! You should have seen the looks on their faces. Have you been to the gallery yet?"

"I have, once. There are some stunning paintings in there. And the quilts are so lovely, like tapestries."

Kitty smiled. "Well, they are a bit different, aren't they?"

"They tell stories. That's what I like about them."

"That is sweet, dear. You know, I'd forgotten that the gallery doesn't open until later this morning. Silly me. I'd hoped to stop in to see Louise before church. She called to tell me about a new painting that was donated anonymously, but she thinks we might be able to guess who painted it."

Lillian raised her eyebrows. "Do you work at the gallery?"

Kitty laughed heartily. She put her hand on Lillian's shoulder and said, "Yes, dear, it's mine!"

Lillian's surprised laughter joined Kitty's. "Of course it is. And why wouldn't it be? You have so many talents. Why wouldn't you own a gallery?"

Lillian paused. "I saw that painting," Lillian said, staring down at her sandals. "*Beauty and the Beast Within*, right?"

"Right! And what did you think of it, dear?"

"I think it's beautiful. That's how I remember the Rose House." Lillian wondered if Kitty would recognize her in the painting. She decided not to mention it yet, not until after Kitty had seen it.

"Well, I can't wait to see it, but now I have to meet my husband for the meeting."

"I thought you were going to church," Lillian said.

"You fit in so well around here that for a second I forgot you aren't a local. It's a Sunday meeting held at my vineyards. It is church!"

"At Frances-DiCamillo?"

"Sure!" Kitty said. "Tourists, vineyard workers, and locals come to our outdoor chapel during the summer. We began by hosting outdoor plays, like *The Taming of the Shrew,* and people would bring picnic lunches. Then someone got the idea of having church too. My husband thought it was a great idea. He is the pastor."

"What a wonderful idea to have church in such a beautiful place."

Kitty's eyes sparkled. "Would you like to come?"

Lillian hesitated. How could she explain to someone like Kitty the feeling she had that God had taken her babies from her? She hadn't been able to sit in church since the accident.

"We sing loudly," Kitty tempted.

Lillian laughed.

"And it's nondenominational. We all just meet under the same canopy of trees and sing about Jesus."

"Maybe," Lillian said, "but I made plans to be alone today." She nodded toward the square. "I borrowed a bike from the Tenneys and thought I'd ride around and see the countryside."

"It's not good to be alone too much," Kitty said. She focused on the bike Lillian had parked in the square. "Oh, you got one of the Tenneys' cruisers." She patted the bike seat beside her. "I love mine. Speaking of which, I better get on it and go!"

Kitty seemed to be in pain when she climbed on the bike, so Lillian offered her hand for support. "Oh, thank you, dear. I know it looks like I'm going to fall, but so far I haven't. Let's have tea soon, okay?"

"I would love that, Kitty."

"Call me and we'll schedule it!"

"Great!" said Lillian. "I would love to hear what you think of that new painting."

"I'll let you know," she said. "I better go. I'm so late for church."

"Of course. I'm sorry to have kept you."

"Don't be sorry, dear. It's not your fault I'm a chatterbox. You have a good day now."

She patted Lillian's arm before she coasted away on her bike. Lillian placed her hand over the warmth that lingered. She tried to remember the painting she'd seen in Kitty's office four years earlier.

What was it Paige had said about how Truman painted his emotions in his paintings? Her mind was so occupied by the painting that she didn't look before she crossed the road to retrieve her bike and found herself face to face with an oncoming scooter. She screamed as it swerved and screeched to a stop beside her.

"Miss Diamon! I'm so sorry!" It was the photographer she'd met in the tower at the B&B. He seemed younger than she remembered.

"You almost hit me!"

"I'm so sorry," he said. "Are you okay?"

He left his scooter parked in the middle of the road and followed her as she stepped onto the sidewalk.

"Are you okay?"

"I'm fine. I didn't mean to yell at you. You just scared me."

"I know. I'm so sorry," he apologized again and climbed on his scooter to leave.

"Hey, Charles!" Lillian interrupted his departure. "Do you paint as well as take pictures, or are you strictly a photographer?"

"I'm just a photographer. It's all I can do to keep track of my camera equipment," he said, nervously. "It would be hard to carry all that painting stuff in my backpack."

"I see. Well, do you know any photographers who also paint?"

He looked up as he thought about it. "Maybe. A few, but I'm not sure." He looked at the ground as a flush spread to his face.

"Thanks. I'll let you go now."

"Not a problem, miss."

"Strange guy," Lillian muttered as he sped away. She walked to her bike and leaned on the handlebars, suddenly tired from her second accident scare of the morning. *Who speeds through the square on a Sunday morning?* Then again, she reminded herself, she had walked into the street without looking. She wasn't usually a walking disaster. That was her sister's department.

Determined to get through the rest of the day without any more disasters, she climbed onto her bike.

16

GEENA PICKED UP LILLIAN'S photograph of the rose-covered house and looked closely. The bed creaked beneath her as she sat down. The odor from the mattress and dingy walls still stung her nostrils, reminding her of a bar, even though she had removed the bedding and replaced the sheets with some she had brought in her suitcase. Since getting clean at Safe Circle, clean had taken on a whole new meaning for her. Some days she found herself behaving more like her sister. She pulled an antibacterial wipe from her purse and cleaned her hands before picking up her cell and dialing.

Aunt Bren answered the call. Her voice sang across the line. "Geena! I am so glad you called, honey."

"Hi, Aunt Bren," Geena said, feeling suddenly comforted by the familiar drawl. As they talked, Geena counted her cash and placed it back in its envelope. Two thousand dollars wouldn't last long. She needed a new job, but first she needed to get to Lillian.

"Pastor and I have been so worried about you. We wish you had stayed to visit for more than three days. We could tell something was wrong when you were here, and you haven't called for a month since you left. Are you okay?"

"I'm a ton better, Aunt Bren. I have most of my energy back."

"Honey, is there something we can do to help you? Can you just tell us what is bothering you?"

Geena felt tears burning her eyelids and swept a finger across her eyes. She wanted to tell Aunt Bren about the attack but was afraid that

Aunt Bren would blame her for being in the wrong place at the wrong time, for working in a bar where such things were possible.

"It's nothing, Aunt Bren. You did help me. I went back to Wild Hollow to be near people who love me, and I got that."

"But three days isn't enough time for us, honey."

Geena's chest felt heavy, and she resisted the urge to hang up. She'd learned so much about herself in her counseling sessions at Safe Circle. One skill she was working on was not pushing her loved ones away.

"Maybe I'll visit again soon," she told Aunt Bren and smiled when she heard the relieved sigh. She had to admit that it was nice to be missed.

"We love you, honey. You and Lillian will always be our girls."

At the mention of Lillian, Geena remembered the reason for her call.

"Aunt Bren, what was it you told me about that picture on the fridge? You know, the one of the house all covered with roses?"

"Oh that! Lillian sent it to me a few years ago. She said it was called the Rose House or something or other. She said she'd visited it and that it had made her feel more hopeful. Why do you ask?"

"I was just wondering. Why do you think it made her feel that way?"

"It was something about the story behind the house. She said it had belonged to a woman who made a big mistake some thirty years ago. Something about a secret."

"What was it? What was the secret?"

"I don't know, honey. Lillian was short on words back then, and I never asked her."

"Aunt Bren, please. I know you talk to her."

"Yes, I do, and you both make me promise not to say anything to the other. I'm tired of it, to be honest."

"I'm sorry, Aunt Bren, but I need to talk to her."

"Oh, honey, I'm so glad to hear that. I hope you two will patch things up."

"That's part of it, but there are other things too."

"Like what, Geena?"

"Just some things I'll tell you later."

"More secrets?"

"It isn't like that, Aunt Bren. It's hard to explain. I went to her place in Sacramento, and she wasn't there, so I went to the restaurant where she works. That grumpy Chef George told me she was on vacation but wouldn't tell me where she'd gone."

"That man does seem grumpy, doesn't he? I always wondered why a man would want to work in a kitchen anyway."

"Oh, Aunt Bren," Geena laughed, "you are so old-fashioned."

"I guess I am."

"You are right about him being a grump. He was so rude and treated me like I was a horrible person."

"He said that?"

"Same as," she said. "He probably has reason to think it, but I still needed to talk to Lillian. To make a long story short, I took Lillian's photo of the Rose House off her employee bulletin board and wondered if she might be there on vacation."

"You mean in La Rosaleda?"

Geena smiled to herself. "Thank you, Aunt Bren."

"Don't mention it, honey. Just make up with your sister so we can all be a family again, okay?"

"Yeah," answered Geena, "that would be nice, wouldn't it?"

"Pastor and I will pray for you, dear."

"It can't hurt."

"Geena, did you say you got that photo off the bulletin board at her work?"

"Yeah," Geena said.

"That's—" She heard Aunt Bren's voice catch.

"Aunt Bren, are you crying?"

"Oh," she sniffed into the phone. "It's just so sad, isn't it? That she would hang that up instead of pictures of family?"

"Yeah." Geena's voice grew very soft. "It's sad."

"She needs us," said Aunt Bren. "She needs you."

Geena's hand started to shake. She laid the photo on the bedside table, wishing she could have a drink. There was a lot Aunt Bren didn't know, but she had such an uncanny ability to see so much.

17

*L*ILLIAN STRUGGLED UP THE HILL on her bicycle and made a mental note to get back in shape after her vacation. She had been riding with no goal in mind, just enjoying the scenery, when she heard singing. She coasted to a stop and listened. A chorus of voices carried out to the road.

"My, they do sing loud," she said. The voices rang out in a refrain of "Amazing Grace" that reminded her of her old church back in Wild Hollow. A sentimental longing rose up.

Curious, she steered her bike onto the driveway of Frances-DiCamillo. She should have accepted Kitty's friendly invitation, if nothing else just to be nice. She coasted down one of the paths and found a small gathering of people standing on a sweep of green grass beneath a canopy of trees.

The pastor, a man who looked to be in his late sixties, stood beside Kitty as they led the congregation in the next song, "In the Sweet By and By," again reminding her of their little country church in Oklahoma.

Lillian parked her bike beside a tree and stood behind a group of older ladies. She tried to join the singing, but her voice cracked with emotion, so she just closed her eyes and let the words pour over her. The music reminded her of attending church even before Pastor and Aunt Bren had taken her in. She recalled singing the gospel hymns with her parents, when Jesus still seemed real to her, holding her mom's hand on one side and Geena's on the other.

Lillian whispered the words now, feeling a peace blanket her heart. She focused on the songs, immersing herself in the moment.

After the singing, Kitty came over and spread a quilt on the grass for them to share.

"So glad you came," she whispered to Lillian as her husband began to speak to the group.

His words rang of sincerity and the sermon was brief. Lillian had to concede that sometimes a short sermon could say as much as a lengthy one.

After more singing, Kitty joined her husband at the podium and announced that there would be coffee and tea served, and everyone followed her to a set of picnic tables in the garden.

Though she felt a bit shy, Lillian made an effort to get acquainted with the others. She poured herself a cup of herb tea in a porcelain teacup and spent a few minutes walking among the people, overhearing snippets of conversation as she studied the garden. It was such a magical place, and she was happy to just enjoy the moment.

She followed a path that spiraled through the greenery, segmenting several garden rooms. The bursts of color drew her eye. She was studying a shrub that had been pruned into a peacock shape when she felt a gentle hand on her shoulder. She flinched and spun around, finding herself face to face with Truman.

He placed his hand at her elbow to steady her wobbling teacup. "Hello, Lillian," he said.

Tucking some stray hair behind one ear, she smiled but couldn't think of what to say. The feel of his hand set her arm to trembling. She softly pulled her elbow free, careful not to spill her tea. He placed his hand in his pocket, not seeming to notice her reticence.

"I didn't know you'd be in church today."

"I didn't know either." She shrugged. "I was riding by and heard the singing."

"What did you think of the service?"

She studied his face, her eyes tracing a small scar along his cheek. "It reminds me of a church I attended as a child."

"You aren't new to church, then."

"Oh no. I was raised by a pastor and his wife. Technically, I was a preacher's kid. And you?"

"I'm new. New, at least, compared to most people here," he explained.

He would have scored points with Aunt Bren by running into her at church, Lillian thought. She could smell his cologne, something leather, as he stepped closer, but before she could fully breathe in the masculine scent, she heard Kitty's voice calling from the center of the garden.

Turning around, she saw Kitty waving her handkerchief. "Attention! Attention!"

Kitty delivered announcements about needing volunteers for a potluck and meals for a pregnant single mother.

"She is so sweet," Lillian whispered. "Yesterday, I helped her tend the roses on the Rose House. Or maybe she told me to," Lillian laughed. "We worked together for a while, and I thoroughly enjoyed it."

"That sounds like Kitty, always trying to find a way to help people."

"I was helping her," Lillian reminded him.

"Believe me," Truman said quietly, "she was helping you. You just didn't realize it."

Lillian shook her head, wondering what he meant. "Then you know her well?"

"I do. We go way back. I was painting the Rose House before anyone had seen my work. You might say that Kitty and Blake gave me my first break when they bought my first piece."

"You mean the one in the office at the tasting room?"

"That's the one," he said. "You've seen it?"

She nodded, smiling to herself at how small her world seemed to be getting. "It's been a while, but I've seen it. I remember that it was lovely. Stunning, actually."

"Thank you," he said. "So what do you say to lunch, Miss Diamon?"

"Lunch? I already said no. We barely know each other." She wished he would stop asking so she wouldn't have to argue with herself about how silly she was to be melting every time he looked at her. She was still trying to get used to the idea that she, a widow who often still felt married, could be so attracted to a man. Especially Truman Clark.

He placed his hand on her elbow. His voice was so low she had to lean in to hear. "But now we go to the same church."

She tried to hold back a smile. "But this isn't really my church. I'm just on vacation."

"Some of the best romances have started during vacations."

"And ended," she said sagely.

"Then there is no pressure. We will just live for today." He winked. "Or the week. How long will you be in town?"

"Until next Sunday," she said, and wondered about why she was so drawn to Truman. She couldn't deny there was an attraction between them.

She looked up at his eyes, so sincere and welcoming. He wasn't offering to whisk her away and marry her, nor did he seem to be suggesting a tryst. He seemed to be offering something slightly above friendship with no strings attached.

As tempted as she was, she decided to slow things down just a little. "We already have a breakfast date," she said. "What if we start there?"

She didn't miss the disappointment on his face, but he didn't push. Instead, he offered her a ride back to the B&B.

"Honestly," she said, "I feel like riding my bike."

He shrugged. "Then let me walk you to the parking lot."

"Okay."

Now that she'd joined him in a flirtatious game, she wondered if she was really ready to play it out. The pain of Robert's death and the secrets he'd hidden from her had left her feeling raw and vulnerable.

He offered his arm, and she walked with him across the grass toward her bicycle, enjoying the warmth of his hand as it pressed her palm against his arm. She was sure in that moment that God had created a man's arm for a woman. Truman reached for her bike and walked it toward the parking lot where he had parked his truck.

Lillian found herself hoping that Truman was not the artist who had painted *Beauty and the Beast Within*. She wanted everything about this moment to be real. She needed a clean slate, to let her secrets unfold when she was ready to trust him.

18

S"SHE IS SO PRETTY," he said to himself as he worked in the dim light of the photo lab, developing pictures. His teacher would be so proud. He remembered the rule about taking pictures of the guests without their permission. This would have to be an exception.

His tongs moved an 8 x 10 sheet around in the bathing solution until the photo deepened and clearly revealed that rare smile he'd seen only a few times. He pulled it from the solution and hung it to dry. In the picture she was bending forward near a weeping willow, talking to a little girl. He'd cut the child out of the photo so that anyone viewing the picture would wonder who was lucky enough to be the recipient of such a smile. In the other half of the photo, he cropped Lillian out and kept the little girl. Her name was Gracie, and she was pretty too. He would frame the two photos side by side.

As he hung the second photograph, he imagined what his teacher would think when he saw them. These might be the photographs that set him apart from the other photographers around La Rosaleda.

He wondered momentarily what the woman would think if he showed her the photo. He didn't want anyone else to see it, only her.

He wondered how he would get her alone to show her his precious photographs. He was sure she would love them. They were his best photos yet. Maybe Gracie could help him. He smiled. It was a good idea.

$\mathcal{A}$T THE B&B, LILLIAN parked the bicycle on her front porch and followed her nose to the kitchen, where she found a large plate of freshly baked oatmeal cookies. Paige sat at one of the café tables, sipping tea.

"Tea?" Paige asked. The aroma of mint mingled in the air with the cookies.

Lillian nodded. "Do you have any Earl Grey or an herb tea?"

"Of course!" Paige stood to make Lillian's tea. When she returned, she looked sheepishly at Lillian and said, "There's something I want to ask you, Lillian."

"Me?"

"Yes, but don't laugh at me. Promise?"

"Of course not."

"It's almost too silly, but I have to ask," Paige said.

"Drop it on me."

"Well, I went over to the gallery today and saw the painting you told me about."

"The one I want to buy?" Lillian tried to hide her excitement.

"It's fascinating, isn't it?"

"It is," said Lillian evenly. "That's why I want to buy it."

"The lady in the painting could be your twin," Paige said. "Did you pose for it?"

"I did not."

"Then how—actually, who—," Paige stammered.

"It's a long story. I don't know who painted it, or even how they knew about that day." Lillian told her how she had first seen the painting in the gallery. She hesitated for a moment, and then told her the condensed version of how she had visited the Rose House soon after becoming a widow and losing her children.

"I wasn't sure that it was me in the painting until now. I was pretty sure, but hearing it from someone else confirms it."

"You've been through a lot, Lillian, and you still seem so together. I had no idea."

Lillian sighed. "I'm better now, but discovering the painting shook me up. It sort of seemed like an invasion of privacy, as if I was spied on."

"I can see where you are coming from, but most of the artists I know are intelligent, good people. I can't even imagine them secretly watching someone and then painting them."

Would anyone who has never been in my shoes really understand? Lillian wondered.

"But it was a private moment," Lillian said. "I thought I was alone."

Paige nodded. "I guess I can understand that. It's like someone read your diary, right?"

"Yes. And then published it in the newspaper for everyone to read."

"Yeah, but it's just the local paper, not the *New York Times*. And not everybody reads the newspaper," Paige teased.

Lillian laughed, realizing that her insecurities sounded trivial. After all, only the people who knew her well would ever recognize her in the painting. "Okay, I see your point, but it's still an invasion of privacy."

Paige gave her a playful look. "I think it's kind of romantic."

"What?"

"Romantic!" she repeated. "This kind of thing always happens to other people, never to me."

"But you're married!"

"I know," Paige laughed, "but Mark and I are so busy. We never have the time for any kind of romantic mystery."

"You are lucky, believe me," said Lillian.

"Why do you want to know who painted it?"

"So I can confront him...or her."

"Oh, it's not a she," said Paige. "It has to be a man. Seriously, I don't know any female artists around here who paint the Rose House. Come on, admit it. You find it a bit romantic to think somebody studied you that closely and thought you were worthy of becoming art."

Lillian tried to maintain her seriousness about it. Paige didn't seem to understand what it all meant to her. "I never thought of it as romantic."

Paige laughed. "Maybe the artist just thought you were pretty. I doubt he ever imagined you would see the painting, much less recognize yourself. What are the chances of that happening?"

"I don't know, but it did."

"Yes, it did, so it must have a divine purpose."

Lillian was not so sure about the divine purpose, but she silently admitted to herself that maybe she was just a bit flattered by the painting.

Suddenly Gracie bounced into the kitchen. "Hi, Diamond Girl. Did you like your surprise?" She reached up to hug Lillian.

"Did you have a good nap?" said Paige.

"Yes, Mommy, I did. And did Miss Diamon like her surprise?"

"I loved the brownies," Lillian told her. "They were the best brownies I've ever had." Lillian plucked another oatmeal cookie from the tray. "The brownies were even better than your mom's cookies."

Gracie beamed and leaned against her mother.

"In fact," Lillian said, "next time I go on a picnic, can I have another surprise?"

"Yes!" said Gracie, who whispered something in her mom's ear. She clapped her hands when her mom said yes.

"This has been fun," said Paige, "but I need to get back to work." She shooed Gracie over to another table where there was a set of crayons and drawing paper.

"Don't worry about the painting, Lillian." She wiped their crumbs from the table. "Do you mind if I help you figure out who the artist is? I love a good mystery."

"Sure," said Lillian, "why not?"

"Good! This is right up my alley. I have a feeling I can narrow it down to a few artists I know."

Lillian's heart quickened at the thought of knowing the artist's identity, and Paige's notions of romance were intriguing. Even though she didn't agree with Paige's silly ideas, it certainly brought a little bit of whimsy to the situation.

20

THE NEXT MORNING, LILLIAN woke to a rap on the door. She threw back the covers and glanced at the clock. It was nine.

"Truman!" Lillian jumped out of bed and rushed to the door. She stopped suddenly, realizing that if it was Truman, she didn't want him to see her with bed head and wearing her jammies. She pressed her ear against the door.

"Who is it?"

"Paige!"

Lillian opened the door. "Don't tell me," she said. "Truman Clark is waiting for me."

"He's been waiting for an hour."

Lillian placed both hands on her cheeks. "I can't believe it," she said. "Since I woke up so early yesterday, I assumed I would wake up at the same time today."

"The church bells don't sound until noon on weekdays."

"I know you're busy, Paige, but would you mind asking him if he can wait for just a few more minutes? I feel so bad. Does he need to get to work?"

Paige shrugged. "He's an artist. He sets his own schedule."

Lillian laughed. "I'll be right over. Thank you so much for waking me. I'm sorry you had to come after me."

Paige smiled. "I didn't mind."

Fifteen minutes later, Lillian found Truman sitting at one of the outdoor tables, a cooler near his feet. He stood to greet her, taking off his hat and fiddling with it. "Hi, sleepyhead."

Lillian came to a stop in front of him, hoping she had remembered to put mascara on both eyes. "Good morning," she said, smiling groggily.

He reached for the cooler. "I hope you don't mind, but since we missed breakfast"—he winked—"I took the liberty of asking Paige to make us a picnic lunch. Will you do me the honor of being my lunch date?"

"That depends," teased Lillian. "Did Gracie put a surprise in the picnic?"

"That she did," he assured her. "She told me herself."

Soon, she was climbing into his truck, all of her reservations tucked away with the questions about the painting. Looking around the cab, she noticed the dashboard was littered with scraps of paper and pencils.

The engine roared to life and he drove past the town square, turned left, and headed down a road lined with vineyards and wineries. The day was warm and they rode with the windows rolled down.

As they rounded a bend in the road, the valley suddenly opened before them, and the vines blanketing the hills tempted Lillian to let her guard down. She leaned toward Truman, resting her weight on one arm in the center of the seat.

"So, Lillian, what brings you to La Rosaleda?"

Lillian almost told him about seeing herself in the painting but decided to wait.

"I needed to get away from my job, and I love how peaceful it is here." She paused, considering how much she should say. "I lost my family four years ago in a car accident, so that's why I'm here alone."

She looked out the window, waiting for his pity. She glanced sideways at his profile, noticing how his chest rose and fell with each breath. She studied his shirt buttons as she waited for his response.

"I didn't mean to be intrusive." He glanced at her. "You must be a strong person, Lillian."

She had seen a lot of pity in other people's eyes over the years, but she had never seen the compassion she now saw in Truman's. It reached inside of her and grabbed so tightly that a small gasp escaped her throat.

Afraid he had noticed, she turned her face away into the breeze, hiding tears that threatened to spill. The temperature cooled noticeably as they descended into a deeper part of the valley where trees bordered the vineyards. They were near water, she could tell. Images of fishing in a creek near their childhood home with Geena flashed into her mind. She pushed the thoughts away. Memories of Geena had intruded more and more lately, and she found it frustrating. She turned back toward Truman.

"So, that's my baggage."

He nodded slowly and she couldn't figure out what was going on in his mind.

She picked at a piece of lint on her pants and tried not to feel awkward.

"Okay," he said and pulled the car to the side of the road. He parked under a huge shade tree. "I'm still glad you decided to have lunch with me."

She smiled and looked around. "Where are we?"

"This is my land."

"This is gorgeous! I had no idea. I didn't know you ran a vineyard, Truman."

"I don't actually run a vineyard. These aren't even my grapes. I just lease the land to Clyde Gray. The vineyard and the winery are his."

Lillian nodded. "So all this is yours?"

"I'll show you."

She climbed out of the truck and looked around. "This tree looks out of place here. It's the only tree by itself."

He patted the tree's thick trunk. "I wouldn't let Clyde cut it down. I have many memories of climbing it when I was a kid."

"This will be a perfect place to have our picnic," said Lillian.

"First," he said, "I want to show you where my land ends. It's a nice walk, and you seem like you could use one."

She took his arm and they walked between a row of grapevines. They walked for a long time, crossing vineyards and fields and even an orchard. Truman explained that not only were the grapes used to make wine but some varieties were used for raisins that would be scattered between the rows to dry in the sun before processing.

"You sure know a lot about grapes for not owning the vines."

"Clyde is an old friend. I usually help him at different times of the year, just for something to do. Plus, I worked the fields when I was a teenager."

"Does managing your land take time away from your art?"

"No, it actually gets me outside, which I love. I stay busy."

As they stepped through the rows of vines, the smell of earth filled Lillian's nostrils. It was hard to believe that all this land belonged to Truman. She admired him for investing in something natural and lasting. At the edge of the vineyard, the land was suddenly covered by trees. Orange wildflowers grew in dappled sunlight, and the quiet was broken only by the twitter of birds and an occasional squirrel scrambling through the branches.

"Wow. This is gorgeous," she whispered, not wanting to disturb the peace that surrounded them. She felt his hand rest on the small of her back as he pointed to a jaybird, its blue feathers visible through the leaves.

"You're fortunate to have such beautiful land in your family."

"Actually," he said, "about five hundred yards through those trees is where I grew up. I live farther out in the country now, but this is my favorite place."

"What do you plan to do with it?"

"I have no idea."

"Then why buy it?" she laughed.

They were shaded by trees now. He removed his hat and rubbed the indentation the hatband had left on his head. "I once thought I was buying it for a girl," he laughed. "It's the oldest story in the world, right?"

Lillian wasn't surprised. "What happened?"

"Oh, she wanted to live in the city. I couldn't give that to her." He said it in a matter-of-fact way but clenched his jaw as he picked up a rock and threw it against a tree.

"That's sad."

"But not as bad as your story, right?"

Lillian shrugged her shoulders. "Pain is pain."

"She was pregnant. We weren't married. Maybe that's why she wasn't ready for a child. She didn't want it."

Lillian's insides clenched and she thought of Sheyenne and Lee.

He picked up another rock, checked its shape, and pelted it toward the forest. The peck of it hitting the tree echoed through the woods. "We fought about it for days." He shoved both hands in his pockets and focused on a hummingbird flitting among the wildflowers that grew in a patch between the trees and the vineyard. "And then one day, when we were driving home from San Francisco in the rain, we were hit by a semi truck."

Lillian held her breath.

"The driver had fallen asleep at the wheel," Truman said, "but he survived. Both Angela and I were relatively unscathed, and Angela decided that she wanted to be a mother after all."

Lillian couldn't help it. She swiped at a tear and let the name roll silently around her tongue, wondering what pull Angela might still have on Truman's heart.

"But she lost the baby that evening."

"I'm so sorry, Truman."

He nodded. "She got it in her head that God was punishing her for wanting an abortion, so she canceled the wedding, packed up, and moved to San Francisco."

"Will she ever come back?"

Even though he wasn't looking at her, the sadness around them was palpable.

"She's not coming back, ever."

Lillian rested a hand on Truman's shoulder. They were silent for a long time, watching the squirrels jump from tree to tree.

Lillian's stomach growled loudly.

Truman laughed. "I think we need to eat. I hope there will be enough to feed you."

Lillian felt warm again as his eyes passed over the length of her body, as if he could gauge how much food she needed at a glance. "I think you need some food before you blow away," he said.

He guided her back through the vines, until the tree and the truck came into view.

"I apologize," he said. "I didn't mean to comment about your figure."

"Oh, goodness," Lillian said, "I haven't exactly kept myself in the best of health these last few years."

"I wasn't actually thinking how unhealthy you look," he cleared his throat. "But I'm too much of a gentleman to tell you how healthy you look right now."

Lillian's face grew hot. She kept her gaze forward as they walked. The touch of his fingertips on her back was reassuring, and she loved the scent of his cologne. The men she worked with usually smelled like oregano or onions, so she wasn't usually treated to the scent of musk that occasionally tickled her nose when she was near Truman.

At the shade tree, they spread a quilt and laid out the food. There were several kinds of cheese, bottled water, juice, and bread. It looked scrumptious. Truman said the best part of the lunch promised to be the egg salad. Paige was famous for it.

Lillian remembered the surprise and reached for the cellophane that was tied with a yellow ribbon. She untied the bow, revealing layers of fudge.

"It's homemade by Gracie!" Lillian said, not able to keep the smile from her face as she remembered the time when Sheyenne and Lee helped her bake chocolate cupcakes. They had all ended up covered with batter.

"Gracie is sweet," said Truman.

"Yes, she is, and she somehow guessed my addiction to chocolate. It's a common addiction among women, you know. Some stereotypes are accurate."

He reached for a piece, and Lillian swatted his hand away. "Before lunch?"

"I'm ravenous," he growled, and Lillian laughed at his silliness.

"Okay, then just one." She picked out a piece and popped it into his mouth.

"Mmm," he growled, "I'm filled with chocolate sensations."

Lillian popped one in her own mouth.

"La Rosaleda is known for its chocolate as much as its wine and cheese." He licked his lips. "Gracie could own a fudge shop some day."

Lillian smiled her agreement, not able to talk through a full mouth.

He leaned on one elbow then and removed his hat, a gesture that already seemed familiar. She tore off a piece of bread and offered it to him.

They ate lunch in silence, the breeze blowing at their napkins, bringing with it a wave of tiredness that caught Lillian by surprise. She stifled a yawn as she watched him devour his sandwich in two bites.

"This is not enough food for you," she said.

"It's fine. It's a myth that men must always eat giant meals."

"You aren't a big eater?"

"I eat a big breakfast. That's why I eat at Carlos's Diner on the plaza. You can get breakfast any time of the day."

"I can't believe you aren't a dinner kind of guy."

"Normally, I'm a microwave guy, but if someone happened to be a really good cook, my mind could be changed."

"Really?" Lillian said.

"I'm not a good cook, but"—he raised one finger—"I make a few good dishes."

Lillian smiled broadly.

"You can't cook either?" he asked.

"Oh, sure, I can cook." She kept her face neutral.

"What do you cook best? Pancakes? Lasagna?"

"No."

"Grilled cheese sandwiches?"

"Huh-uh."

"PB&J?"

"Have you ever heard of Chef George Ballenta?" she asked.

"Of course!"

"I work at his restaurant."

His face broke into a surprised grin. "So you are a chef?"

She shrugged. "I could be. I went to culinary arts school a long time ago. Chef George said he would promote me when I come back. I don't know what that means, though."

He shook her hand. "Congratulations! Next time I'm in Sacramento, I'll stop by for dinner."

"I chop a mean carrot!"

"Scary!"

She brandished the butter knife in front of him, and he playfully wrenched it from her fingers and then handed it back, their hands lingering together for a moment. It reminded her of the day before in the plaza, which now seemed like such a long time ago.

"Yesterday, in the plaza—" He paused. "I hope I didn't come on too strong."

Her pulse raced as his fingers brushed the inside of her palm, and her fingers tightened around the plastic knife, clasping his fingers against the smooth edge.

"It's a good thing this is a plastic knife," he teased.

She dropped the knife and stared at their hands, still clasped together.

He sat up and leaned close. Tears broke through her eyelids as his hands caressed hers. For a moment she didn't breathe.

Her voice came in a whisper, "I feel like I have known you forever, Tru."

"I feel the same way. In fact, my soul has already kissed yours many times."

A small smile touched her lips. "Ah, the poet Heinrich Heine—almost."

Truman's hands tightened around hers. He looked into her eyes until she couldn't bear his penetrating stare any longer. She closed her eyes against the overwhelming urge to forget herself. His hands moved slowly up her arms, and she wrapped hers around him, letting him draw her closer, pulling her away from bittersweet memories of another.

Their lips met, first grazing lightly, and then more familiarly, as if they had known each other for a long time. Lillian's head was spinning. Their lips brushed and caressed more intimately than she'd known was possible. When she pulled her lips away, he tightened his embrace, his lips traveling up her face and into her hair. They stayed like that for a long time.

The kiss had been filled with longing too long restrained, pain too long hidden. A newly discovered affection stirred between them.

No words were needed.

⁓❁

It was dark when Lillian returned to her cottage. She switched off the porch light and sat on the swing in her pajamas with a cup of fruity herbal tea, compliments of Paige. Thoughts of Truman filled her mind, and she mused at how quickly the day had passed while she was lost in a sort of heaven with him.

She checked her voice mail. The first message was from Kitty, saying she needed to talk to her as soon as possible about the painting.

The second message was from Geena. She pressed to listen. "Hey, sis." Geena sounded out of breath. "I can't talk about this in a phone message, but I need to tell you something very important. Stay away from men you don't know until we talk, okay? Please call me as soon as you get this."

21

LILLIAN SNAPPED HER CELL PHONE shut and curled her legs beneath her in the swing. What did Geena mean by not talking to strange men? She glanced toward the tower of the B&B, remembering the person with the camera who had seemed to be watching her earlier. The room was lit up now, and it looked like somebody was seated near the window reading a book.

Lillian pushed away uneasy thoughts of being followed and sipped her tea. It had only been a photographer taking pictures of the cottages. And as for Geena, she had always been overly dramatic about things. Her cryptic message was probably just her way to get Lillian to talk to her. Lillian had no reason to trust Geena.

She sighed, dismissed Geena from her thoughts, and tried to think of more pleasant things, such as Tru's lips on hers that afternoon. Her defenses had easily crumbled around him, and it left her feeling a bit mystified. It had been easier than she'd expected to give in to an experience she would have previously considered impulsive.

Lillian absently brought her cross pendant to her lips and kissed it, trying to concentrate only on Tru, but Geena's intruding message kept working its way back into her thoughts. Was Geena trying to scare her? Lillian's mind searched for answers to old questions and sifted through troubling memories of the personal effects of her family that had poured out of a manila envelope and landed with a clatter on the kitchen table four years earlier.

These were the things that had been salvaged from the accident, from the bodies of her loved ones. Sheyenne's cross pendant with the red gemstone had twinkled up at Lillian, its chain missing, telling a story of the violence Sheyenne had suffered. Lee's favorite toy race car, one of the tires conspicuously missing, had rolled across the tabletop. And she'd nearly lost all control when she spotted Robert's wedding band, the diamonds still sparkling, which she later sent to the funeral home to be placed back on his hand.

All of these things had been precious to her, except for Robert's leather wallet, which she had burned that evening in the backyard.

She remembered with an ache how she'd found the photo tucked neatly behind a crisp hundred-dollar bill. The beautiful woman in the photo was sitting demurely in the sand, laughing, her arms crossed over her chest in a playful effort to hide the absence of her bikini top. In the background was the beach house where Lillian and Robert had spent countless romantic weekends in the early years, before Sheyenne and Lee had required so much of their time.

She had immediately recognized the woman in the photo. Even with sunglasses and her reddish-brown hair swept up into a loose twist, she would have recognized her anywhere. Watching the image burn as the flames licked their way along the photo and wallet had made her feel somehow vindicated.

She sighed. Shaking off her grogginess, she stared at the night sky. With Tru seeming so eager to get to know her, maybe it was finally a good time to accept the truth.

Why didn't You stop them? she prayed, but heaven seemed so distant, even more distant as the years went by. She didn't know how to close that gap any more than she knew how to close the distance between her and Geena. Nor was she sure she wanted to. Her sister was guilty of betraying her. If not for Geena's selfish acts, maybe the accident would have never happened.

The truth tapped at her heart, forcing her to acknowledge Robert's actions. Geena had not been the only traitor. To accept that truth would mean acknowledging that her husband had cared very little about her.

With Tru's kisses still warm on her lips, the truth began to unfold against her will, encircling her heart in a bittersweet hold that tempted her to let go of her grief. She wrapped her arms across her chest and watched the moon's slow path until it slid behind a magnolia tree.

Lillian decided truth was complicated. Keeping it at bay would be easier than admitting that she had been callously betrayed by her husband. That their marriage had been a charade.

Truth might unlock doors she had kept bolted shut. Once opened, those doors might allow someone new, perhaps Tru, to betray her, to enter the deepest corridors of her heart.

Lillian seriously considered hurling her cell phone across the room. She had been talking on the phone to Kitty when Geena had called again. She had called six times during the morning and had left a strange message each time.

She had really had enough of Geena's games as she flipped open the phone and punched in the code to retrieve yet another voice mail message.

Geena's voice sounded hysterical. "Lillian! *Please* call me! Somebody might be following us!"

Lillian's blood turned cold. "Oh, my God," she said, as she dialed Geena's number.

"What is going on?" she said before Geena could say hello.

"Sis!"

"Geena!" Lillian tried to calm her voice. "What is going on?"

"Lil, I received a phone call a few days ago, and I've been trying to reach you." Lillian's heart raced as she listened to Geena's breathless description of the call.

"Lil, I don't know who it was. He was calling from a restricted number, but he said lurid things about us both. He said he wanted to find me and make me tell him where Robert spent the money."

"What money?" asked Lillian, wondering what else Robert had done to betray their marriage.

"I don't know," said Geena. "I don't know about all of it, but this guy must have been involved, either with Robert or against Robert. Or maybe it's just a crank caller. I'm just not sure."

"What are you talking about, Geena?"

"You don't know about any of Robert's"—Geena paused—"dealings. Do you?"

"No," said Lillian. "I only suspect, but nothing has ever been proven."

"Lillian," Geena said, "he said he would get back at Robert. He said he would find you and…"

Lillian's blood ran cold. "And what?"

With Geena's tearful description, Lillian fell heavily into a nearby chair. She wanted to hang up, to shut out the words, but she sat frozen with the phone pressed to her ear.

"And then," Geena finished, "he said, 'Have you seen your sister lately? She's so pretty.'"

Lillian's heart battered her chest. "We have to call the police," she said.

"No!" Geena said.

Lillian stared incredulously at the phone, and then put it back to her ear.

"I mean, I don't want to alarm them. What if it's nothing?"

"Are you crazy? You are trying to scare me."

"I'm not."

Lillian was quiet, then asked, "Is this related to the accident?"

Geena was silent.

"Geena, you have to tell me! I deserve to know."

"You might hate me even more when you know."

"That is not possible," Lillian snapped.

"Sis, just trust me that it's possibly related. Maybe it's a prankster, but I'm just worried. Either way, you don't want to know the details."

"I do want to know, and I think maybe we should talk to those who investigated the accident."

"No," Geena said.

"Why not?"

"What if it is a prank?"

"What if it's not?" Lillian exclaimed.

"Listen, I don't know everything, Lillian, just bits and pieces, but Robert told me that some of the cops might be dirty. He saw some cops he recognized at times and didn't think they were undercover for the police department."

Lillian gasped. The idea was too big for her. She didn't understand the workings of the police, but she immediately thought of all the times she'd tried to get investigators to do something on the case, and all the times they'd said there were no leads.

"Are you sure about that?" asked Lillian.

"No," Geena said. "I'm not sure about anything." Well, that made two of them, Lillian thought.

Silence.

"Lil, are you still there?"

"I'm here," she said. "I just don't know what to say, Geena. Tell me what happened at the accident. I know you were in the car."

Geena was silent.

"I saw you on the news. The police saw you."

"Then why didn't they look for me?"

"They did, until they decided there was no cause to arrest you."

"They didn't even want to question me?"

"I think so." Lillian was confused, remembering the delays she had assumed were just part of normal police business.

"I've been worried about you, Lil."

"I could tell," Lillian replied dryly. "Tell me how it happened."

"Are you sure?"

"Absolutely."

"Where are you?"

"In La Rosaleda. Where are you?"

"La Rosaleda."

"What?"

"I was looking for you."

There was a knock on the door. Lillian put her hand on the knob "Who is it?"

"Geena!"

Lillian drew in a deep breath and swung wide the door.

22

THE TWO SISTERS STOOD FROZEN. The first thing Geena noticed were Lillian's eyes. So sad, and yet more beautiful, set in a face that was thinner than she remembered. If Robert had been seeking beauty alone, he would never have strayed from Lillian.

"Hello, Lillian." Geena's voice was barely audible. For a second, Geena thought Lillian was going to hug her, but instead she turned sharply away. Geena shrugged off the rejection, but being so close and not able to embrace her sister reminded her of the gulf that stood between them.

She silently followed Lillian into the cottage and looked around. She held back tears of joy at seeing her sister again, sensing by Lillian's demeanor that she was hardly glad to see her in return.

The cottage was cute, with lace curtains and a crisp décor; just the kind of place Lillian would choose. They sat across from each other at the table. Lillian wouldn't meet Geena's eyes as she sat ramrod straight, her hands clasped tightly together on the tabletop.

Geena could feel the hatred emanating from her sister. Desperately needing to break the silence, she slapped both hands down on the table. "Mind if I make some coffee? Or tea?"

Lillian shrugged but still refused to meet her eyes, so Geena picked up Lillian's cup and emptied the cold liquid into the sink. She rifled through the cabinet and pulled out a box of mint tea.

Lillian's voice was icy. "Not that one."

"Okay, then," Geena said, slightly bewildered. "How about this fruity one?"

Lillian said nothing, so Geena took it as a yes. She put the kettle on the stove and pretended to be unaffected by the silence. It seemed to take forever for the water to boil, but finally Geena set two steaming mugs on the table and sat down.

When Lillian finally raised her eyes to look at Geena, a single tear trickled down her cheek, revealing the weight of her suffering. The heaviness in Geena's heart expanded. If only her sister knew how sorry she was, but she couldn't think of anything to say. She didn't dare apologize before giving Lillian what she had asked for: the truth about the accident.

Another tear trailed down Lillian's cheek. Geena reached across the small table to wipe it away, but Lillian flinched. Geena's palm hovered, longing to comfort her sister, but slowly, awkwardly, she pulled away and pressed it between her knees.

Geena cleared her throat. "Okay, you aren't going to talk to me. I understand." She watched Lillian's face and wondered if she would be able to handle what she was about to tell her.

"You sure you want to hear this?"

Lillian's nod was barely discernible.

"Okay. Just tell me to stop if you change your mind."

Unconvinced that Lillian would be able to handle the full revelation, Geena decided to tell only part of the story.

Lillian raised her eyes to meet her sister's. They were steely now and seemed to bore a hole into Geena.

Geena fixed her eyes on Lillian's clenched hands, the details of that day coming back to her. Mosquito Road led into a more rural area, so she had felt a million miles away. It had been raining because the road shimmered with moisture and the grass beside the road had felt wet on her bare feet. She'd wondered where her sandals were as she stood in the center of the wreckage, trying to remember how she got there.

"The roads were so wet," she began. "When I eased onto the interstate, I noticed that a car seemed to be following us. I thought it was strange that Robert ducked down and looked in the passenger side mirror. He told me that maybe they were just impatient, to switch lanes and see if they would go around us.

"I did as he instructed, but the other car switched lanes too and pulled closer behind us. I swerved back into the right lane, but the car nearly rear-ended us. I screamed at Robert."

Geena swallowed, remembering how Robert had gently squeezed her thigh. "You're doing fine," he had told her. "Just drive." He had run his fingers through his hair then and said, "We'll be fine. I just need to think."

"I wanted to cry," Geena continued, "but he told me to just stay calm and take the next exit. I asked him if he meant Mosquito Road." She took a ragged breath.

" 'Yeah,' he said, 'and don't slow down.' I asked him who was following us. He glanced in the mirror again and said he thought they were the people he owed. I didn't know what he meant.

"Then he raised his voice and said, 'Oh, come on, Geena. Don't pretend you don't know.'

"I didn't know what to think. I was struggling to keep the car steady on the wet pavement. Robert kept beating his fist on the dashboard. The other car rammed us from behind, and I swerved, barely managing to stay on the road. The children and I were crying, so Robert told Sheyenne and Lee not to worry, that nothing was wrong and to duck down low.

"Lee asked why, and I told him, 'It's a fun game! Are you both buckled in like a big boy and girl?'

"Sheyenne cried, 'Daddy is supposed to buckle us, and he forgot.'

"Robert freaked out, then he unbuckled his belt and leaned into the backseat to buckle them in.

"At that moment, the car rammed us again, and the windshield shattered.

"I slammed on the brakes, but the car swerved, then hydroplaned into the ditch. Everything became chaotic. The children were screaming as the car rolled over and over again. It stopped when we slammed into a tree.

"I remember everything got deathly quiet, except for the squeak of the car rocking back and forth.

"The next thing I knew, I was standing in my bare feet beside the road. I stared at the wreckage, trying to remember how I got there. The police and ambulances arrived. A paramedic asked my name. I couldn't speak at all, so I shoved her away. I remember rushing toward the bloody sheets. The police yelled for me to stay back, but I couldn't."

Geena kept the next part of the story to herself as she recalled how she had knelt down and lifted away one of the sheets. It was one of the twins, but she couldn't tell which one. She had vomited, and two policemen took her to an ambulance.

"The paramedics bandaged my cuts and then left me alone in the ambulance, but after a few minutes, I climbed out and made my way across the road and hitched a ride on the first semi truck I saw."

Geena swiped a tear away as she remembered hearing the sad whine of gears shifting just before the truck carried her far away from the horrible thing that she had done.

23

LILLIAN HADN'T EXPECTED HER emotional reaction to Geena's story to be so strong. She tried to remember what the police had said: "There is more to this than you think, Mrs. Hastings. We think your family might have been murdered." She thought of Geena's excuse—dirty cops—and it all seemed too scary to consider. She wanted to leave it all behind, to just forget it, but her grief still felt fresh.

When Lillian looked up at Geena, who was fighting back tears, anger boiled inside her.

The next hour was a blur as Geena and Lillian argued. Lillian called Geena a murderer and a liar, and she ranted about how Geena had abandoned her. With the truth now told, Lillian found her voice, and it rose with a fury Geena would have admired if it had not been directed at her.

"I thought you hated me!" Geena said. "I didn't think you wanted me to be there after what I did."

Lillian jerked away toward the window. "I didn't know what you had done!" She shook her head. "I kept thinking that maybe you were in the car because you needed a ride. I certainly didn't know you were driving! You lied to the cops!"

"I didn't!" Geena said. "I just left before they could question me."

"I know you left. You left me to deal with everything alone! And what were you doing in the car? Did you or did you not have an affair with Robert?" Lillian demanded.

Geena couldn't confess to Lillian what she had so easily confessed to

Edna in the bar, so she didn't answer. It wasn't an admission she could make without an explanation.

Lillian rifled through the cabinet for more tea, but all she found was mint. Where was the fruit tea? She growled and threw the box of mint into the trash can, slammed the lid, and reached for a water glass.

"Don't like mint?" asked Geena.

Lillian shook her head. "You are amazing, Geena. You really are. How can you be so trivial about this?"

"I just meant that I don't remember your having such an aversion to mint. In fact, you seemed to love growing the stuff. Don't you remember? We had mint tea all the time, and when I helped you thin it out of the garden, we hung it on your ceiling to dry."

"Yes," Lillian said. "I remember."

Geena and Lillian had spent the better part of an afternoon pulling seemingly endless clumps of mint from the flower beds around Lillian's back porch. They'd chatted and laughed as they bundled the greenery with jute and hung it from pushpins on the kitchen ceiling. Drying it had been Geena's idea.

Robert complained that they marred the ceiling with pinholes. When Geena giggled from her place at the table, Robert gave her a curious look, then they both erupted in laughter. Lillian never figured out what was so funny.

A few minutes later, Geena offered him a cup of mint tea, and he looked at her so strangely that Lillian felt a swirling in her stomach that she couldn't explain. Grabbing the broom from the pantry, she had hastily brushed the silly thoughts away, along with the mint cuttings that had fallen on the tile floor.

"I do remember the mint," Lillian said. "And there was a joke between you and my husband that I never understood." She pinned Geena with a glare. "Is this something else that I don't want to know?" she asked.

Geena fiddled with a clasp on her sandal. "Yes, it is," she said quietly.

Lillian grabbed her purse. "I have a meeting at the gallery. Don't be here when I return." She slammed the door.

Geena opened the trash can, pulled out the box of mint tea, and turned on the stove under the kettle. She'd been more transparent about her feelings for Robert than she'd planned to be. She sipped her tea, wishing it was something stronger. She tried to brush the desire away.

The mint had hung in bunches for months, gathering dust. Its fragrance waned over time, and eventually neither Robert nor Lillian noticed it hanging there anymore. It became invisible, until Robert died and Lillian was preparing the house for sale. When she took the bundles down, the holes in the ceiling seemed like a metaphor of their marriage, forgotten and marred, and no amount of spackle would be able to fill those holes.

Lillian had hated mint ever since.

24

THE BELL TINKLED ABOVE THE door as Lillian and Paige breezed into the gallery.

"Lillian!" Kitty exclaimed. "And Paige! My, don't you both look lovely today!"

"Thank you, Kitty," Lillian said.

"I just couldn't stay away," Paige said. "I love a good mystery. I hope I'm not imposing."

Lillian shook her head and laughed. "I'm grateful for the support. It makes me feel less crazy."

Kitty patted her arm. "You certainly aren't crazy, dear." She motioned toward the counter. "Do you remember Louise and Kara?"

Kara, who was flipping through a bride magazine, waved from her seat behind the desk, and Louise walked out from behind the counter and shook Lillian's hand.

Kitty clasped her hands together. "Well, now, let's not waste any time. Lillian, we asked you here because when I saw the painting, I recognized you."

Lillian sighed. "So I'm not crazy after all."

Paige smiled broadly. "I thought I was crazy when I first saw it."

"We're all here together," Kitty said. "Three of us can't be wrong. And now that Louise can study Lillian and the painting side by side, we'll see what she thinks."

Louise smiled. "So you are Beauty from the painting. Now I know why you wanted so much to buy it when you were here."

Lillian frowned. "It's a picture of an intimate moment, the importance of which is known only to me."

"But, dear," Kitty said, "except for us, nobody knows that it is you."

"I guess that's true," Lillian nodded, still reticent, regardless of how romantic it seemed to the others.

"When Kitty told me your name," Louise said, "I remembered meeting you just moments after the painting was donated to the gallery. I remembered that you wanted to buy the painting, but I didn't remember exactly what you looked like."

"Unlike the artist who painted you," said Paige with a wink. "He remembered you quite well."

"Exactly," Kitty said.

"Do you know who the artist is?" Lillian asked.

"We have a pretty good idea."

Paige squealed. "This is just too romantic!"

Kitty studied Lillian. "Do you think this is romantic, Lillian?"

Lillian shrugged. "I wish I did, but I don't know what to think yet."

"Well, let's take a look," Kitty said, reaching for Lillian's arm. They walked to the back of the gallery where racks of paintings and quilts were stored.

Kitty pulled out the painting in question and everyone grew silent. Her hand flew to her throat. *Beauty and the Beast Within* was even more stunning than Lillian remembered, and her face flushed. She had seen the painting only once before, and her memory had not done it justice. Not only was the Rose House an exact replica, but the woman gazing at the roses seemed fully dimensional.

The artist had painted her in detail, as if he'd studied her closely. The image was so lifelike that it brought heat to her cheeks; he had captured every nuance and curve in her form and on her face. She could actually see that she was crying in the painting! Lillian reached out to touch the tears on the woman's cheeks, but Louise stopped her.

"I'm sorry," Lillian said. "It's just that—"

"I know," Louise said, then she pointed to Lillian's necklace. "Where did you get that pendant?"

Lillian's hand went to the cross, feeling its familiar lines between her fingers. "It was my daughter's."

"It's beautiful," Louise said. "And it's the same pendant in the painting."

Kitty and Louise spoke in hushed tones as they compared other details in the painting.

"Kitty and I have been comparing other paintings against this one," Louise said. "We want to show you what we've figured out about who the artist of this painting might be."

They began pulling out other paintings of the Rose House and various landscapes in the region. There were breathtaking paintings of vineyards, houses, and roses. They all looked a little bit similar to Lillian's eye, but Louise and Kitty identified unique techniques in each one, pointing out differences in the petals of a flower or the profile of an animal while describing how these distinctions could indicate a particular artist's style. Several of the paintings were Tru's.

Louise explained that Truman used special colors and tones in his paintings. "Lots of gold, red, orange, and burgundy," she said. "See?" She pulled out a painting that Lillian recognized.

"I've seen this," Lillian said glancing at Kitty. "It was at your office at Frances-DiCamillo. It is the one you showed to me when we first met."

Kitty's eyes brightened. "Yes, I remember. And if I recall correctly, you loved it."

"I did," Lillian said, admiring its beauty with renewed interest.

Louise placed the painting on an easel next to *Beauty and the Beast*

Within, and then she glanced knowingly at Kitty. Louise and Kitty pointed out that both paintings contained the colors and tones and other specifics that characterized Tru's style.

"How in the Good Lord's name did Tru paint Lillian before he had even met her?" Kitty asked.

"Yes," whispered Lillian, "how?"

"I remember when the painting was donated," Louise said, pinching her chin as she recalled the events. "It was less than a month ago. You came in that day, Lillian. I didn't know the man who donated it." She shrugged. "I had never met him before."

Lillian peered closer at *Beauty and the Beast Within,* remembering the moment she first saw it. Before spotting the painting that day, she had bumped into a man on his way out, but she couldn't remember what he looked like, just his hands. "His hands were smudged with paint," Lillian said.

Kitty walked to a file cabinet and pulled out a folder. "You'd remember him, Louise, if you had seen him." She winked. "He's a sight for sore eyes, isn't he, Lillian?"

Lillian tried to smile.

Kitty carried the folder of clippings to a table and quickly flipped through them. She stopped on a photo of a ribbon-cutting ceremony.

"The gallery opening," Louise said. "I couldn't make it. I was working in Sacramento that day."

"Correct," Kitty said, "but Truman made it. Here he is cutting the ribbon with me."

"That's him!" Louise exclaimed. "That's the man who donated the painting. I remember he seemed to be messing with me, maybe teasing me. It's definitely him." She nodded her head, seemingly pleased with her memory. She called for Kara to take a look.

"What is it?" Kara asked.

"Isn't this the man who came in that day to donate *Beauty and the Beast Within*? The one who wouldn't identify the artist?"

Kara peered closely at the photo and smiled. "Of course. It's Truman."

"Kara," Kitty said, "if you knew, why on earth didn't you tell us?"

She shrugged. "He didn't want Louise to know who he was."

"But she would have eventually figured it out," Kitty said.

"I know, but I wasn't sure what Truman was up to that day. He is kind of shy, you know. I just figured he would work it out with you later."

"And perhaps he still intends to," Kitty said. "It hasn't been that long ago."

"Maybe that's it," Louise said. "Perhaps he wasn't trying to be mysterious, but when he saw Lillian, he got worried and became secretive. Maybe that's why he hasn't mentioned it yet to you, Kitty."

"But Truman and I are friends," Kitty said.

Paige smiled. "Maybe he randomly painted Lillian by the Rose House, and now that he's fallen for her, he doesn't know how to explain it to her."

Lillian's face grew hot.

"Or," Kitty said, "maybe it didn't happen by chance."

"That's what I tried to tell Lillian," Paige said. "There are too many coincidences, so maybe something bigger is at work here."

Kitty winked. "God does work in mysterious ways."

"Stop it!" Lillian said, thrusting out her arms.

The women stopped talking and gaped at her.

"I'm sorry," Lillian said, "but how is this romantic? You all don't know the whole story." She looked pointedly at Paige. "You know the most, Paige, so why are you making light of this?"

Paige frowned, trying to place her hand on Lillian's shoulder. "Relax, Lillian."

Lillian shrugged her away and Paige's eyes darkened. Lillian knew she might feel bad later, but at the moment she was angry. Nothing was going the way she wanted it to.

"And now," Lillian said, "my crazy sister showed up this morning to tell me she thinks some crank caller is trying to terrorize us." She jerked her hands up in frustration. "And if that's not bad enough, she confessed to me that she was the one driving when my husband and children were killed four years ago. After that she ran away, and now she wants to be friends!"

Silence and shock wrapped around the gathering.

"So," Lillian continued, "maybe this has nothing to do with anything, but do you see why I'm having trouble seeing the romance today? It's not romantic. I hoped it might be, but it's too confusing. Too much is happening at once." She began to pace. "So does Truman care about me, or am I just the girl in his painting? Is he just trying to have a tryst with me?"

"He's not like that!" Paige said. "He isn't just trying to have some tryst."

"And he's not crazy," Kitty said. "So he can't be your crank caller, if that's what you're thinking."

Lillian had thought of that, but she silently agreed Kitty was probably right about that much.

"He's a good person," said Paige. "I don't know how he came to paint you, but I'm sure that, given a chance, he will explain it. I have to take up for him, Lil."

"Me too," Kara said. "He even volunteers at the school my brother attends."

Lillian was confused. "Tru volunteers?"

"At Sunshine House," Kitty said. "Do you remember when I mentioned that people from the school come to help me in the gardens?"

Lillian sat down on a stool, burying her face in her hands. She groaned. "What about the way he invaded my privacy?"

"Lillian," Paige said, "you were in a public place."

"But I did not give him permission to paint me. It was private. It was—"

"Lillian," Louise said in an attempt to bring them back to identifying the artist, "do you remember seeing Tru the day he donated the painting? I am positive you came in right as he was leaving. Was it him?"

Lillian tried to remember more than the blotches of paint on his hands, a flash of satin and ribbons, her purse falling to the floor. She remembered a dashing man who'd gotten his fingers tangled in the purse ribbons when he tried to help her retrieve it. She'd been flustered at his presence and the way their fingers had touched, but her attention had been pulled away from him when she saw the painting. His face hovered in a fog just out of her grasp.

"I don't remember," Lillian said. "I guess it could have been him, but I don't remember his face. I do remember that he was holding a hat, or maybe he had laid it down for a minute to help retrieve my purse. Could it have been his fedora?"

Paige gave Lillian a hug from the side. "It was him," she said. "Accept it. Part of the mystery is solved."

Lillian stood, ready to leave. "That's what I'm afraid of." She didn't try to hide the tears that slid down her cheeks. "So why did he lie to me about it?"

25

GEENA WAS CLOSING HER CELL phone after talking to Aunt Bren when she heard a knock on the door. She crossed the floor and started to swing it open, but then stopped herself. She walked to the window and peered out. It was just a little girl.

Geena swung the door open and greeted the child with a warm smile. "Hello there, sweetie. May I help you?"

"Is my Diamon Girl here?"

Geena smiled, realizing she meant Lillian. "Well, no, but my last name is Diamon too. Does that help?"

The child leaned in conspiratorially. "Okay, then, I can trust you." She thrust a large envelope forward.

"What's this, sweetie?"

"It's for Miss Diamon. The other Miss Diamon."

"Do you want me to give it to her?"

She nodded.

"What is your name?"

"Gracie."

"Ah, Gracie. Would you like to come in for a cookie? I found some in the cookie jar."

Gracie looked like she was tempted, but then she glanced toward the tower room. "I have to go. I am getting a new doll."

"That's great. Thanks for stopping by. I'll give this to Lillian." She started to shut the door, then opened it again. "Gracie?"

Gracie turned around, her curls bobbing around her face. "Yes?" Her smile made Geena think of Sheyenne and Lee.

"Where are your parents, sweetie?"

Gracie looked to the side and closed her eyes, as if trying to remember what to say. "Mommy is at a meeting and Daddy is working in the bike shed."

"Where is the bike shed?"

Gracie pointed to a small building nearby with its doors open. Geena could see Mark Tenney in the shed.

"Okay," Geena said. "I just wanted to make sure you weren't alone."

Gracie waved. "Bye, miss!" She ran off toward the B&B before Geena could ask her any more questions.

Geena closed the door and tossed the package on the kitchen table.

꧁

Gracie hurried upstairs to the tower room, where she knew her doll would be waiting. It would be a cowgirl doll, the one she had been wanting for so long. How did he know she wanted it? The doll was so pretty with her soft brown hair, just like her own, blue jeans, a pink vest, and matching cowgirl hat.

When Mommy sees the doll, she won't be mad at me for keeping a secret, Gracie thought. He had told her not to tell Mommy about it. And he had told her not to tell Miss Diamon his name. He promised that he would tell them later, and then her mommy would understand.

She had smiled at him and promised. She liked him so much. He was a nice friend.

26

"THANK YOU, PAIGE." Lillian climbed out of the car and stood at the end of a gravel path.

"Don't mention it," Paige said. "Just go easy on him, Lil." She looked concerned. "Sometimes things aren't what we think they are."

"Apparently," said Lillian.

Paige shook her head sadly. "That's not what I meant, really." She looked down at the steering wheel. "He's a wonderful man. He'll have a good explanation for all this."

"Okay," Lillian said. "I will try to give him a chance." But her heart thundered with betrayal.

"That's all I'm asking," Paige said, placing her hands on the steering wheel. "I care about Tru." She paused. "And I care about you too."

Lillian smiled. "I feel the same way."

Paige's smile lit up her face. "I'm glad to hear it." She shifted the car into reverse and waved at Lillian. "Maybe he will drive you back to town, but call me if you need a ride. I'm hoping you won't!"

Lillian stood before a large farmhouse. Its simplicity didn't surprise her. Truman was an easygoing man who liked a trouble-free lifestyle. The three-story house was located a few miles outside of town and sat half a mile from the road, surrounded by pastureland and trees beyond that. Lillian thought it was beautiful.

Two horses grazed in a corral between the barn and an abundant vegetable garden. She climbed up the white porch and was greeted by a lazy chocolate lab who raised his head and barked halfheartedly. She patted him on the head, which enlivened him enough that he sat up and licked her face. Lillian heard the door creak slowly open.

"Cody!" Truman's voice was quiet and grainy. "Leave her alone, old boy."

"He's fine," she said, dusting off her dress. At the sight of Truman's face, she almost forgot why she had come. His lazy smile lit the corners of his groggy eyes. She had woken him.

"This is a pleasant surprise," he said through the screen door.

"I tried to call."

"I worked late, so I unplugged the phone to take a nap. I didn't intend to sleep so long."

"Sorry to wake you. I hope you don't mind my popping in."

He shook his head. "Of course not! Have you come to tell me your vacation has been too short and you plan to extend it?" He winked and motioned for her to step inside.

The house was clean and tidy, except where he'd tossed his hat on the antique-looking coffee table in the center of the living room. There was no television in sight, and Lillian was surprised to see higher-end appliances in the kitchen. She wondered if Angela had been a good cook, since Truman had confessed that he wasn't.

The kitchen was decorated simply with a country garden motif. "It doesn't get used much anymore," Truman said. "Just before my grandmother died, I bought her these appliances."

"How long has she been gone?"

"Three years last week."

"I'm sorry," Lillian said.

He sat on a barstool. "Yeah, it was hard. She was my only family. Everyone else has been gone for years, and just a few years before that, Angela…" His voice trailed off. He suddenly stood up and steered her out of the kitchen. "Let me show you around."

The house seemed enormous. His studio sat just off the kitchen, separated by a window with curtains drawn tight.

"Top secret," he said, leading her past it and upstairs. The rooms were cozy, decorated with colorful quilts and lacy curtains.

"My grandmother was a fan of Kitty's quilts," he explained as they entered another room, "so they are everywhere."

"Kitty made these? They are lovely." She ran her hand over an Irish chain–pattern quilt. "They're like tapestries."

"She's a true artist. She made all of them in the house except for this one." He patted the quilt on the bed beside him. "My grandmother made this one."

She looked around at the room, realizing that it was his bedroom. It was rugged, compared to the other rooms, and very neat. The furniture was made of lodgepole pine complimented with a few southwestern pieces with rusty hinges. She ran her hand over a carving on the dresser drawers painted with bright green, yellow, and orange.

"Did you paint this?"

"With the help of my students."

"Students? From Sunshine House?"

"One of them is. They like art. It gives them something to do."

She was intrigued and wondered how he had time for so many activities. No wonder he was tired.

"I am sorry. I just remembered I woke you up. I'll go so you can get back to your nap." She turned to leave.

He caught her elbow and drew her to his chest. He smiled playfully. "You can wake me up anytime you want."

She looked up, lost in the intensity of his eyes. She wasn't sure what she wanted to say. That she knew he'd painted her? That she was falling for him? That she was angry he had lied?

His lips met hers, sweeping her into a swirl of emotion. He wrapped his arms around her, and she melted into them, telling herself that she just wanted this one kiss before she said good-bye, just one more embrace.

He was tall, his shoulders towering and powerful, as he leaned toward her. She allowed her hands to venture up his toned arms and reach around his neck, eagerly returning his embrace. He held her tenderly, tempting her to forget the real reason for her visit

Lillian felt her body shiver as Truman pressed his lips against the cleft of her neck and began to lower her toward the bed. She wanted to let herself sink into its softness, letting his lips ease away the years of loneliness and hurt.

"Tru!" Lillian gasped for air. She gently pushed him away.

His chest rose and fell rapidly as he sat down on the bed. "It's okay. You can relax," he said and pulled her around to stand in front of him. "I understand." They were eye to eye, his hands clasping hers, tenderly.

Taking a deep breath, he broke into a wide smile. "Wow."

She squeezed his hands in return, not sure what to say.

"Sorry about that," he said, running his hands up her arms and back down to her hands. "You are just so beautiful, I forgot myself."

Heat filled her chest, and she tried to think of how she could bring up the painting without destroying the moment. "Listen, Tru," her voice was a whisper, "I just can't."

He nodded. "I know. We barely know each other, right?"

She nodded.

"And besides," he continued, "we have plenty of time." He pulled her into a playful hug, but she gently pushed away.

She shook her head. "No, Tru, we don't."

"Don't what?" he said. He pulled her close again. She didn't pull away this time, so he kissed her, one hand smoothing her hair around her face as his lips caressed hers. "You don't leave until Sunday," he whispered.

"And you can come back. Or I can come to Sacramento." He pulled back to look at her. "If that's okay with you, of course."

She buried her face in his neck, unable to answer. It would have been more than okay, she wanted to say, if only he had not lied to her about the painting.

"I want you to come back," he said, his voice low and quiet. He caught her lips again. "Lillian, I am not usually so"—he breathed heavily—"so taken with women as I am with you." He placed his hands on her shoulders. "By the way, why did you come here today? Do you need something? Or did you just miss me?" He winked.

Lillian gently extracted herself from his embrace and sat down beside him. "Tru, I had a meeting today with Paige, Kitty, and Louise. Someone named Kara was there too." She turned to look at him, her pulse racing. It was hard to read his profile, but she thought she saw his jaw clench. His easy smile faded.

Suddenly, he stood and offered his hand. When she reluctantly took it, he walked her back downstairs to the living room. She sat on the couch, but he avoided sitting beside her, choosing instead an oversized chair.

"I'm sorry I didn't tell you about the painting," he said gravely. "As soon as I realized who you were, I should have said something, but I worried that you would think I'm crazy. And when Paige told me you have been followed in the past, I didn't want to frighten you or make it look as if—"

"She told you that?"

He shook his head. "She meant no harm, but it worries me that you've been followed. I couldn't blame you if having a mysterious person paint you might unsettle you."

"Don't worry about that," she said with a flick of her wrist, "but you should have told me about the painting. Why didn't you?"

His face was somber and regret clouded his features. "Because—I felt like an intruder. I could tell when we talked about the painting that day in front of the gallery that you weren't fully comfortable about it."

"You knew who I was then?"

He leaned over then, resting his elbows on his knees, his head cradled in his hands. She watched him nervously.

"I am not some obsessed artist like you see in the movies, Lillian."

"It was you that day in the gallery a few weeks ago, wasn't it?" she asked.

"Yes."

"And you knew that it was me?"

"No!" he said seriously. "Not then. I didn't know you were you, but—"

She swallowed, not understanding why he was struggling to answer her questions.

"I did realize you were the woman I'd seen by the Rose House four years ago."

"And painted," she accused.

His face and scalp turned slightly red. "I guess it does sound crazy, but yes."

"Why?"

He shook his head and held his hands out, palms up. "I don't exactly know, Lillian. I'm sorry."

She believed him, but for some reason she couldn't stop asking him questions. She didn't want to say it was okay that he'd spied on her privately and decided to paint her feelings in a painting he chose to make public—however beautiful the painting was.

"I don't understand how this could have happened," she said. "It makes no sense."

"I'm sorry, Lillian." He stared at the floor. "If I could go back and not paint you, not watch you, I would."

"Wouldn't you?"

He took a deep breath and sighed. "It would be hard not to notice you, Lillian." His eyes burned with desire when he looked at her. "But if I knew you would feel so invaded, I would choose not to paint you." His voice caught. "I'm sorry."

"There has to be more to it than this," Lillian said. "It's got to be more than coincidence. It just can't be some random thing."

He risked taking her hand and seemed surprised when she returned his grasp. "You're right, Lillian. It can't be just chance."

She frowned, "It can't? But you just said—"

"Listen, Lillian. Four years ago, I saw you at the Rose House. As an artist, I was drawn to you for how lovely you looked, but the emotion pouring out of you also intrigued me. With the backdrop of the Rose House, I guess my imagination was inspired." He raised his hands in defense. "I never imagined seeing you again." He cleared his throat. "It was a perfect scene. It expressed what so many people can't put into words, you know?"

She shook her head. "No, I don't."

He sighed, suddenly short on words. This was the Truman she'd first met. Quiet, thoughtful, shy.

"Grief. It's difficult to articulate, but the picture of you and the house— Well, I just understood how you might have been feeling."

Lillian was silent, amazed at how closely his observations mirrored how she had felt that day.

"The look on your face," he continued, "it was exactly how I felt when Angela and I lost—"

"What about the camera?" she asked.

"What camera?"

"Weren't you taking pictures? Isn't that how you remembered me so well?"

"I painted you from memory."

Her pulse quickened. "Then who were the men taking pictures of me?"

He shook his head. "What men?"

"I saw a man photographing me and another one who seemed to be following me," she explained. "One was talking on a cell phone."

"I left before you did." He shrugged. "I wanted to give you space." He squinted as if trying to remember. "I don't recall if there were other people around or not, but I can tell you that I don't have a cell phone. I never have."

"Someone using a professional camera with a zoom lens?"

"The only camera I have is a small digital one. I rarely use it. I have a student who is a photographer, but we use his camera during sessions."

She tried to think back. After her driver had dropped her off, she'd walked the grounds. At what point had she gone to the Rose House?

"Did you visit the Rose House twice during your visit to the vineyard?" asked Truman. "Maybe you visited, then walked around, and visited again?"

"You know," she said. "I might have. Maybe I walked around and then returned to the house before leaving. I can't remember."

He shrugged. "Sorry. I didn't see anyone else there, but photographers love to photograph the Rose House."

"What about that day at the gallery?" she asked. "Did you follow me there?"

He turned bright red.

"I was there to donate the painting," he said, "which I now regret.

"So you *were* watching me that day at the Rose House."

He sighed, exasperated. "I wasn't there to watch you. I was there to study the roses for a new painting. You just happened to be standing by the Rose House."

"I was alone."

"It is a public place. You didn't even notice me."

"My husband and Sheyenne and Lee had just died."

"Yes, I know. At least, now I do."

Lillian's voice was a whispered plea. "You really didn't know who I was, did you?"

"Of course not! How could I have known? I was there to paint the roses," he sputtered. "Truth be told, you were in my way!"

She sat up straighter, feeling color flush along her cheeks. Truman stood and began to pace.

"I was shocked when I saw you a few weeks ago in the gallery. You were my muse come to life before my eyes; the inspiration standing in front of the masterpiece." He rubbed his hands along his scalp again. "In fact, you became the masterpiece. Of course I had to meet you when I saw you. What artist wouldn't be intrigued? But when we met, you were even more than the woman in the painting."

He walked to her chair and sat on the coffee table, facing her. "When you became real, Lillian, you became more than paint and canvas."

She said nothing, but she felt a space in her heart soften. Too much had happened in the past week to go from falling in love to hating him. She wanted to blame Robert for her fears of getting close with Truman, but it was getting harder to do when she was the one having the foolish thoughts.

"I didn't know who you really were until you told me." He reached to touch her cheek, a question in his eyes. "You are afraid of getting close to me, to anybody."

She sat, silent, unable to believe he had just voiced one of her biggest fears.

"Lillian, I promise you"—he ran one finger along the curve of her cheek—"I am as surprised by the way we have come together as you are." The smoothness of his voice tugged at her heart, but then she remembered other promises. *Lillian, I promise you. I was in surgery…in a meeting…called back to the hospital…*

She leaned away. "I am not your muse."

He withdrew his hand as if she had slapped it. She felt him stiffen beside her. "Maybe not *you*, Lillian. But that day, your likeness, that moment, it was. And I painted what might be the most excellent portrait of my life because of it."

She rubbed the back of her neck and sighed deeply. "If it was such an amazing piece, then why did you give it away?"

"I don't know," he said. "I've asked myself that question a million times." He rubbed his chin. "I guess the painting begged to be seen, to be enjoyed by others."

"But why donate it anonymously?"

"Because I put so much of myself into that painting, my feelings, my grief. It's all on the canvas," he sighed. "Why would I want anyone to know?"

"But what about me?" she said. "What about *my* grief displayed to the public?"

He shook his head. "I didn't mean to embarrass you. I didn't intend to invade your privacy. But Lillian, nobody would have ever known it was you if you hadn't walked into the gallery that day."

He was right, just like Kitty had said. "What are the chances this could ever have happened?" she asked softly.

"Slim to none."

Lillian's eyes met his, her gaze level. "You looked into my soul, Tru, and you painted it, uninvited."

He closed his eyes, and when he opened them, they were sincere and determined. "Your soul," he whispered, "was beautiful."

Lillian's heart leapt to her throat, and she struggled to stifle a sob. She thought about what he'd said during their picnic a few days earlier. It was something about his soul kissing hers. Her hands reached for his as a laugh escaped her throat.

"When did you paint it?" she asked.

His face brightened and he grew more animated. "I started the night after I saw you. I was inspired."

Passion poured from the excitement in his voice, the flush on his cheeks, and the gestures of his hands, and Lillian suddenly felt honored to be part of a process that was beautiful, yet fortuitous.

"I've never had a painting come so easily," he said. "Your eyes, your dress, your hair, your skin, the expression on your face, I couldn't get the images out of my head. You stood there so long that you became part of the Rose House."

Tears trailed down Lillian's cheeks, and Truman reached out and whisked them away.

He whispered, "I never meant to make you cry. You might wake up tomorrow and hate me for the painting."

"If I do, then I don't want tomorrow to come."

"Lil, please trust me."

"I want to," she said.

Lillian needed a man she could trust. She felt so tired of worrying. She wished they could return to when they had first met and just start over. She scooted aside, letting Truman sit beside her, but he pulled her up on his lap. She leaned in to brush her lips lightly against his just one more time.

His breath shuddered as her lips sank into his, exploring the sweetness of newfound affection. Not knowing how to end their interlude, she simply laid her head against his chest.

After a few minutes, she asked, "Do you think you could give me a ride back to the cottage?"

He smoothed back her hair. "Do you have to go?"

"I think I need some space."

"Will you come back?"

"I need to work some things out in my mind first."

He hugged her to him but didn't say the words she wanted to hear, that he understood, that he would wait for her to figure things out.

They didn't speak on the drive back to town.

At the cottage, Lillian unlocked the door and held it open for Truman. She motioned for him to come in. "Just for a minute," she explained.

He followed her and shut the door behind them. They stood facing each other.

"Lil, I don't know how you are going to feel about this tomorrow, but I want you to know that whatever happens, this week has been—" He shook his head. "Well, it has been nothing like I've ever experienced."

She nodded.

"And," he said, "I promise, I haven't been trying to create some artist's fantasy around you."

"So I'm not the girl with a pearl earring?" she teased.

He shook his head. "No, of course not."

He placed his hands on her shoulders and looked directly into her eyes. "I'd be lying if I said that meeting you in the flesh didn't ignite powerful feelings, but it surprises me as much as you. The way it happened is a kind of miracle to me." He cupped her face in his hands. "But as soon as you opened your mouth and became real, you were more than I could have ever dreamed you would be." He ran his finger along the edge of her jaw. "I'm glad to discover your beauty runs inside and out."

They kissed again. His hands glided slowly down the length of her back and rested on her hips. When she wrapped her arms around the back of his neck, his hands grazed her rib cage. Abruptly, he fumbled behind him with one hand for the doorknob.

"I'm afraid you will regret it if I don't leave now." He cleared his throat. "I don't want you to have regrets."

She stood and watched him put his hat on his head. He tipped it in a good-bye, just before he closed the door.

27

LILLIAN STOOD WITH HER BACK against the door. Suddenly, a tapping on the door disturbed her reverie. She peeked through the window, expecting to see Truman. It was Geena. She swung the door open.

"I thought you were leaving."

"I didn't say that," Geena said. "Besides, I'm staying in La Rosaleda, remember?"

Lillian turned and walked into the kitchen, leaving the door open behind her.

Geena followed. "Lillian, we need to talk."

Lillian waved her hand. "I've had enough talking to last all year. No more, Geena, please."

Geena slapped a brown envelope down on the table.

"What's that?" Lillian asked.

Geena opened the envelope and a stack of pictures slid out.

Lillian gasped. "Where did you get these?" She sat down at the table, her hands reaching to touch the photos. "Oh my gosh, Geena. Who took these?"

"I was hoping you knew."

Lillian shook her head. "I have no idea." She picked up one photo of her by the magnolia tree, and then another of Gracie.

Geena sat down and they both shuffled through the black and white photos, their disagreement forgotten for the moment.

"Look at this one," Geena said. She held up a photo of Lillian standing by the Rose House and then another of her running away from the camera. Shivers pricked her arms as she recalled the men.

"I was right," Lillian whispered. "I was being followed."

"Paige called the police," Geena said.

Lillian's eyes widened. "I thought that creep on the phone told you not to."

Geena shook her head. "I know, Lil, but we don't even know if it's the same guy, or if it's connected at all. He hasn't called back. But with these pictures, with Gracie involved—"

Lillian reached for the photo of Gracie. She remembered the day when she and Gracie had been talking near the magnolia tree.

"I wonder why he would take a picture of her?" asked Lillian.

"It gets worse," Geena said. She told Lillian how Gracie had knocked on the door to give her the envelope and then ran off to get her new doll.

"It wasn't even thirty minutes later that her dad knocked on the cottage door. He had been frantically looking for Gracie. When I told him about her stopping by, we both raced to the B&B. We found her in the tower, sitting on a couch, playing with a brand-new doll that neither Mark nor Paige had given her."

"Oh, my goodness, Geena." Tears gathered in her eyes. "I feel terrible. I shouldn't have ever come here. This is because of me!"

"What do you mean?"

Lillian flipped the pictures facedown on the table. "I can't look at them. What if this is related to Robert's mess? It's my fault!"

Geena reached for her sister's hands, but Lillian pulled away. "Don't touch me."

"Okay, but will you please calm down? The police have already been here and questioned Gracie. She said that the man who gave her the photos is her friend, and that she can't tell anyone his name because of the surprise."

"What surprise?"

"I don't know," Geena shrugged.

Dark thoughts invaded Lillian's mind. "Was Gracie hurt?"

"She's at the hospital with her parents now, but as far as they know, she wasn't harmed in any way. It's so strange."

"Why didn't somebody call me?"

"You left your phone in Paige's car. We tried Truman, but he didn't answer."

"His phone was unplugged," she said as she rummaged through her purse. She headed toward the door. "I can't hang around here."

"Where are you going? I'm supposed to take you to the police station to give a statement."

"Fine," said Lillian. "Do you have a car?"

"I sold mine, but I'm renting one," Geena said.

"Let's go."

At the police station, Lillian gave a short statement about her time in La Rosaleda. She briefly mentioned that she might have been followed in the past, but that she hadn't ever been able to prove it.

"Probably just my imagination," she joked.

Halfway through the interview, the phone rang.

"Excuse me," said the officer. He turned away from Geena and Lillian, grunting into the phone. His bald spot shone under the fluorescent lights as he bobbed his head up and down. "You did," he said. "Good. Charles?" He sat forward. "You have got to be kidding me. I'll call Truman Clark and get him in here right away." He slammed the phone down and swiveled around to look at Geena and Lillian.

"The little girl told her momma who it was." He reached into his desk and pulled out a toothpick, which he tucked between his teeth.

"Who was it?" they asked in unison.

"Can't say right now, but don't worry. It was somebody harmless. He's going to be in a bit of trouble, but he isn't dangerous. Now, if you'll excuse me, I have work to do."

Geena and Lillian stood to leave. Lillian's mind was racing. She was halfway out the door when she spun around and called after the officer.

"Why are you calling Truman in?"

He gave her a pointed look and slid the toothpick to the corner of his mouth. "Now, ma'am, you know I can't tell you details, but no need to worry about your boyfriend."

Lillian's jaw dropped and Paige smirked.

Lillian's heart felt like it would leap out of her throat as she climbed into Geena's car. Geena slid behind the steering wheel and stared at Lillian.

"What is going on, sis? Why did he call Truman Clark your boyfriend?"

Lillian shook her head. "You wouldn't understand. Anyway, I don't trust you enough to tell you anything, Geena."

Geena shrugged. "You can, Lil."

"How?"

"I stopped drinking. I've changed."

"Since when?"

"Since a month ago. I quit after some difficult things happened to me."

"Difficult things?" Lillian wanted to shout, but she struggled to keep her voice level. "What difficult things have you gone through, Geena? What could have happened in your life that measures up to an ounce of what I have suffered?"

Geena started the car. "Nothing," she said. "Nothing as bad as what you have suffered, Lillian."

Lillian crossed her hands in front of her, strangely satisfied that she'd put Geena in her place. She was sick of her sister's antics and all the drama. She didn't believe for a minute that Geena had stopped drinking. She had abused alcohol since high school, and it had only gotten worse over the years.

Geena put the car in gear and took off too fast. The tires squealed as she drove out of the parking lot. Lillian didn't comment. It would have required her to speak to Geena, and she was growing angrier by the minute, remembering Geena's alcoholic binges. *Only white wine in a glass at a dinner party, nothing else. Never let it get empty, but never keep it too full. That way nobody will notice how much you drink.*

"You're turning into a drunk," she had heard Robert say to Geena one night after a dinner party at their home.

"Well, if I'm a drunk, I'm a classy drunk," Geena had replied, "and *you* know it."

With that, she'd dropped a cluster of wine glasses into the sink and laughed at the sound of shattering glass. Then she'd passed out on the couch. It usually wasn't a problem to let her sleep it off, but one time Lillian found her sleeping in Robert's office. When Lillian questioned her about it, she'd said the children would wake her up if she slept in the living room. On another occasion, Geena had been nearly naked when she walked through the living room to the guest bathroom, seemingly unconcerned about whether Robert or the children were in the room.

Geena's behavior had baffled Lillian at the time. Now, the memory made Lillian's blood boil. How could she have been so stupid?

"Robert thought you were a drunk," Lillian said.

Geena's head swiveled to look at Lillian and then back to the road. Her lips pursed, but she said nothing.

"Slow down," Lillian snapped.

Geena eased off on the gas but still said nothing.

"You could kill somebody," Lillian said.

Neither one of them articulated what they were thinking: that Geena might have been responsible for the deaths of Lillian's family that fateful day on Mosquito Road.

"You and Robert," Lillian said, her voice cracking from the tension between them, "you had an affair, didn't you?"

"I can't talk about that right now, Lil."

"Yes, you can!"

"No. Right now it's all I can do to stay sober and take care of you." Geena turned into the B&B driveway and parked.

Lillian laughed sarcastically. "Take care of me? Are you nuts? You have never taken care of me. I've always taken care of you!"

They climbed out of the car and stared at each other across the roof, neither of them caring that they were being observed by other B&B guests on the front porch.

"I know!" Geena yelled. "I know it's always been you taking care of me! That's why I owe it to you to make things right."

"Of course," said Lillian, "but that doesn't change what you are, Geena."

Geena spun around and headed toward the cottage. "I know, Lillian. I'm sure if I forget, you'll be happy to remind me. I'm a drunk, and a bunch of other things you are too ladylike to say out loud."

Lillian watched Geena stride toward the cottage. Geena had a physical appeal that was the result of minimal effort that seemed like no effort at all. Lillian had always admired this trait in her sister, but she had never envied it until now, as she realized her husband's attraction to this quality in Geena.

Lillian started toward the cottage, then she remembered that Paige had her cell phone, so instead she hurried into the B&B, grabbed the phone on the desk, and dialed Truman's number.

"Hello, Paige?" Truman said.

"It's Lillian."

"Lil! What's going on? The sheriff just called and said I need to come in."

"I don't know," she said. "I thought you would know."

"Me? No! What happened?"

Lillian filled him in, careful to leave out nothing.

"Charles? Are you sure he said Charles's name?"

"Yes, does he mean Charles who sometimes takes photos here at the B&B?"

"He's just one of many photographers who use the B&B. Why would they mention him? And why me?"

"They said whoever gave Gracie the doll was harmless. Could it be Charles? Are you and Charles friends?" Lillian asked.

"He's a student. I'm sort of a mentor to him. He attends the Sunshine House school."

Lillian took a deep breath as realization dawned. "Wow, lots of things make sense now."

"Yes, but he will still be in some trouble," Truman said. "I better go see what I can do to help. I'm sure his sister, Kara, is worried."

"Kara is his sister?"

"Yeah, she's basically all he's got, and those of us who are his friends."

Lillian felt a new respect growing in her heart. This was more than she had expected. She felt terrible for their earlier conversation.

"Before you go, Tru, I want you to know that as soon as I can get my cell phone from Paige and call my driver, I have to get going."

"Lillian, don't leave today. Wait."

"I don't know if I can," she said.

"Stay," said Truman.

But she knew she wouldn't. She hung up without giving Truman a chance to say anything further. She was confused about Truman, happy that Gracie was fine, curious about Charles, and livid at Geena for showing up in La Rosaleda to complicate everything in her own special way. She needed to get home. She swung open the door to the cottage and glared at her sister.

"Just because you came back from wherever you've been hiding for all these years doesn't mean I've forgiven you."

Geena stood quickly, nodding her head. "I know," she said. "I understand."

"And someday soon, I want to know the truth, Geena. I want to know everything there is to know about you and Robert, so I can bury it with him and move on with my life."

Geena nodded. "Okay."

Lillian sat on the couch, suddenly feeling exhausted. There was just too much information to process.

"What should we do?" Lillian asked Geena.

"Go back to Sacramento and focus on your job for a while. I'm planning to go back too, as soon as I tie up a few things here."

"Tie up what?" Lillian asked.

"Just some stuff."

Lillian shook her head. "More secrets?"

"I'll be there the next day."

"I assume you have your own place?"

"Yes, I lined up a place in Sacramento before I came here, and a waitressing job."

"Good." Lillian walked in the bedroom to pack her suitcase.

Lillian shuddered to think that the event with the pictures and Gracie could have ended much differently. Charles must have taken the photographs for reasons yet to be explained, but she assumed Paige would fill her in. She didn't blame Truman. After all, how could he be responsible for his student's behavior? The idea that Charles had been watching her was baffling, but knowing he lived at Sunshine House explained a lot of it.

"I'm glad this picture thing is over," Lillian said, explaining the situation to Geena.

"I don't trust him," she said.

"You've got to be kidding me, Geena."

"Well, there are pictures to prove he was following you, right?"

"I'm not worried. It was all in innocence," Lillian said.

"How can you be so sure? It seems like men are lining up to spy on you."

"Geena, it's a coincidence. There is nothing sinister about Charles or Truman."

Geena looked at her quizzically. "There's something going on between you and this Truman guy, isn't there?"

Lillian nodded. "Sort of."

"Tell me."

"Why should I tell you?"

Geena reached a hand toward hers, but Lillian pulled away. Geena suddenly stood, stomped across the floor, and slammed the front door behind her.

~⦿~

"Lillian, you just arrived," Paige said, hanging up the phone at her desk. "You're checking out already?"

"Don't worry. I'll call you and Gracie."

"I appreciate that, but I'm worried about you. You have had a lot to think about the past few days."

"Yes, but I'll be fine. Besides, Geena will be nearby. We will check on each other."

"Sounds comforting."

Lillian ignored Paige's sarcasm, sensing she had read Geena pretty well so far.

Gracie chimed in. "Will you come back and see us?"

Lillian looked down at Gracie. The corners of her mouth were turned down in a frown.

"Of course I will, sweetie. Maybe in a few months. Maybe sooner." Gracie squealed and applauded. She reached out and fluffed Gracie's curls. Gracie didn't understand what had happened. It was the grownups who had been scared.

"Tru called," Paige said.

"What did he say?"

"That they just had some questions for him, but that Charles wasn't in any trouble. Tru sounded mortified that Charles took pictures of you without your permission."

Lillian's eyes widened. "I hardly think Truman is in a position to be so shocked at Charles, when that's exactly what he did when he painted *Beauty and the Beast.*"

"*Within,*" Paige said. "*Beauty and the Beast Within.*"

"Whatever."

Paige's face went blank.

"It's just that I am really confused about all of this, Paige. I need to think about Truman. It's been a long time since I've been in a relationship. The last one didn't go so well. I can't even grieve properly since I'm always learning something new about what a jerk my husband was." A wave of emotion rose to Lillian's eyes, but she fought back the tears.

"Truman isn't responsible for any of that."

"I know." Lillian hugged Paige. "But I still need to think. He doesn't need my baggage. Let's not allow this to come between us, okay?" She ruffled Gracie's hair.

Lillian walked through the lobby and paused in front of *The Rose House in Winter.* Its bare brambles and cold, dark house mirrored exactly how she felt. An ache grew in her heart as she walked out the door, down the front steps, and slid into the car's backseat.

Jake was already backing the car out of the driveway when a beat-up blue truck pulled past and stopped near the mailbox. The truck door swung open and Truman jumped out.

"Can you stop for just a minute, Jake?"

"Sure, Miss Diamon. Just let me know when you are ready."

"Thank you, Jake." She rolled down her window and stared at Truman standing beside the truck in a pair of faded blue jeans, a black T-shirt, and his trademark hat. The sight filled her with doubt.

His eyes questioned her as he raised his hand and crooked one finger.

She waved back and noticed that he looked tormented as he leaned against his truck and crossed his arms over his chest.

Common sense told Lillian that she was not yet ready for a relationship, but seeing him made her want it anyway. A reckless abandon welled up inside her heart, that panicking pump of deception. She longed for him to stride across the driveway to the car. It almost compelled her out of the car, but instead she shrank back.

When Truman made no move, she said, "We can go now."

Jake glanced surreptitiously toward Truman. "Are you sure, ma'am?"

"I'm certain."

Jake put the car in drive.

As they rolled slowly away, Lillian nodded at Truman. He pulled his hat down low and saluted like a lazy soldier; the brim of his hat concealing any expression that might betray his mood.

Lillian adjusted her position so that she could look into Jake's rearview mirror as they pulled onto the road. Truman was still leaning against his truck, and he still had not moved when they turned the corner onto the highway that would carry her away from him.

28

GEENA WALKED DOWN THE COBBLESTONE alley in search of the café where Truman Clark had agreed to meet her. Something about Truman still didn't feel right. And after that creepy call, she owed it to her sister to look out for her, whether Lillian realized it or not. What Paige had told her about *Beauty and the Beast Within* made Geena distrust him even more, though Paige had insisted that the painting had come about through a series of unlikely circumstances.

Truman had said there was a garden at the end of the alley that nestled an outdoor café. Geena nervously made her way between historic buildings and shops decorated with hanging baskets of flowers and wine barrels filled with pink and red impatiens.

She found him seated in the garden beneath an arch of roses that hid the table from passersby. He balanced his masculine posture on a small wrought-iron chair that didn't seem to suit him. He stood when she approached.

"You must be Truman. I'm Lillian's sister, Geena."

His voice was flat. "Nice to meet you." He pulled a chair out for her.

As the waitress poured her a glass of iced tea, she glanced around. Truman shifted in his seat, leaning his elbow on one knee. His fedora rested on the other; an old-fashioned hat, she thought, for a man who appeared to be in his late thirties. From the set of his jaw, she could tell he wouldn't be much of a talker.

Geena waited for him to speak first. He looked coolly at her and then away, studying a hummingbird that flitted among the yellow and lavender gladioluses. "Why are we here?" he said, finally.

"To find out why you are following Lillian."

"She knows I am not following her."

Geena glared. "Then where did those photographs come from?"

"I'm sure you know as well as I do that my student took them."

"Yes. Charles."

He twirled his hat in both hands, his mouth drawn in a thin line. "Listen," he said, "Charles didn't mean any harm. Paige knows this, Lillian knows it, and so do I. You would do well to drop the whole thing."

"Why would I do that?"

"Charles is a good kid, so he gets extra privileges. Or at least he did before this happened." He shook his head. "I talked to the director of his home today. Charles is losing his privileges for a few months, which I think is unfair, but it could have been worse."

Geena sat back in her chair and cursed softly. "I can't believe this." She stared at Truman. "I think maybe you are using Charles for your own strange obsessions with my sister."

"That's ridiculous." He seemed unruffled by her accusation. "What are you trying to say?"

"Just that maybe he was doing what you told him to do. I know about the painting. It makes sense that you would want to photograph her too."

Truman was scowling now. "You don't know anything about the painting," he said intently. "I certainly never intended to invade Lillian's privacy. I didn't even know who she was when I painted her." He rubbed his head. "But it stopped there. I would never have followed her, or used Charles, let alone Gracie, to get to Lillian. And besides, I don't have to."

Geena leaned in. "Lillian has never enjoyed being the center of attention."

"I'm sorry," Truman said, "but what does any of this have to do with you? You waltz in here at the last minute and think you know what's going on. I wonder why." He shook his head. "How do I know you didn't come back to meddle in your sister's life? You have caused her much pain already, I understand."

Geena looked shocked.

"I seem to recall that the two of you have been estranged since she lost her family in the accident. You ran away, right?"

"You don't know anything," Geena said. She wondered silently how much he did know.

"That's what I'm saying to you. This is between me and Lillian. She knows I would never hurt her or anyone else. If she doesn't know that, then she's not who I think she is." He stood. "I don't mean to be rude, but I have to go."

"Where are you going?"

"To church."

"At night? I find that hard to believe. Where are you really going?"

He chuckled and seemed amazed that she was still going on about it. "You are desperate to make something out of nothing, Ms. Diamon."

"I just don't trust you, that's all."

"Not that it's any of your business, but I'm meeting Gracie and her parents for a special service at Frances-DiCamillo Vineyards. Maybe you should go too. It might help you be a little less unpleasant, less of a witch."

Geena jumped to her feet, blocking his path. "You don't have to be such a gentleman. Just say what you really think of me, Mr. Clark."

Too late, Geena realized that she had broken a cardinal rule: when a man is mad, don't invade his space. "Just hear me out," she said.

"I already did." From the steely glint in his eyes and the slight way the space between his eyebrows crinkled, he looked furious.

"I didn't plan to engage in name-calling. It's just that I care about my sister, and it looks like you were following her before she knew you. She has been followed before, and I need to know if you are involved."

"I'm not," Truman said.

"Did you know Robert Hastings?"

"Lillian's late husband? No, I never met the man, but it sounds like he was quite a jerk."

Geena froze. Truman didn't know Robert; what right did he have to say such a thing? "You didn't even know him."

"I know he was a criminal and probably a womanizer, among other things."

Geena felt her ears get hot. Despite his many faults, he had been a good person on the inside.

"Mr. Clark, I'm just trying to help my sister. If you were me, wouldn't you want to protect Lillian?"

"I'm not you, Ms. Diamon. I want to protect her too, but I'm wondering if I need to protect her from you. Now, if you'll excuse me."

Geena watched him walk away in long strides. The church thing was a nice touch, but she still didn't trust him or that Charles. The circumstances appeared too coincidental, and Truman's ire toward Robert was totally unfounded. Her thoughts made her shiver.

29

TWO MONTHS HAD PASSED SINCE Lillian and Geena had returned to Sacramento. Lillian went back to her work with Chef George, and Geena started a new job as a waitress at a family restaurant downtown. There had been no indications that either of them was being followed since leaving La Rosaleda. They both hoped the caller had moved on.

Geena had suggested more than once that maybe the caller had been Truman. Lillian had only laughed.

"That's ridiculous, Geena. He didn't even know Robert," Lillian told her, dismissing the idea. "I think everything that happened in La Rosaleda is circumstantial and that the person, or people, who followed me all those years ago were mixed up in Robert's illegal dealings. They were just trying to scare us. Now they've stopped."

They were sitting on Lillian's couch, folding Geena's laundry, since Geena had yet to buy a washing machine and dryer for her new place.

"I don't know," Geena said. "What about the call?"

Lillian pinned Geena with a glare. "You know more than I do, don't you, Geena? Why ask me?"

"It just doesn't add up. There is still something bothering me about all of this. I simply can't believe that everything that happened in La Rosaleda was just happenstance. That place has some kind of curse on it."

"That's silly, Geena. La Rosaleda is a wonderful town. It was all a mix-up. You know Charles didn't mean any harm. His intentions were not dangerous."

"How do you know?" Geena asked. "Maybe he can't be trusted the way Sunshine House seems to think. It's still possible that Truman used him."

"Even though Tru lied to me about the painting, he wouldn't do something like that. He didn't need to go through someone else to get to me. I was there for the taking."

"He seduced you into thinking he was harmless. And now Paige, who is too trusting for her own good, has convinced you that Charles is harmless too, even though he endangered her daughter."

"No, he didn't," said Lillian. "Not really. You should give the kid a break."

"Yeah, well, I'll give him a break when that school takes his privileges away for good. I don't think he needs to be running around scaring people. And he's not a kid."

"Some people would say you are prejudiced toward Charles, Geena."

"I don't care about political correctness, Lillian. I care about our safety."

"You know what, sis? You are talking crazy, trying to make connections where there aren't any. What has made you so paranoid? What do you know that makes your mind jump to the ridiculous? This isn't some crime to be solved."

"Maybe it is!" Geena retorted. "Maybe if you knew everything that I do, you'd have the good sense to be scared!"

"But I don't know, because you won't tell me!"

"Some things are better left alone," Geena said.

"No! No, they aren't. You just said if I knew, I would be scared. Tell me what is turning you into such a detective! Or maybe all of this talk about being in danger is just your way to deflect the real truth."

"What truth is that?" Geena's face was impassive now.

Lillian's voice was barely audible as she whispered, "The truth about you and Robert."

"Every wife knows, so why do you need to hear it?"

"I want you to confirm it!"

Geena grabbed her laundry basket and walked toward the door. "I'm sorry, sis. I can't today." She started to walk out and then turned back. "You know, Lillian, you run around like you are Miss Perfect and everyone thinks you are so sweet and innocent."

"Geena, don't start this."

Geena's knuckles turned white as she gripped the basket tighter. "See? That's what I mean. You are so condescending, but you"—she jabbed a finger in Lillian's direction—"you hold a grudge forever! You cannot forgive, can you? So what if someone is following us, you just want to set the record straight, to make sure I know what an awful person I am. You will never forgive me, will you?"

Lillian crossed her arms over her chest. She had reasons. Anyone would have a problem forgiving the sins that divided the two of them.

"Lil, I don't think you really want me to explain about me and Robert. What you really want is to keep rubbing my face in it."

Before Lillian could protest, Geena walked away and slammed the door shut behind her. Lillian wondered how long Geena would be gone this time.

-❦-

Lillian walked into the dining room of the restaurant. The smile on Chef George's face told her he was up to something.

"What?" She threw her hands up. "Am I in trouble?" Lillian's short time away from the restaurant had somehow changed the way Chef

George interacted with her. She wasn't sure if it was the promotion he had given her, her improved attitude or his, but she liked the change.

Still smiling, he turned her toward the wall. She gasped, placing her hands on her knees as if to balance herself.

"Holy—" Lillian drew in a breath as she gaped at a large new painting of the Rose House that now hung behind the VIP dining area. The thorns looked sharper than Truman usually would paint, but their danger seemed diminished by the softness of the petals. A feeling as warm as the muted tones of ruby, burgundy, and scarlet spread over her. Claret roses leapt off the canvas, their brambles twining up and over the house through the latticework. Gold glinted off the edges of the house, lighting up the roses. She stepped closer and felt enveloped by the size of it.

Lillian didn't need to look at the signature to know who the artist was, but she looked anyway. Seeing his name scrawled on the canvas brought back the memories of their time together a few months earlier. She studied the painting as if it would reveal what Truman was thinking, how he was doing.

Maybe it was just her melancholy memories of Truman, but as she studied the Rose House, it looked expectant in the way the roses reached out toward the viewer. Her eyes traveled from rose to rose, reveling in how intricate each one was. Her eyes moved to the brambles on one side of the house, and a soft gasp slipped through her lips. A woman dressed in golden silk hid in the roses. Lillian couldn't tell whether the hair was brown or blond because the woman's image shone like the sun reflecting off the roses.

"Lillian?"

She turned toward Chef George, with an indifferent glance. "It's beautiful."

"It is," he said. "And it's interesting how the girl appears within the roses." He gestured to the shining image of the woman. "It could easily be missed, couldn't it?"

"It is very intriguing," she said.

"I've heard that Truman Clark is a talented artist, but of course you know this." Chef George turned to look at her. "You do know him, don't you?"

"Sort of." She felt her face turning pink. "How did you know?"

"The painting came yesterday as a gift to the restaurant, along with a card that read: To Mr. and Mrs. George Ballenta and Lillian Diamon." He snorted. "I thought it was odd for an artist to give a gift to one of my employees, even if you are a good employee."

Lillian knitted her eyebrows together, trying not to show surprise.

"It reminded me of that picture you put on the bulletin board a few months ago."

Lillian turned to look at him as he studied the picture.

"Where is my picture, by the way?"

"I thought you took it down."

"No, I don't know what happened to it."

"Well, this is better than that photo, don't you think? So how well do you know each other?"

"We have met."

"Hmm," mused Chef George. "You have only just met, and he sent you a painting? Who can explain the quirkiness of artists? You must have made quite an impression on him." He winked.

Lillian was glad when he left, and she took the moment to peer deeper into the painting. It was so large that it seemed to sweep her into it its colors and hues. Her visit to La Rosaleda had renewed her love affair with art.

A sadness swept over her as she reflected on how artless her life had become since the accident, how beauty had eluded her consciousness. At least in the restaurant she'd been around the scents and sounds of life. The art of a dessert perfectly plated and the delicate blending of flavors and colors kept her senses satiated, but her home was almost void of art and beauty.

She hungered for that beauty now. She'd started to feel it when she spent time with Truman, but her confusion had torn it away. Now, the portrait before her brought the feeling back. She remembered it was this hunger that had caused her to fall in love with the Rose House, and maybe it was even the reason she'd been attracted to Truman. As an artist, he had the ability to create beauty. If only she could put Robert to rest and move on.

She tried to push the swelling of her heart down, but it grabbed toward the lifeline Tru had so obviously extended through the painting. What would happen if she went back to La Rosaleda?

When she walked into the kitchen, Chef George's voice traveled from the break room.

"Yes, dear," he said into the phone, "make the gift certificate to Truman Clark at no price limit. And sign Lillian's name too."

"No!" Lillian said.

Chef George looked surprised. "Never mind, Barbara. Make it from us and all the employees." He hung up and shook his head. "Does this have anything to do with why you cut your vacation short?"

"I thought I was needed here, so I came back."

"Of course that is true, but I gave you a vacation. I don't want to hurt your feelings, but we can survive without you." He grabbed a towel and began wiping down the counter. "And this Truman Clark has a thing for you, doesn't he?"

Lillian cleared her throat and shrugged.

"Why don't you take some time off? Give the poor guy a chance. Or at least just say thank you on the card."

Lillian didn't respond.

"Oh, come on, Lil, do you think I have always been old? It's okay to have some fun once in a while. You are a widow, but you are not dead."

They stared at each other, his eyes revealing the old stubbornness that Lillian didn't have the energy to argue with. Instead, she walked to the counter and began whisking eggs.

"You don't need to kill the eggs, Lillian," Chef George said with a laugh. "Take the afternoon off and enjoy your weekend. It will make up for your shortened vacation."

She set the eggs next to the intern. "I think I will."

—∽—

Opposite the bookcases in Lillian's apartment hung a painting of the Rose House that she'd picked up for a pittance during her first visit to La Rosaleda. The Rose House was such a popular destination that it wasn't difficult to find it on postcards, coffee cups, and cheaply framed prints. This print was an impulse buy, purchased at the height of her grief, when looking at the print helped calm her spirit.

The only other piece of art was a print of *Beauty and the Beast Within* that Louise and Kitty had sent. It was magnificently framed and hung behind the dining room table.

She still had not convinced Kitty and Louise to sell her the original, but they had promised it to Lillian if it was ever offered for sale. Lillian reached out to straighten the painting's frame. Maybe Truman could acquire the original for her. Now that the gallery knew he was the artist, how could they refuse him?

Lillian clicked through the selections on her sound system until the mellow sound of Botti's trumpet danced through the room. She opened the curtains halfway to let light in and settled onto the couch with a cup of Earl Grey, pondering the new painting at the restaurant.

Truman hadn't forgotten about her, and even from afar he had found another way to bring new beauty into her tiny world. What had he meant by placing the woman in the new painting? She wondered if she was the girl peeking out between the thorns and roses, and knew somehow that she was. The woman had been seeking something. Maybe she was afraid to come out, to grasp the beauty around the Rose House. Is that how Truman saw Lillian?

Was she afraid to face the future? Maybe her life before the accident had not been as perfect as she'd thought, but she missed it. At least she had known beauty in the creamy complexions of Sheyenne and Lee, and in watching them chase butterflies in the garden, and in their kisses on her cheek.

Life now was lonely, the giggles and sweet voices of her children still absent, the bouquets of flowers they gathered from the garden non-existent around the house. In contrast, her apartment was void of any other living thing, even a plant. If she was honest with herself, the Rose House really had been the only source of beauty she had welcomed into her life since the accident, and somehow Truman knew more. In some ways, what he had seen and painted of her soul wasn't possible, but the painting existed. The truth was, she loved it.

She gazed across the room at *Beauty and the Beast Within*. The painting brought warmth into the house. Every time she looked at it, her eyes would mist. Each time she saw it, there were things about it she hadn't noticed before, that could only have been noticed by an attentive observer.

Sipping her tea, she tried to imagine Truman standing somewhere off to the side, making mental notes about how she looked and felt. He had studied her inside and out, recorded every detail of her appearance and demeanor with precision. He had painted her likeness exactly as it had been that day, except that it was more beautiful through his eyes. The thought that he'd seen such loveliness in her swirled and formed an ache that she knew Tru could soothe, if only she would let him. Perhaps she should at least return his calls.

Lillian longed to see him again, if only for a little while. She pictured him with his brush in hand, dabbing and stroking the canvas until her image appeared.

She could still feel his kiss on her lips, a kiss filled with a longing she had not expected, as if he'd been waiting for years to kiss her. And maybe in his artist's mind, he had. He'd been with her on that day four years ago, when she'd felt so alone, and he'd painted her each day as she'd trudged through her pain. She had not been alone in her grief, and that realization settled softly around her heart.

She set her teacup in the sink as she felt a wave of inspiration from her memories of Truman and the Rose House. Her apartment needed life. Maybe the presence of flowers would enliven her.

As she drove to the neighborhood nursery, a smile played on her face. Perhaps, she thought, purple cosmos and daisies could salve her wounds. And maybe a few pink carnations.

Peace began to settle around her in soft ripples as she envisioned pots of petunias on the porch and vases of blooms in the house. She wondered how she had ever managed to live in such stark, mundane conditions. How could she have suppressed the very things that had always brought her happiness in the past?

Thanks to Truman, Beauty had returned. She smiled at the cleverness of Truman's title, *Beauty and the Beast Within*. She hadn't actually slayed the beast yet, but thanks to Truman, it had been subdued.

If anyone had seen the abundance of flower-filled vases in her apartment later that day, they might have thought she had finally slipped over the edge. But since Geena had disappeared again, nobody would be visiting. Her eccentricities would remain a secret.

She chuckled out loud as she arranged a bouquet of daisies. Then she carried pots of flowers onto the porch. The sight of blue tricycles and brightly colored toys littering the neighborhood's yards surprised her. How could she not have noticed them before? She must have walked past them daily.

In that instant, she felt joy that there were kids living in her own neighborhood. She would always miss her own children, but as she knelt to dig holes for the flowers, she felt comforted by the knowledge that the kids in her neighborhood were safe.

She didn't mind that images of her own lost children still kept her company as she worked her hands into the damp soil of her meager flower beds. It would always be this way, she decided. From then on, she would welcome the thoughts and think only of the happy times she'd had with them, like when they had helped her garden.

"It's just the way things are," Aunt Bren had once told her over the phone. "Our loved ones live in our minds when they go, honey. That's a good thing. That's what your grandma always told me when your mom died."

The smell of fertile earth and plants wafted around her as she planted, and in a few hours the flower beds were filled with color, much like the gardens she had once planted with Sheyenne and Lee.

"Excuse me, miss." She turned to see a teenage boy peeking at her from behind a bouquet of orange, gold, red, and burgundy roses.

"Oh, my!" She laughed at the irony. "Flowers!"

"It must be a big day for you," he said.

Thinking about the flowers that filled the rooms of her house, she laughed. "A very big day indeed."

"Chef George asked me to deliver these to you here."

"They're from Chef George?"

"No, but you weren't there, so he sent me here."

"Oh, my, you came all this way across town? This can't be your normal delivery area." She dug in her pockets and produced a tip.

"No ma'am, Chef George already tipped me."

"How much?" she asked.

His face reddened. "Enough."

Inside, she set the vase of roses in the center of the coffee table. The card was simply a thank-you note, but the familiar handwriting tinged her cheeks pink.

My soul has kissed yours. Must I forget it?

30

LILLIAN'S CELL PHONE RANG.

"Geena?"

"Lily Bug? Can you come, please?" She sounded drunk.

Lillian's heart fell. It was just like Geena to suddenly reappear and bring trouble just when good things were starting to happen.

"Where are you?"

"La Rosaleda."

"La Rosaleda? What are you doing there?"

"I don't know." Her words were slurred.

"Geena, can you get a ride home and just sleep it off? We can talk later." Geena sobbed.

"Where are you?"

"The Sunset Hoootell."

"What are you doing there?"

"I don't know. I just woke up here. What time is it?"

"It's evening, Geena. How long have you been sleeping?"

"Oh," she said, "off and on."

"Have you been doing something besides drinking?"

"Maybe," she said. "I can't remember." Something rustled in the background. Geena's voice was muffled when she came back on the line. "Yep, from the looks of it, I took one other thing."

Lillian sighed, wondering if she should call an ambulance or drive there herself.

"Geena, do you need to go to the hospital?"

"No, I just don't want to be alone. Please come, Lillian."

"Okay," Lillian said. "But don't go anywhere, okay? I'll see you in a little while."

Lillian called Paige from the car. "I'm sorry for the late notice, but do you have a room or a cottage for two?"

"Of course, Lil. We always have a room for you. I'm excited you are coming!"

"Well, it's not for happy reasons," Lillian explained and launched into a diatribe about Geena's drinking problem.

Paige stopped her about halfway through the story. "You don't have to explain anything to me."

Relief washed through Lillian. "She frustrates me so much. This is one of the reasons we don't speak."

⟣

When Lillian arrived, Mark Tenney met her to help with her bags.

"We gave you a cottage with twin beds," he said. "We've reserved it for the week in case you are staying awhile."

Lillian nodded.

"You need help?"

He glanced at the backseat where Geena slumped against the window, her feet twisted beneath her in the leather seat of the sedan.

"Yes, please."

He said nothing as they walked Geena to the cottage. Lillian was grateful when he ignored Geena's off-color comments about how cute he was as they laid her across one of the beds.

Mark paused just inside the door on his way out. "Paige said to have you come in for coffee."

"It's late for caffeine."

"Maybe you could use some."

"Tell her I'll just have tea."

He nodded and then closed the door. For a moment, she envied Paige. What would it be like to have someone like Mark around every day?

She peeked in on Geena. The rise and fall of her chest was the only sign of life. Lillian didn't know whether to feel sorry for her or to be angry. She decided to be angry. It was easier.

～◈～

Lillian accepted a warm cup of herb tea.

"You don't have to explain anything," Paige said.

Lillian nodded. "Thanks. I didn't know where else to go, and there was no way I was staying where I found her. It was a skanky hotel, but I don't want to talk about Geena, so tell me, how was your day going before I called?"

Paige smiled. "Wonderful. Gracie can tie her shoes now!"

Lillian remembered how proud she had been when Sheyenne and Lee had learned to tie their shoes. "That's so neat!" she exclaimed. "I'll congratulate her tomorrow."

"She'll be so excited to see you."

"I'll be looking for a Gracie hug."

"Guess who else might be glad to see you?"

Lillian wondered if the racing pulse in her temples was visible. "Let me guess," she whispered. "Tru?"

Paige nodded, smiling.

"But how did he know I was here?"

Paige's face grew serious as she pulled her long legs underneath her. The movement reminded Lillian of Geena.

"He was here when you called this evening."

"You told him it was me?"

"He was sitting right beside me and guessed it was you." She shrugged an apology. "He always asks about you when he's here."

"What did you tell him tonight?"

"That I'd call when you got here."

"He knows I'm here?"

She nodded. "He said he'd drop by tomorrow."

Lillian shook her head. "Geena and I will be gone early in the morning."

Paige glanced out the window toward the cottage where they both knew Geena was passed out cold. She gave Lillian a questioning look.

"Okay, maybe not," Lillian said, "but that doesn't mean I'm going to see him."

"Why don't you just stay for the week and see what happens? You could stay as a guest of the family. No charge."

"I can pay. It's not a problem."

"That's fine, but I'm taking some days off and I'd love to have the company. You don't have to tell me anything, but if you want to talk, I am here."

Lillian sighed heavily. "It's such a long, sad story. You don't want to know."

"I certainly understand." Paige carried the teacups to the sink. "You don't have to share, but I have crazier things I could tell you, if it makes you feel any better."

"They couldn't be worse, I assure you." Lillian stood to leave. "I'm sorry I kept you up so late."

Paige glanced at the rooster clock on the wall. "It's only ten. Stay."

Lillian stood by the door, considering the offer. "Okay," she said, happy to delay whatever unpleasantness she would encounter with Geena at the cottage.

31

GEENA WAS SPRAWLED FACEDOWN across the bed in only her cartoon panties and a red tank top with the same absence of modesty she'd always had. Lillian draped a sheet over Geena's legs against the cool breeze coming through the cottage window.

Geena flung the sheet off and said in a thick voice, "No, I'm hot."

An image of them as little girls lying side by side at Grandma's house flashed through Lillian's mind, the acrid smell of smoke burning their nostrils.

Moisture pooled in her eyes as she sat on the bed, leaned forward, and cried into her hands. "God," she whispered, "please help us."

"Lily Bug?"

Lillian swiped the back of her hand across her face and looked at her sister through blurry eyes. Geena sat up. Her red hair splayed around her, making her look like a mermaid in an animated film. She was beautiful, even in her drunkenness.

Lillian blinked away more familiar images of them as little girls, their hair pulled back into french braids. Had Geena always been this beautiful? Lillian tried to remember. Lillian had never been jealous of Geena's looks, but now that she knew about Robert's attraction to her, Lillian couldn't help viewing Geena as a man might see her.

"It's always the letters and the pictures that give cheaters away," Lillian said, not meaning to say the words out loud.

Geena's face turned ashen. Her regret was evident even in the dim moonlight that poured through the window. She looked so vulnerable that Lillian was tempted to feel sorry for her. She started to apologize for her bluntness, but then her eyes fell on the cleavage that peeked out of Geena's tank top. Jealousy pumped through Lillian's veins as she tried not to think of her sister's indiscretions with Robert.

"I am sorry, Lillian."

Lillian cringed at Geena's hands suddenly on her shoulders. This was not how she wanted to make up. She didn't want Geena to touch her with compassion. Jerking away, Lillian turned from Geena, slipped into her bed, and closed her eyes against the betrayal.

The smell of bacon from the B&B woke Lillian early. She remained still, refusing to open her eyes, and remembered how Geena had come to her bedside several times during the night to rub her back or smooth her hair. She'd tried to soothe her, but Lillian had covered her ears each time she tried.

Feeling emotionally raw and sleep-deprived, Lillian turned over in her bed and called Geena's name, but she found Geena's bed empty.

Lillian looked out the window and saw Gracie striding down the pathway into the garden. She grabbed her robe and stepped onto the porch.

"Gracie!" she called out, jogging in bare feet on the smooth pebbles that paved the driveway.

"Lily!" Gracie called out, bounding toward Lillian. "Hi, Lily Diamond! I have something for you!"

Lillian smiled and accepted a hug from the curly-headed girl. "Do you remember my sister, Geena? Have you seen her?"

"She went in the car," Gracie said.

"She what?"

"She got in a black car." Gracie pointed toward the road.

Lillian shaded her eyes against the glare of morning sun. *Where has she gone?* Lillian huffed. It was so like Geena to stir things up and then just disappear.

"Don't you want your present?"

Lillian glanced down at Gracie, expecting to receive a childhood craft or drawing. Her smile faded when Gracie held out the tattered photo of the Rose House, the same photo that had disappeared from the restaurant bulletin board.

"She told me to give you this."

GEENA STARED OUT THE WINDOW at the vineyards as they drove through the valley. She had been stupid to think Lillian would want to help her. To think Lillian would be able to forgive her was an even crazier idea.

She'd always known that Lillian might have read the letters, seen the pictures from the beach house. Robert had been a meticulous businessman who never threw away anything. Lillian had complained about it more than once to her. *"He even saves his old girlfriend's letters from nine years ago. Why on earth does he need those?"*

Of course he would have saved her letters and maybe the photos too. She tried to remember what had attracted her to him. Was it the bad boy buried beneath his white doctor's coat? Was it the contrast of the bad boy and the good boy his parents had raised? Or the Stanford graduate? Or maybe it was the James Dean rebel who daringly gave her permission to use his beeper number but was too cowardly to tell Lillian he had fallen in love with her sister. The same man bold enough to save their mementos but not leave his wife.

Geena watched the vineyards roll by, thinking of the visit she had made to the Rose House on her way out of town. The fragrance of the blooms had wafted into her soul, and she had become overwhelmed with shame. Why had she traded her sister for a salacious affair? What was in her blood that made her so bad?

"HOW COULD I HAVE LET her manipulate me again?"

Paige was busy in the kitchen, preparing for breakfast. As she checked the coffee canister and organized ingredients for blueberry pancakes, she pressed her mouth into a thin line.

Lillian complained about what an idiot she had been. When she got to the part about the nude photo, Paige raised her eyebrows, and Lillian suddenly felt she had said too much.

"I'm sorry, Paige. We haven't known each other long and here I am sharing intimate details about my family. I must sound petty and bitter."

Paige tossed the dishrag into the sink. "True, you sound bitter."

Lillian stared into the mug Paige had given her.

Paige grasped Lillian's hands in hers. "Don't be embarrassed, Lillian. You sound bitter, but you don't sound petty. Being angry about these things isn't petty." She let go of Lillian's hands, grabbed a towel, and turned her attention to wiping down tables. "We can't control when our hearts burst open for the entire world to see. I am sorry you have had to endure so much. You've had a hard time."

"Thanks," the word sounded empty and flat.

Paige moved behind the counter and began pouring batter onto the hot griddle.

"Can I help you with that?" Lillian asked, reaching for an apron.

"Of course. Mark is busy with a repair, so I would appreciate your help serving, if you want to." She handed Lillian a coffeepot.

"You've dealt with this alone since your husband died. Now your heart is reaching out. What's the harm in that?"

"I don't want to burden you," Lillian answered.

"Maybe I want to be burdened," Paige said. "Maybe I'm honored to be burdened! And I suspect Truman would like to be burdened too!"

After breakfast slowed, the two women stood leaning against the counter with mugs of coffee. "My goodness," Lillian said, "that's a lot of work! You do this every day?"

"In the summer I do," Paige said, "but I've been thinking about switching to a continental breakfast on Sundays. We are always late to church."

"My Aunt Bren was a big breakfast person. She didn't have a B&B to run, but she always served a cold breakfast on Sunday since we couldn't be late to church."

"Do you miss it?"

"Church? Sure. I used to love it. We grew up in a small country church in Oklahoma. We were the pastor's kids, so we had to attend. I didn't mind. The singing is what I miss the most."

"Where do you attend now?"

"Nowhere. I went to a big church in Sacramento for a while, but after the accident, I quit going."

"But you really liked it when you were a kid? You are lucky you grew up that way."

Lillian chuckled. "Maybe. I remember how Pastor didn't have real church employees, so Geena and I would go early to make sure the pews had a Bible, pencils, and hymnals." Lillian smiled. "But it seemed real back then. When you are a teenager on fire for God, you feel invincible. That's before you grow up and meet the devil."

After a long silence, they both laughed.

"The devil indeed," Paige said.

A deep voice penetrated the room. "Good morning, ladies!"

"Hi, honey!" Paige offered her husband a peck on the cheek. "You two are just in time to give Lillian a break and help with cleanup." She tossed Gracie a wet sponge, which caused her to erupt into giggles.

"I think I'll head back to my cottage. I need to make some calls."

"Come see me this evening," Paige said. "Let me know if you are staying longer."

Lillian said good-bye and walked onto the terrace. As she paused beside a table to dig for her keys, she felt a warm hand on her shoulder. She turned to find slate blue eyes staring down at her.

Her hand flew to her hair in an attempt to smooth the strands that had slipped from her bun. "Tru," she whispered. The memory of their last kiss flooded her thoughts. She glanced down at her feet to hide the flush that she felt in her neck.

He sat down in a patio chair and pulled her into the one next to him. He dangled his hat between his knees, his eyes never leaving hers.

"Hi," she whispered.

"Rough night?" he said, placing a hand on her knee.

She nodded but didn't elaborate. The intensity of his gaze dissolved the little resistance she had left.

His deep voice cracked. "It's so good to see you."

She smiled.

"If I can't hug you right this minute, I'm going to ignite."

He stood and his gaze grew serious. She allowed herself to be lifted into an embrace and pressed her cheek into the warmth of his chest. She had missed him. She knew he wanted to kiss her, but it certainly wasn't the right place, even if it did feel like the right time. He gave her a squeeze before releasing her.

"Time for lunch?" he asked, his eyes hopeful.

"I just had breakfast, but I would love to have lunch with you," she assured him.

"In the meantime, we could take a walk."

"I was just heading over to the cottage to make a quick phone call. Can we meet back here in, say, half an hour?"

He let her go, slowly. "I guess I can," he teased, hooking his thumbs in his pockets. "I'll just help myself to some brew." He walked over to the pot of gourmet coffee and poured himself a mug while she walked the path back to the cottage.

~∅~

Lillian tried to remove Truman from her thoughts for the next few minutes as she dealt with Geena. As tired as she was of her antics, she had to make sure her sister was okay. If for no other reason, then for Aunt Bren.

"Geena, please call me," Lillian breathed into the phone. As soon as she flipped the phone shut, she saw Geena's name light up the screen.

"Geena?"

"Sis, I am so sorry. I know there's nothing I can do to—"

Lillian was silent.

"I miss how we used to be," Geena whispered.

"Where are you?"

"Not in La Rosaleda."

They argued for a few minutes before Geena's voice rose above Lillian's. "I know, I know! Please stop it!" There was a long pause. "I just wish you didn't have to know every little detail. How will that help?"

"What *really* happened, Geena? I have a photograph of you half naked! I found it in my dead husband's wallet. I think that warrants an explanation!"

"I was just tanning on the beach. It was nothing."

"Nothing? Are you saying you never had sex with Robert?"

She was quiet for a minute. "I cannot say that, but—"

Lillian's heart ripped open again. Of course she already knew, but hearing it from Geena's lips was harsher than she had expected.

"I *can* tell you he didn't mean to—"

"What? Isn't that what all men say?"

"I mean he really didn't mean to, and neither did I, at least the first time—"

Lillian cut in, the edge in her voice growing sharper. "At least the first time? Were you two drunk the first time? High? Isn't that the typical excuse? How many times were there?"

Her silence told Lillian that it hadn't been a mere slip but an ongoing affair.

If Lillian's heart had not already been broken, it shattered now; everything she had held pure in her marriage became tainted.

"I'm sorry, Lily Bug. I know this is hard. I will just get out of your life. I'm at the airport now."

The realization that Geena was going to disappear again set off an alarm in Lillian. On one hand, she wanted Geena to feel pain for what she'd done to her, but on the other, the idea of losing her sister again made her panic.

"What kind of tramp are you?"

"I don't need your judgment! You're not perfect, either. High and mighty, flawless Lillian. If you are so wonderful, then why did Robert want me?"

Lillian's chest felt like it would implode. She couldn't speak. She wanted to fling the phone across the room. Geena had just said out loud what Lillian had worried about since finding the photo in Robert's wallet.

"Lillian," Geena whispered, "I'm so sorry. I didn't mean—"

Lillian was no longer listening. Garish images from the newspapers of her babies and the man she thought was her husband, covered by bloody sheets on Mosquito Road, flashed across her mind.

"Lillian, I'm so sorry. I hate myself for being involved. That's why I ran away."

Lillian sat down at the kitchen table. Staring out the window at the cherry blossom trees, she saw Tru strolling around the pathways, studying flowers and picking a few here and there, waiting for her.

"Tell me this, Geena. Did you love him?"

"Maybe," Geena answered. "Yes, we loved each other."

Lillian drew in a shaky breath and brought her hand to her mouth.

"You know," Geena said, "he loved you more than he loved me. I hated that he would never have left you."

"Even if he was a scoundrel who cheated on me."

"He just lost his way and got involved in some really bad stuff, including me."

The phone grew heavy with silence. Images of Robert and Geena filled Lillian's mind. She recalled the two of them sitting together at dinner parties, talking intimately on the back porch, Robert giving Geena rides, and, ultimately, the ride on Mosquito Road with her children, Robert too distracted with his girlfriend to remember to buckle the children's seat belts.

"If I had taken them to their lessons that day," Lillian said, "maybe I would still have Sheyenne and Lee with me." Lillian remembered Robert heading out of the house that day, how she had complained that he was always leaving when she needed him the most. Just once, couldn't he take the children to their lessons and then pick them up, so she could start planning their birthday party the following week? She'd hounded him.

"I'll do it," he finally said, "but then I have an errand to run." He'd

mumbled an apology for being cranky and offered her a kiss. She had
watched him leave with the children.

A clinking of glasses brought Lillian's attention back to the present.
"Geena, are you at a bar?"

"I'm at a coffee bar in the airport, thank you very much," Geena said
dryly.

"Sorry."

"Yeah, whatever." Geena's voice had changed. "I know what you
think of me, Lillian, and I don't blame you." The line went dead.

Lillian flipped the phone shut. Her feet felt like bricks as she walked
into the bathroom to freshen up. She stared at her face in the mirror, a
stranger's face, gaunt and hollow. Reaching for her makeup bag, she wondered if foundation and lipstick would help, but she applied it anyway;
painting over the blemishes of her life, hoping they wouldn't show when
Tru saw her.

◦⬯

When Lillian walked out of her cottage, Truman was waiting for her on
the terrace with a bouquet of flowers in hand. He didn't ask for an explanation. He set the bouquet on a table beside him and opened his arms to
her. What an amazing sight it was, a man inviting her to come in and be
comforted. She stared into his worried eyes, expectant but not demand-
ing. What else could she possibly lose by accepting his affection?

She felt stripped bare before him in a way that physical intimacy
could never emulate. He'd known her heart well enough to paint it without a word or even a touch. Soul-kissed, is what he'd called it.

She tucked her head into his chest, pressing her cheek where his
heart thundered. Was she the reason his breath came so rapidly? His lips

touched her forehead and then her lips, soft and tentative, smoothing sad thoughts away, pressing them into the holding part of her heart to deal with later.

They pulled themselves apart when shrieking children ran past, waking them from their reverie. Lillian ran her fingers across her lips as if she could wipe away the evidence. Tru pulled her close to his side, like they were old friends, as they walked away from the B&B and toward the plaza.

"If you ever want an ear, I'm here," he said.

She shook her head. "I'm okay for now. And, honestly, I want to talk about you for a change."

"I'm boring," he teased. "Let's talk about you. Tell me everything."

They walked hand in hand past shop windows and gazed at a sprinkling of families picnicking around the fountain in the park.

"My favorite color happens to be purple," Lillian said.

"Really? I had you pegged as a lover of blue."

"What's your favorite color?"

"Orange."

"Seriously? Why?"

He laughed. "I don't know. Maybe because it's more masculine than purple, but I love all colors for different reasons."

"Of course," she giggled, "you are an artist."

His stomach growled, and they both laughed. "I'm starving," Truman said.

"We should feed you," Lillian said.

"Why don't you teach me how to cook?" Truman suggested.

"I love that idea."

They walked back to the Tenneys' B&B, and he helped her into the truck. She wrinkled her nose at the mixture of scents from oil, dust, and the pine tree air freshener. The truck was so untidy compared to his house. He buckled her in and she laughed. "Such a romantic gesture. Will you do this forever?"

"If you'll have me forever," he said teasingly and closed the door.

As Lillian settled comfortably in the seat, her eyes fell on a snapshot of *Beauty and the Beast Within* tucked into the driver-side visor. She had not noticed it before and wondered when Truman had put it there. It was wrinkled and curled at the corners, similar to her own snapshot of the Rose House. She reached into her purse, pulled out the snapshot, and tucked it into the visor beside his photo.

When Truman settled behind the wheel, his eyes fell on the Rose House photo and a smile spread across his face. He turned to her, like he wanted to say something, but apparently changing his mind, he turned and started the truck. When they were driving through the valley toward his house, he reached across the seat and squeezed her hand.

34

LILLIAN STAYED LONGER IN La Rosaleda than she had expected. She had called Chef George to tell him that she needed more time away from the restaurant. "Will you be spending time with your artist admirer?" he had asked.

"Yes," she had answered.

"Why don't you take the whole month off?" he had suggested. "Your job will be waiting for you."

And so Lillian found herself indulging in a brief sabbatical. She extended her stay at the Tenneys' cottage and treasured lazy days getting to know Truman. When he wasn't painting or managing his land, they spent their time driving around the valley and visiting the vineyards that surrounded La Rosaleda. The lush hills of grapevines and forests spread for miles in every direction. Truman seemed to know most of the growers in the region and many of the migrant workers as well.

He introduced her to the best Mexican restaurants, where she reveled in the authenticity of the cuisine. She even started experimenting with Mexican recipes in his kitchen. He finally told her that if she continued to feed him fresh avocado every day, he'd have to take up jogging, so they began hiking on the weekends.

Tru drove them to places like Bodega Bay, where the craggy cliffs seemed to drop dangerously into the rolling sea, through the giant redwoods of Muir Woods, and to Point Reyes, where they walked to a lighthouse and watched for whales. The history of the lighthouse amazed her, and the first time she saw the hump of a whale breaking the ocean's surface, its spray shooting into the air, Truman had to remind her to breathe.

Before their outings, they would stop to eat breakfast at Carlos's Diner, where Carlos and his friends acted like Lillian was already engaged to their friend.

"You like this young man?" Carlos inquired in a heavy accent, a cheerful smile pasted on his lined face.

"Kind of," she teased.

He leaned close and said, "This one would make you a good husband, señorita."

Truman had laughed when he saw her eyes widen. He shook his head at Carlos, but the amused smile didn't leave his face. "Now, don't scare away my señorita."

They reveled in getting to know everyday things about each other, and after such a dramatic start, they enjoyed the unhurried way their relationship was unfolding. For all of Carlos's teasing, there was really no rush. In La Rosaleda, life moved slowly. There were no expectations about what would come next, so they talked as if they had already reached their destination.

Each night they stayed up late talking, either together or on the phone, exploring each other's hopes, dreams, and losses. She learned that his parents had died in a car accident when he was a teenager and that he had been an only child. After his grandma died, he had formed his family ties around the folks at the diner and those he worked with in La Rosaleda. After Angela, he'd promised himself that he would stay away from romantic entanglements.

"You came along and dissolved my plan," he teased during a late-night conversation.

"Mmm," she said, "should I apologize for ruining your plans?"

She expected to hear his usual low chuckle, but instead he whispered, "No. I made them before I knew there was a Diamon out there for me."

"A Diamon in the rough, right?"

"Not at all, Lil. It was me who was in the rough before you came on the scene."

"Ah." She hugged him and smiled. "You are too good to me. And you have excellent come-on lines to boot."

His laughter joined hers as he reached to tickle her rib cage. When their laughter settled, he pulled her close. "But seriously, Lil. It's true. Before you, I was a different man. Being with you makes me a better person."

"You're a great person," she said.

"Your sister doesn't think so."

Lillian sighed. "Well, that doesn't mean much."

35

"GEENA, WHERE ARE YOU GETTING all this money for plane tickets?" Aunt Bren asked. "We've seen you more in the past few months than in the past ten years, honey."

"I've been waitressing here and there. And Lillian gave me a little money before I left."

"You took her money and left?"

"No, Aunt Bren. It wasn't like that. I didn't plan to take it and leave, but we got into an argument and—"

"Did you tell your sister what you told me?"

Aunt Bren smelled so strongly of lilacs that she could have bottled it, but Geena didn't mind. It was Aunt Bren's trademark.

"I told her everything, except about the attack, which you now know."

"You should have told her." Aunt Bren said.

"She doesn't need to know about it, Aunt Bren. She's already filled with anguish, and much of it is my doing."

Aunt Bren walked into the kitchen and poured fresh coffee into two John Deere mugs. It was three in the afternoon, but as always, she had kept the pot warm.

Geena studied her aunt, noticing for the first time the spider-web lines that stretched from the outer edges of her eyes to the apples of her cheeks. Her brown hair was pulled back into a bun, the same way she'd always worn it. Her glasses were out-of-date and had slipped down her nose. She wore a pair of loose-fitting jeans and a floral cotton top that she had purchased on sale in three different colors.

Aunt Bren crossed her legs and twirled the toe of her brown loafer as she talked. "You need to go back to your sister and patch things up. She's your family."

"Oh, Aunt Bren, I don't know this time. Besides, I'm here now. Isn't that enough for you? You are my family too. I'm sorry I haven't treated you like family. I was a stupid kid and now—"

"Don't you talk like that."

"I have prayed and prayed, Aunt Bren, but I can't forgive myself for what I've done to you—to Pastor—to Lillian." Geena placed her hands over her face to cover her shame. "Especially what I've done to Lillian," she cried. "Her poor babies."

"Their deaths weren't your fault, honey."

"They were, Aunt Bren. If I hadn't gotten involved with Robert…"

"It might still have happened, only maybe with someone else."

Geena had never thought she might have been just the girl of the moment. "If only I hadn't believed he could love me more than my own sister—"

Aunt Bren patted her hand. "Sweetheart, it might not seem like it now, but you will get through this."

"I feel like I've wasted so much time, even with you and Pastor."

"Oh," Aunt Bren said, dabbing at tears, "don't look back, sweetie. You and Lillian had a time of it with your family gone. We always expected you to have a harder time than other girls. Your grandmother tried to prepare me for this, but I was too young to absorb it."

Geena grasped Aunt Bren's hand. "You were great to us."

"I don't know, honey. Maybe you still would have made difficult choices, even if your mom and dad had lived. It's normal, but you and Lillian had it harder than most. I never really knew what to do for you."

"If Momma were here, she'd say you've been a great mom to her daughters."

Aunt Bren hiccuped and wiped her eyes. "You just go back and make up with Lillian, okay? You two are meant to be together. Not all sisters have a good relationship. My own sister and I never got along. Good Lord, rest her soul. She never even liked me."

"Really?"

"It's true. Oh, sure, we managed to get along for our mother's sake, but my sister never liked being around me, and I never knew why."

"She never told you?"

"Never. I'll wonder about it until the day I join her in heaven. At least I know I will see her there."

"That's really sad, Aunt Bren. I bet it was hard, losing your sister. If I ever lost Lillian—" Geena sighed. "I've felt dead inside for the past four years since I haven't been with Lillian." Geena handed Aunt Bren a tissue, realizing that she had never thought of her adoptive mother as someone who understood hard times.

"It was difficult," Aunt Bren said, taking another sip of her coffee, "but not as hard as the day I lost your mother. She was my real sister, Geena. Blood is thick, but it's not true what they say about it being thicker than water."

"Really?" asked Geena. "I guess I always thought blood came first."

Aunt Bren smiled knowingly. "Water can seem thick too when it ebbs around the love people have for each other. How else is it that adoptive parents love their children so much?"

"Like us," said Geena. "You came to Grandma's house to help us the night of the fire, didn't you? I remember now."

"It was horrible. When your grandma and I woke you girls the next morning, you had already figured out the truth on your own. I'll never forget how you both sat up straight, your arms around each other, as I confirmed your worst fears. Your eyes were so wide and scared, but I had to tell you the truth."

Her voice cracked and Geena blinked through the moisture in her own eyes. Silence filled the room as they remembered what had happened. Geena had always thought of it as their loss and had never considered how it had affected Aunt Bren.

"You girls, you sobbed and screamed, fighting the truth, and me, and your grandma. You were both inconsolable until you exhausted yourselves."

"I remember," said Geena. "I couldn't believe that my mom, my dad, and both of my brothers were gone. I was so angry at everyone, even at God."

"Are you still mad at Him, honey?"

Geena shrugged, "I think so, but I'm trying not to be. Did you know that when I lay my head on the pillow every night, your words and Pastor's words still echo in my mind? I can't get your words out of my head!"

Aunt Bren laughed. "Like what?"

Geena grabbed a pillow off the couch and hugged it to her chest. "You wanna hear the best ones?"

Aunt Bren nodded. "Tell me."

"Well," said Geena, eyebrows raised, "the attitude of obedience is more important than the act."

"I said that?"

"Yes, you did," Geena said, "along with something about a child's cry to God—"

Aunt Bren finished the phrase, "—is sweetness to His ears."

"Yeah, that," said Geena. "There are so many things you or Pastor said that never left me. Jesus this and Jesus that, but mostly I remember the story about the prodigal son."

"That's my favorite too," Aunt Bren said.

"I always thought there should be one about a prodigal daughter," said Geena with a quiet laugh.

Aunt Bren smiled knowingly. "I suppose it applies to both genders."

"But it was hard to believe that the father didn't yell at his son for running off and messing things up. A human father couldn't do that."

"Yep," said Aunt Bren, "unless that father is mirroring a father that isn't human."

"I know where you are going, Aunt Bren."

Aunt Bren sighed. "I'm sorry, Geena. I don't mean to preach."

Geena rubbed Aunt Bren's shoulder. "It's okay. You're a preacher's wife. You can't help it."

Aunt Bren roared with laughter, then she grew serious. "Sweetie, do you realize that if you hadn't gone to stay with your grandma that night, you would have died in the fire too. He had a plan for you girls."

"Why is that, Aunt Bren? Why them and not us?"

Aunt Bren stood to refill their cups and Geena followed her. She ran her hands along the Formica countertop and the painted cabinets stenciled with daisies. She loved how familiar the kitchen felt, realizing it had not changed since she was a kid.

"I don't know, sweetie. I guess they had accomplished their purpose here on earth. You and Lillian hadn't. God wasn't yet finished with the two of you. Your grandma said the same thing when she asked Pastor and me to take care of you when she was gone."

"Grandma died less than a year later, didn't she? It's hard for me to remember."

"Because you were so young, sweetie."

They slipped into silence, until a shudder caused Aunt Bren to look over at her.

"So Lillian's babies were meant to die and not me? And Robert—" She sobbed at the mention of Robert's name. She couldn't change the fact that she had loved him, even if it hadn't been right. She couldn't stick around to help Lillian with the funeral and everything that followed,

because not only did she feel it was all her fault but she had been grieving for Robert too.

"I'm sorry, Aunt Bren, but I miss him. I know it's wrong and that he
was not a good person, but I do. No matter how wrong it is, I feel a deep
loss." She gasped for air. "I didn't mean for it to happen, but I loved him
and he died!" Regret and loss that she had never revealed to anyone
poured forth.

Aunt Bren wrapped her arm around Geena and walked her back to
the couch. They sat close as Aunt Bren began to whisper in Geena's ear,
but while the words comforted Geena, they were not said to her.

Aunt Bren, well-versed in what needed to be done when a broken
person came to her for help, continued to whisper the soul-southing
words as Geena sobbed into her shoulder.

"See," Geena hiccupped and tried to smile, "you can't help it, Aunt
Bren."

They laughed together, and Aunt Bren patted Geena's head. "You're
right, sweetie, I can't."

⁓◐⁓

They were still laughing when the front door opened and Pastor walked
in. Geena was struck by how small he seemed. She had always thought
of him as a more formidable man. Even though she'd seen him during visits, she hadn't allowed herself to look at him for fear of judgment, but she
looked straight at him now.

He stood only five and a half feet tall and he was balding. What was
left of his white hair stood up when he removed his cap. She tried to
merge this image with the dignified image of him behind the pulpit she'd
grown up with. He'd seemed tall back then, even imposing.

A grin spread across his face as if he knew this time was different. He tossed his cap onto the coffee table. "Geena, bright Diamon girl. Welcome home, kiddo."

She walked quickly into his arms, accepting his embrace. It was that of a loving father, and it made her feel like she really was home.

"Welcome home, little sister," Pastor said, and she knew he meant it. He held her out at arm's length. "Now, what are we gonna do about big sister?"

36

SEVERAL TIMES, LILLIAN HAD tried to get Truman to show her his studio, but he always said he was working on a surprise for her and didn't want her to see it just yet. Every time she had gone to his house, his studio had remained locked.

He worked several hours each morning, so Lillian would sometimes drive to his house and let herself in. She would knock on his studio door and wait for him to open it and find her standing there, usually wearing one of the lightweight sundresses he loved and holding a tray of iced tea and something gourmet she had whipped up in his kitchen.

"Can I come in and play?" she would tease. He would give her a quick kiss, take the lunch, and with a wink shut the door behind him. While she waited, Lillian would settle into an oversized couch draped with quilts and read a book.

Sometimes she could finish a book in a day. She noticed that in the love stories, their heroines rarely enjoyed a happy household and passion at the same time. That was disappointing, so she tried to imagine a marriage to Truman as both domestic and filled with a fervor for each other that would only grow stronger over time.

Sometimes she would fall asleep reading, and sad dreams of Robert would haunt her. She didn't tell Truman about the dreams or of the lingering sad feelings for Robert, just as she never asked him about Angela. These were private pains they didn't need to talk about. They simply knew the pain was there and tried to ease it.

On this day, she had just given Truman his lunch and was reclining on the couch with a book when the studio door swung open. He walked purposely toward the couch, reached down and pulled her to her feet, and swept her into a hungry embrace.

His mouth on hers was gentle yet eager as he eased onto the couch, pulling her onto his lap. His hands cupped her rib cage as his mouth grazed her neck. Her hands stroked the smoothness of his head, pressing his mouth closer to hers, then moved to massage the firmness of his shoulders. She was trying to turn her body to more easily face his when a loud knock on the screen door startled them. She nearly jumped out of his lap. They both erupted in awkward laughter.

"Wow. Um, hmm." He cleared his throat, and they both stood, his eyes penetrating hers with a question. He leaned down and drank in another kiss. His voice came out in a low growl. "Should I answer that?" he asked, his hands massaging her spine.

She pushed him gently away and tried to hide the smile on her face. Folding her arms across her chest, she whispered, "You should answer it."

He nodded and shoved his thumbs in his pockets, a gesture he used when he was trying to keep from touching her. She watched him walk toward the door, his jeans and T-shirt covered with paint. She glanced down at her dress. It was covered with smudges of blue, red, and brown.

Sighing, she glanced at the open door of the studio. Truman was busy signing for a package, so she walked stealthily into the studio. Unable to hold back the playful smile from her face, she looked around and found herself surrounded by easels and paints. Soft jazz tunes filled the room, and the smells of paint and turpentine tickled her nose. Unlike the rest of his house, which was always organized and neat, the studio was cluttered with canvases: some blank and several partially covered with paint.

Tables were strewn with paint tubes. Several jars held brushes. Large sheets of paper and drawings were tacked up on the walls next to finished paintings of roses and vineyards. A ceiling fan slowly rotated, and the studio was surrounded by windows covered with heavy drapes, some of them drawn back. Studio lamps were set up around the room but turned off. Lillian could see that he had designed the studio so that he could let light from the windows in at various angles or black out the room completely.

Several easels had been turned away from the door or draped with cloths. The painting he was working on faced away from her. She wanted so badly to look, but she had promised not to snoop, so she turned back toward the door, satisfied that she had seen where he spent the bulk of his time.

Truman stood leaning against the doorjamb. Caught in the act, she gasped, covering her mouth like a child who had just been caught snooping under the Christmas tree.

"I'm sorry," she whispered.

"Like Eve, you just couldn't stay away from temptation, huh?"

She laughed. "It was Adam who didn't keep an eye on Eve. If he had, maybe she never would have tasted the apple."

His eyes sparkled. "If not for Eve, maybe Adam would never have been tempted."

His eyes swept over her, and she knew they weren't talking about apples. He didn't move from his place in the doorway.

"I ruined your dress." His face held mock regret. "I love that dress too."

"It's okay," she said. "I'll just save it as a souvenir."

He laughed and then walked toward her, sweeping her into his arms. "A souvenir of what? To remind you of what a scoundrel I am?" His fingers tickled her ribs.

"You aren't!" she shrieked.

He held her at arm's length, his eyes earnest. "I am. If that delivery man hadn't knocked when he did—"

"We would have made love." Her words came out fast, in a whisper, surprising both of them with the truth, spoken out loud. So there it was, the truth in all its glory, and her face as red as the splatters of paint on her clothes.

She looked down, smoothing her dress. Should a widow even think such things?

"Lillian," he tipped up her chin, but she looked away. "Please, sweetheart, look at me."

Robert's face flashed before her mind's eye. It was one of the nicknames he'd called her; a name that a husband calls his wife. She looked at Truman through the memory.

"Have you ever been married?" she asked.

"No. Angela and I never got there, remember? I told you."

"But I have."

He stared at her, confused at the obvious, but waited for her to finish. She looked down. "I am a widow, remember?"

He cupped her face in his hands and kissed her lovingly. "Lil, you are a widow, but you aren't dead."

She choked back a sob that pressed against her throat. "But sometimes I feel like I am."

Truman ran his thumb softly along her cheek. He sighed, and it broke her heart.

"Just because you are a widow doesn't mean you can't feel or experience love again. You are alive." He leaned down, his breath warm in her hair. "Believe me, Lil, you are very alive." He inhaled deeply. "We don't have to go down that road right now, but someday, Lil, you will want to." He tipped her chin up again. "Especially if I can get you to stay forever."

She nodded, afraid of what he was proposing. He pulled her close to his chest. She couldn't imagine being married to anyone right now, and wondered if she would always feel like Robert's wife.

She relaxed into his chest, listening to his heartbeat. "It is probably wrong for me to allow myself to get so serious, but when I'm with you, it feels—"

"It feels right because it seems like we have become much closer than we should be, doesn't it?"

She wrapped her arms tighter around his chest. "Yes, it does."

"So then, where do we go from here?" he asked.

She laughed. "Well, not there, even though it would be fun, wouldn't it?"

He laughed loudly. "I can't believe you said that, my prim and proper Lillian."

She laughed with him. "It's true! And it feels good to get it out!" She rolled her eyes. "Now that it's said, maybe it will lessen the desire a bit."

He shook his head. "Not for me, my sweetheart. Not for me. Come and sit down here." He walked her to a couch and arranged her arms and legs into a pose where she rested against a pillow, one hand on her chin, her legs tucked beneath her dress.

He set up an easel and began to work, his brush stroking the canvas, his eyes focused on creating an image with his paints.

"You're painting me again?"

"Yes. It is consensual this time, isn't it?"

Her cheeks warmed. "Yes, it is this time." She smiled.

"Don't smile, just rest and let me paint."

She watched him study her as he worked, his eyes bright, energy emanating from his movements, and for a moment she was embarrassed. How many people their age waited to make love? She wondered what Truman really thought of her prim and proper behavior. She was attracted to him on the deepest level, but she wondered if she could ever be intimate with him after Robert had left her feeling undesirable and inadequate.

She readjusted her hips on the couch and took a moment to stretch one leg.

"You should call this painting *Waiting*," she teased.

"Shh," he whispered, "be still." He gazed at her face and turned back toward the canvas.

"Sorry," she whispered.

He kept painting, his movements quick behind the canvas, eyes darting back and forth between her and the canvas. "Maybe I should call it *The Frustrated Artist's Muse*."

She giggled. "What about the paint on my dress? You won't paint the smudges, will you?"

"I have to paint it the way it is."

"But it will look strange."

"No, it just complements the rest of how you look."

"How's that?"

"Well, it matches the smudge of paint in your hair and on your hands."

She glanced down and realized it was true. She had smears of blue paint on her hands from the caresses she had lavished on him during their passionate kissing.

He walked over to her and readjusted her chin to rest on her hand, and then he kissed her nose. "Shh."

He returned to the easel and dabbed at the canvas. "And somehow you ended up with a smudge of paint on your chin and your cheek."

"I'll look disheveled."

He breathed deeply and sighed. "Like you've just been kissed by a frustrated, albeit patient, artist."

37

DURING THEIR FREQUENT WALKS in the town square, Lillian noticed that people would occasionally step out of their shops, nodding and smiling at them as they watched them pass.

"What are they looking at?" Lillian asked during one of their strolls. "Did you get paint on me again?"

He hugged her to his side. "I think they just want to look at you. Some of them are always trying to fix me up with someone. They probably thought I would be a bachelor forever."

"Do you think they all know about the painting?"

"Yes. Didn't Kitty tell you? Louise is advertising the story behind the painting. She hopes it will increase traffic from visitors to La Rosaleda. Does that bother you?"

She shrugged and decided to answer honestly. "I guess it does. It still feels like a private thing to me. I wish she would have asked."

"I'm sorry you feel that way. I thought it was a good idea. I like our story." He let go of her as they walked, slipping his hands into his pockets.

Lillian regretted the curtain that slipped between them.

"On a positive note," he said tentatively, "the story behind the painting has also intrigued new people to show an interest in my work. I feel more motivated than ever to go deeper in my painting. I know my work can be better."

"Your old work is good too. I saw *Rose House in Winter* at the B&B. I love it. It is so gripping. So real."

"Thank you." He slipped his hand into hers, and relief washed over her.

"The Tenneys were the only collectors interested in that one. I suppose it was because they knew me. Most collectors looking for florals or landscapes of the area weren't interested in a house covered with dead roses to sell in their gift shops."

"But it was more than dead roses. It was winter," Lillian said. "That's what roses look like in winter."

"Doesn't matter. Some people perpetually live in summer." He laughed, but she didn't think he really thought it was funny.

She couldn't help smiling at the children who galloped in front of them as their parents tried to keep up. It saddened her, but she'd decided to let her memories of Sheyenne and Lee live, even when it meant the recollections brought pain.

"What about the painting you gave to the restaurant? Did it turn out as you envisioned?"

"Ms. Diamon, if that painting meant anything at all, it was a message to you. Didn't you receive it?"

They stopped under the awning of the gallery. She chose her words carefully. "When I first saw the painting, I was confused, but when I noticed the golden woman painted in the roses, I realized you'd again painted me without my knowing."

He frowned. "I was lost when I painted it. Having just found you and lost you, it was a way to express myself, a way to communicate with you." He glanced at the sidewalk and back at Lillian, holding her gaze. "You wouldn't return my calls."

She squeezed his arm. "I was so happy about the painting. All I could think about all day was you."

Relief flooded his features. "So you got the message?"

"I think so, or I wouldn't be here now. Of course, you are welcome to translate."

"The message went like this: 'I'm sorry I invaded your space to paint your portrait, but I'm not sorry we met. Please come back to me.'"

He leaned down to kiss her cheek, then jerked back at the sound of camera shutter clicks.

"Charles!" Truman exclaimed. "What do you think you're doing?"

Charles dropped his camera to his side, suddenly looking contrite.

"Charles, I asked what you are doing."

"I'm sorry, Mr. Clark." Charles glanced to the side and then down at his feet. "I was hanging out with Kara today, and when I saw you and Miss Diamon, I thought you would make a good picture." He shrugged. "I thought you would like it."

Lillian stepped into the gallery and came face to face with Kara, who looked panic-stricken.

"I am so sorry, Lillian!" Kara said. "He didn't mean anything by it."

"It's okay," Lillian mumbled.

"I was hoping I could bring him here to spend the day with me, but I was in the back for just a second talking to my fiancé on the phone and—"

"Truly, Kara," Lillian said, "I understand. Tru is dealing with him. I understand he is Charles's mentor."

"Yeah," Kara said, sounding relieved as she walked behind the counter. "He is. He's great with Charles. Goodness, when I saw him taking your picture, I was worried. He doesn't mean to be rude. He's just enthusiastic about his camera."

Charles entered the gallery with Truman close behind.

"I'm sorry," Truman said. "Charles sometimes forgets to ask people if they mind when he takes their picture."

Lillian watched as Charles sat in a chair behind the desk and busied himself putting away his camera equipment.

"A camera is a sort of canvas, and you are his teacher, after all," Lillian teased. She noticed Truman's face redden as he offered her a guilty smile.

"Kara," Lillian said, "as long as we're here, can we see *Beauty and the Beast Within*?" She gestured toward the other paintings. "I don't see it here. Did Louise put it away?"

Kara cleared her throat. "Yes," she said, "Louise put it away. I can't bring it out just now. Can we do it later? Maybe sometime next week? Will you still be in town?"

"The question is," Truman winked at Kara, "is she ever leaving?"

Truman again brought up the idea of Lillian staying in La Rosaleda that evening in the cobblestone alley café, as they were enjoying a young man singing classic Frank Sinatra songs.

"I'll think about it," Lillian said, "but if I stay, I'll have to find a house or an apartment, because I can't stay at the cottage forever."

"Paige wouldn't mind if you stayed forever. She doesn't want you to leave either."

The waitress appeared with two glasses of mango passion iced tea.

The evening was still warm from the day's heat, and they drank their tea before the ice could melt in their glasses. Lillian gazed up at a small, dimly lit balcony filled with pots of colorful flowers. She couldn't help smiling at the picture-perfect scene.

"What a romantic spot," she said.

"That's Kitty's balcony."

"It is?"

"There's a story behind it," he said.

"One of Kitty's stories. I love to hear her talk about the Rose House, her daughter and granddaughter, and her romance with Blake."

"As long as you aren't one of those crazy followers who think they see dead people on the Rose House porch." Truman shivered.

"No, I don't believe in ghosts," Lillian laughed. "I'm just interested. The story about the Rose House inspires me. To me, the Rose House is the antithesis of what happened on Mosquito Road, especially when you consider the story behind it. The beauty of it moved me from the first time I saw it."

"Yes, I know." He winked at her. "The idea that it was tended for so many years as a way to keep hope alive is extraordinary."

"Yes, it is."

"Is that why you carried a picture of it in your purse?"

"You might think me strange, but before you ever painted me by the Rose House, I kept that snapshot either in my purse or pinned to the bulletin board at work. It made me dream that I might be happy too someday."

"The Rose House changes people," he said, "but Kitty says it only changes the ones who can see beyond the roses."

"Look at us!" Lillian exclaimed. "Was it the Rose House? Was it fate?"

"That depends on your idea of fate. I would prefer to think of it as divine intervention."

She gazed up at the balcony. "I would like to believe in divine intervention."

He squeezed her hand. "You've never experienced it?"

She remembered the smell of smoke as the fire took her parents and brothers. She recalled the news clips from the car accident, images of the bloody sheets, Geena tiptoeing among them, the photo of Geena in Robert's wallet.

"I never experienced it, but I was raised to believe that it's possible."

"What about how I came to paint you?" he asked. He reached across the table and took her hand.

She glanced up at the balcony and thought of the Rose House painting. "The title you chose, *Beauty and the Beast Within*...it's a little sardonic."

"It was telling. By now, you know you are Beauty in the painting. Not just the image of a woman."

She smiled. "And I understand the part about the beast. How strange that I never thought of grief as a beast, but it is. It's like a monster that eats away at your sanity."

They placed their orders and began to work on a dish of nachos and corn mango salsa when a flash illuminated their corner.

"Charles!" Truman exclaimed, but it wasn't Charles. It was a dark woman about Lillian's age with curly brown hair and a cameraman.

"Laura Balmain. What are you doing?" Truman demanded, standing to his feet. "We are trying to have dinner!"

The woman looked frightened for a moment, and Lillian wondered if she was another of Truman's students, but it soon became apparent that she was a local reporter for the small-town newspaper.

Laura stared at Truman's imposing frame but held her ground. She waved her cameraman closer.

"Truman Clark, is this your girlfriend?"

Lillian stood and waved Truman away. She hoped to intervene and avoid causing a scene. Tourists were starting to stare.

"I am Lillian," she said. "I guess you could call me Truman's significant other."

"Is it true?" Laura asked Truman.

"Okay, it's true. This woman is my"—he winked at Lillian—"fiancée."

Lillian's mouth dropped open. "Your what?"

Truman said, "Now, if you'll excuse us, we're having a little celebration dinner," and he grabbed the tape recorder from the reporter's hand. "Laura, go bother somebody else. You don't work for *People* magazine. Surely you can find something more interesting to report than who I'm having dinner with."

"I was just trying to get all the facts before I ask you my big question," she said smugly.

Truman's hands flew into the air. "Laura, please go away!"

"Truman Clark, do you know who stole the painting titled *Beauty and the Beast Within* from the La Rosaleda Gallery?"

"What?"

"Stolen?" Lillian exclaimed.

"Oh, you didn't know, Miss Diamon?" Laura eagerly swiped the tape recorder and held it in front of Lillian.

"Of course not. What are you talking about?"

"Rumor has it the painting was stolen today. We heard that maybe Truman—" She suddenly looked stricken. "Well, it was suggested by someone that maybe Truman has it and is hiding it—or something."

"Why in the world would you say that?" Lillian retorted.

"Because Kitty DiCamillo wouldn't let him have it back. It just makes sense that Truman could be involved." Laura shrugged, looking slightly embarrassed.

"No, it doesn't," said Lillian.

"This is preposterous," Truman exclaimed. "Laura, I know your dad, and when I talk to him—"

"Is it even worth enough for somebody to steal?" Lillian asked. Truman looked at her like she was a traitor. "Just asking," she said. "I know it's worth millions to us, but—"

"It might be worth something," said Laura, picking up the thread, "or they wouldn't have taken it, right?"

"No! Not right," Truman interjected. "You are just trying to make a story out of nothing. Now please leave us. You are interrupting my dinner."

"With his fiancée," said Lillian, her eyes twinkling. Truman sent her a questioning glance. She forced back a smile.

Lillian looked past Truman and saw the manager approaching the table.

"Laura Balmain," he chided, "that's enough. This is my restaurant, and I want you to leave."

"Sorry, Bob," Laura said and motioned for her cameraman to follow her out. She called back over her shoulder. "And congratulations on your engagement!"

Lillian sat down across from Truman. "I can't believe this," she said.

"I can't believe it either," Truman said. "The painting has been stolen?"

"No," Lillian said. "I can't believe we are getting married."

A slow smile spread across his face. "I'm sorry I said that," he said. "I was only teasing."

She tried to look injured. "So you don't want to marry me?"

His gaze swept over her appreciatively. "Now, that's not what I said at all."

-ᗡ-

The next morning, the five-page *La Rosaleda Sun* emblazoned a gossipy headline announcing the robbery of the gallery: "Engaged Couple Mourns Loss of Painting."

Lillian slapped the newspaper down on the table in front of her as Paige poured another cup of coffee. "This is ridiculous."

"Don't worry," Paige said. "Nobody around here takes the paper seriously."

"But Tru will be embarrassed," Lillian moaned.

Paige smiled knowingly. "I doubt it."

Mark walked in and opened up an independent paper from nearby Santa Rosa. The article about the stolen painting hadn't made it to the front page, but it was mentioned, and it reported that the artist and the muse who inspired the painting were engaged.

"Do I need to get fitted for a tuxedo?" Mark teased.

Lillian stood quickly. "So you both find this amusing?"

They both nodded. "I'm afraid we do," said Paige. "Besides, we would love it if the two of you got married."

"He hasn't exactly proposed," said Lillian, turning to leave. She whirled back around. "How many papers is this in?"

"Just these two," Paige said. "Look at this way. If it gets people talking about the painting, then maybe it will be located more quickly."

Lillian sat down again. "I hadn't thought of that." Her mind searched for answers. Who could have stolen it? And why?

38

A FEW DAYS LATER, Lillian gazed over the garden from Kitty's sitting room. Her eyes sought out and found the path where Truman had first approached her after the church service. So much had happened since that day.

Truman shifted in his seat, perched on the edge as if the rattan might not hold his weight.

"Now, everyone," Kitty said, "the police aren't here to accuse any of us of taking the painting." She toyed with the walking stick that was propped against her chair.

Louise Roy sat nearby, nodding her agreement.

"They just want to get additional information that might help us get the painting back," Kitty said.

Kitty looked at Truman. "I am so sorry your painting has been stolen, Truman. Since we found out it was donated by you, we have been especially proud to display it."

"But," the young officer chimed in, "we do need to question all of you." He glanced dramatically around the room at each individual, reminding Lillian of Barney Fife.

"For starters," he began, "where were each of you the night the crime occurred?"

Kitty glared at the officer. "Young man, I thought you were only here to gather information. It sounds like you are asking us each to provide some kind of alibi."

The officer colored and cleared his throat. "I'm just gathering information."

Each person answered dutifully. When it was Truman's turn, he twirled his hat between his hands. Lillian thought it strange how the officer observed him more closely than the others.

"I was in my studio at home, painting," Truman said.

"Where is your studio, Mr. Clark?" the officer asked.

"It's a few miles outside of town. You know where it is, Peter." Truman rubbed the stubble on his chin, looking bored.

"Was anyone with you in your studio?" Peter glanced at Lillian. "Perhaps Ms. Diamon?"

"Me?"

"Were you with him in his studio that night?"

"No, I was in my cottage at the B&B. We had dinner around six, as usual, and then Truman dropped me off."

"How late did he drop you off, Ms. Diamon? And did he stay?"

Kitty interrupted. "Peter, is that really a necessary question?"

Peter sighed and set his pen on the coffee table. "If I can establish where Truman was, then I can squelch those crazy rumors that Truman might have stolen the painting himself."

Kitty rocked restlessly in her chair. "Have you been talking to Laura, that reporter?"

"The paper called this morning and raised the question."

Lillian leaned forward in her seat. "It's okay. We want to help. Truman dropped me off at eight."

Peter looked at Truman. "Then you went home to work in your studio?"

"Yes."

Peter continued. "Truman, you know Kitty well. Perhaps you have a key to the gallery, or maybe someone who knew about the painting stole a key."

"There are no keys missing, young man!" Kitty was reaching for her cane to stand.

Peter motioned for her to remain seated. "I'm just asking questions, Kitty," he said. "Don't worry." He turned to Truman. "Was anyone else at your home that night? Someone to say you were home?"

"Yes. I had a client until about ten. I was painting her."

Lillian felt her face grow warm. What woman would Truman have in his house late at night? Insecurities she'd tried to bury with Robert forced their way to the surface.

"This person was the subject of a painting you are working on?"

Truman looked at Lillian. He must have noticed her distress, because worry lines creased his brow.

"Yes," Truman said. "It was Paige."

What is wrong with me, Lillian thought. She wanted to shake off her insecurities, but they only grew by the minute. She stood, confused, and looked down at Truman. She softly shrugged his hand away, turned, and walked out of the room.

"Wait up, Lillian," Kitty called after her as she swept down the hallway toward the front door.

"Young lady, I have arthritis!" Kitty shrieked. "You cannot expect me to chase after you!"

Lillian stopped. "I'm sorry, Kitty."

"Calm down, child. I think there is something you are misunderstanding here. Truman and Paige are friends, but not like that. Truman was painting Paige as a surprise for her husband for their anniversary."

"How do you know?" Lillian asked.

"How do I know?" She laid a hand on Lillian's arm. "If I can be so bold, Lillian, I think you might be overreacting."

Lillian crossed her arms, embarrassed. "Do you think I am?"

"I do."

Lillian looked past Kitty and spotted Truman walking briskly toward her.

"Can you please tell Truman I will speak to him later? Maybe I just need a little space before dinner tonight."

⟋⟍

Truman tried to follow Lillian, but Kitty placed her arm in front of him.

"Let her go, dear. Even if you can explain this, she isn't going to hear it right now. She needs some space."

Truman took a deep breath and sighed heavily. "It seems I can't do anything right with Lillian, Kitty. From the moment I invaded her privacy at the Rose House, I've found chance after chance to say or do the wrong thing."

"Just give her space," Kitty repeated. "Sometimes it's the best thing for a woman like her. She's not used to the attention you have lavished on her." She linked arms with Truman and led him back to the group. "Give her time."

"Maybe I need time too, Kitty," Truman said.

"Maybe you both do."

⟋⟍

Lillian paused in front of the house, not sure how to get home since she'd ridden there with Truman.

"Ms. Diamon. It looks like you are ready to leave and Truman isn't."

She whirled around. It was Kitty's husband, Blake, dangling a set of car keys in front of him.

"Do you need a ride?"

"Please, Mr. Birkirt, if you don't mind."

Lillian's heart raced in her chest, but she was too angry to cry. Blake flipped on the radio, and she tried to focus on the Sinatra tune that filled the cab. Was Kitty right? Had she overreacted to Truman's story? She was reasonably sure that Truman would never have an affair with a married woman, nor would Paige do that to her husband. Yet her mind had automatically jumped to Robert and Geena's affair. She felt terrible for her thoughts and planned to explain her fears and apologize to Truman later that evening when they met for dinner.

"Would you like to stop anywhere before the Tenneys'?" Blake asked.

"No, thank you," she said. "I think I would just like to go back to the cottage, Mr. Birkirt."

"Just call me Blake."

She laughed softly. "Okay, but it feels a little bit strange to call you by your first name when you are a pastor."

Blake's truck was a far cry from Tru's beat-up jalopy. The cab's black interior was meticulously clean and uncluttered, and smelled of polished leather, which seemed in sharp contrast to its driver. Blake was dressed in a denim work shirt, and his weathered hands were placed firmly on the steering wheel. She could indeed imagine him driving a truck, but not such a fancy one. He reminded her more of the pastor who had raised her than someone who owned a vineyard.

Blake caught her studying him and smiled. She ducked her head. "I was just thinking how I enjoy your sermons on Sunday mornings," she said. "You are a good preacher."

"Thanks, but I'm not really a preacher, just a teacher. Preachers go to seminary school and study things like theology. I just lead a Bible study."

She reached forward to rub a nonexistent smudge from the dashboard. "I think it's more than a Bible study. With all the singing it seems more like church. My adoptive father is a preacher, and you remind me of him."

"How so?"

"He's a simple preacher," she said. "His sermons are easy to understand but delivered with conviction. Like yours."

"Well, thank you. Where does your father preach?"

Lillian didn't bother to mention that she called him Pastor and not Father as she told Blake about the countryside church she grew up in, describing the music, the sermons, and the people.

"I miss the people the most," she said. "I miss how down-to-earth they were. They were always there to help." She smiled to herself, remembering the women who always offered a cheery lipstick smile, and the friendly men who were quick to offer a helping hand.

He nodded knowingly. "Then I can see how you and Truman got together. He's about as down-to-earth as you get, and he especially has a soft heart for people in need."

The way he had suddenly turned the conversation to Truman caught her off guard. "He does," she agreed and then, not knowing what else to say, gazed out the window at the passing houses. Meeting Truman had caught her off guard too. She had come to La Rosaleda to escape her problems, but letting Truman into her life had only invited more.

As they entered town, she glanced at Blake, who was staring intently at the road in front of him. He was the man responsible for how the Rose House now looked. It had been his labor and care that had created it, from the first nail driven into the wood. Lillian wondered what he thought of the numerous stories, photographs, and paintings that existed of the Rose House.

"Do you ever get tired of all the attention the Rose House gets?"

"Yes and no," he said. "I do get tired of those who make it a mockery by seeing ghosts and the like."

"You don't believe in ghosts?"

He snickered. "Do you?"

"No," she said, "but I guess I can see why people do, especially when they see loved ones they have lost." She thought of how the memories of Sheyenne and Lee lived in her mind. They were only mirages, but she would have loved to speak to them if God would let her.

"Well," he said, "I guess I don't want to think of Ruby, the daughter I lost, as hanging around in this world when she could be in heaven. I see it this way: why would she hang out here when heaven is so much better?"

Lillian smiled and thought of her own children who, she was sure, lived happily with God in heaven. They would be unaware that she was so sad without them.

"Most folks who come to the Rose House are sincere. I'm glad that something I built for my wife could be meaningful in so many ways to so many people. I guess God does work in mysterious ways, even through roses sometimes."

"Maybe," Lillian said.

"I especially like the letters people send us," he said.

"You get letters?"

"Sure. Our granddaughter sifts through the letters when she comes to visit and then Kitty reads me the best ones."

"What was the best one you ever received?" she asked, happy to be distracted from her frustrations with Tru and the painting.

Blake stared intently at the road, as if carefully considering the question. "It came from a woman in Arkansas. She said that her mother had died from cancer when she was very young and that she had never gotten over it. Visiting the Rose House had inspired her to live life more fully."

She sighed, knowing how the woman might have felt. She needed to let go of Robert, but she never wanted to let go of Sheyenne and Lee.

They pulled into the B&B and sat with the truck idling in the driveway.

"It turned out this woman was a children's author. She sent a picture book she had written. It was about a little girl who lived in a house of roses that had grown so thick that the little girl became trapped."

Lillian was captivated. This sounded like a story her children would have loved. "How did the little girl get out?"

"Not for a long time," he said. "Each week when her mother went to market, she told the little girl not to leave the house unless she heard exactly three knocks, lest she be eaten or taken away by the wolf. One day her mother didn't return. The girl worried that maybe the wolf had eaten her mother, but she stayed in the house because she had promised her mother she would. Her mother never returned, and as time went by, the roses her mother had planted around the house grew out of control, covering the doorway."

"Oh, my goodness," Lillian said. "Was she afraid?"

"Well, no," he said. "The rose brambles actually served to protect her from many intruders, including the wolf. Of course, since the little girl couldn't leave the house, she couldn't play with the children in the dell. Instead, she sang to them as they played. In time, the children grew up and forgot that a little girl had ever lived there, and the house was overcome by brambles."

"And she just had to stay in it?" Lillian asked, impressed that the author had created a fairy tale from her visit to the Rose House.

"Yes, she had to stay inside the house for a long time, until one day, after many years had passed, a young knight happened by."

Lillian's face broke into a smile. "The fairy-tale part!"

"Right," Blake said. "And the knight heard a lovely voice coming from a huge mound of rose brambles. The voice reminded him of the little girl who used to sing from the roses by the dell. Jumping off his steed, he grabbed his sword and cut through the endless brambles one by one until he exposed a door."

"Was it locked?" she asked, feeling like a child.

Blake smiled at her. "Yes, so the knight knocked—"

"—three times." Lillian finished his sentence.

"Right. Then the surprised and lovely young maiden opened the door to find the knight holding a bouquet of roses."

Lillian sighed. "And then they lived happily ever after."

"They did," Blake said.

"That is sweet," Lillian said. "If only we all had a Prince Charming to rescue us."

Blake chuckled. "True, but sometimes the prince needs a little help. It's a good thing the girl was singing or he would have passed right by."

"Or if she had a good pair of gardening shears, she might have been able to cut herself out and avoided the whole thing!"

That made Blake laugh so hard his face turned red. "Lillian, you just reminded me of my granddaughter, Lucy. She said the same thing after we showed her the book."

Lillian laughed with him. "Maybe your granddaughter and I are both the impatient types. All we need are some good garden shears to cut ourselves out."

They shared another laugh. "But really, I think the moral to the story is how we keep doing the same old thing because it's what we've always done, and pretty soon we're all wrapped up in our troubles."

"I would love to see the book sometime."

"Kitty says the illustrations are enchanting. We carry the book in our gift shop, so I'll set aside a copy for you as a gift." With that, he walked around and opened her door. She wished she didn't have to get out, preferring to stay longer in Blake's fairy-tale world and not have to face Paige, who was standing on the porch.

"Thank you," Lillian said. "It was a pleasure getting to know you. And the story made me smile."

"It was a pleasure to see you smile," he said. "Now have a good day."

He waved at Paige and climbed into his truck, leaving Lillian no other choice than to talk to Paige.

Lillian stopped at the bottom step and looked up at Paige, who held her arms folded across her chest. Her mouth was pressed into a thin line. Lillian's heart thundered.

"You heard about the big inquisition, didn't you?" Lillian asked, trying to lighten the moment with a small smile. "I misjudged something Tru said about you."

"I just heard," she said. "Truman called to tell me he thought you were on your way here." She uncrossed her arms and held the door open. "I think we need to talk."

~⟳~

The camera zoomed in on Lillian as she approached the porch. The sun glinting off her honey-colored hair was one of the best parts about how she photographed. It was easy to see why Truman had become so captivated by her beauty. She must have been a splendid subject to paint. The camera zoomed back out and panned across the yard. Little Gracie had not come home with her. That's too bad. They were both so pretty that they were a joy to photograph together. The way they played together, the way they smiled at each other, made them seem like mother and daughter.

The camera zoomed in again on Lillian's face as she stood by the porch. She looked upset, but she looked pretty even when she was sad. Truman had proven that in the painting, the magnificent painting.

People might notice the photograph as they had the painting, *Beauty and the Beast Within.* Maybe it would even win an award.

The lens captured a half smile on her confused face. Maybe just one shot.

Click.

GEENA TURNED AWAY FROM the window and let her eyes scan the hotel room. There was an antique brass bed, crystal knobs on the doors, and an old-fashioned claw-foot tub that welcomed her from the corner of the room. The thought of a personal spa day beckoned her, but there would be no time for that today. She simply had too much to accomplish.

Most important, she had to find a job. The hotel was expensive and would dig into her wallet if she stayed. She had been afraid to stay at the more affordable B&B, certain that Paige wouldn't welcome her there. She flipped through the classified ads. Finding an apartment would help, but she couldn't qualify without a job.

She flipped to the employment section, and her eyes landed on an ad for Carlos's Diner. With any luck, she might have a job sooner than later.

Changing into the only pair of designer jeans she owned, Geena dashed on some lip gloss, grabbed her purse, and reached for the crystal doorknob.

"I hope you forgive me, Lillian," she said. "But I promised Aunt Bren that we would make up."

LILLIAN LOOKED AROUND AS she entered the B&B. "Where's Gracie?"

"It just so happens," Paige said, leading her up the steps to the tower room, "that Gracie and Mark are at Frances-DiCamillo. They wanted to have a picnic, and Kitty invited them to make themselves at home. That was before she knew she would be hosting Truman and the police."

They stepped into the room, and the brightness caused them both to squint. Lillian pulled the sheer lace curtains together, and they both started at a shuffling sound in the hallway.

"Charles?" Paige called, walking into the hallway in the direction of the backstairs that led down to the kitchen. When she came back into the room, she said, "Hmm. Maybe it was nobody."

Lillian walked over to the windows and looked down at the gardens. "I thought Charles wasn't allowed to go anywhere without a guardian for a while."

"He's not," Paige said. "It's just that I didn't think anybody was up here, so when I heard the scuffling, Charles came to mind. He's shy. I feel kind of bad that he automatically came to mind, instead of someone else."

"Does Tru ever use this room?" Lillian asked.

"Rarely, unless he is helping Charles with something."

Paige touched Lillian's arm. "Lil, come and sit down."

Lillian allowed Paige to lead her to the settee that faced the front of the B&B. She let her eyes rest on the part of the plaza that was visible through the magnolia trees.

"Lil, will you please look at me?"

Lillian's eyes glistened as she focused on Paige's face. "Don't worry about me," she said. "I just panicked. Old feelings and fears just hit me out of nowhere."

"Lillian," Paige said, "I'm sorry you are going through this, but I can relate. I don't think I've ever told you this before, but before I met Mark, I was married to somebody else."

"Why haven't you ever mentioned it?"

"I put that part of my life behind me, and now I focus only on Mark and Gracie. But when I found out you misunderstood about Truman and me, I thought it would help."

Paige patted Lillian's knee and stood to stare out the window. "The reason I mention it is because my first husband had an affair with a dear friend of mine."

Lillian's heart swelled. She certainly knew how that felt.

"And even though it's part of my past and I have a wonderful life now, I didn't trust Mark at first. In fact, the first few years of our marriage were riddled with insecurities and petty jealousies. He couldn't even drive to the store without me accusing him of going to meet another woman."

"Mark?" Lillian asked. "Are we talking about the same Mark that I know?"

"Exactly. It wasn't anything he did; it was just me. I was so wounded by my first husband's affair that I was afraid it would happen again. Do you know what I mean?"

Lillian gave a heavy sigh, thinking of Robert and Geena. "I think I know exactly what you mean. Once it has happened to you, you know how easily it could happen again."

Paige draped her arm across Lillian's shoulder. "Mark has never cheated on me, Lillian, and I have chosen to trust him."

"It's hard to trust someone new after that," Lillian whispered.

"Yeah, it sure is. On days when I'm weighed down by mountains of doubt, I just decide to trust God. I can't control Mark. I just have to trust."

"So you brought me up here because you want me to give Tru a break."

"Not just Truman," Paige said. "Yourself, and me too."

Lillian turned to hug her friend. "Oh, Paige, I'm so sorry to have doubted you. It was awful of me."

"It's okay. I understand how you feel. Just know that I would never do something like that to you. I would never do something like that to Mark or Gracie. Why would I? I know how it feels to be betrayed."

"I'm sorry, Paige. Really."

"It's okay. I want you to know that Truman was painting me for a surprise portrait to give to Mark for our anniversary. We've been married ten years, and I wanted a gift that would be something special."

"What a wonderful idea," Lillian said. "I know with Tru painting it, it will be a beautiful portrait."

"It will be," she said. "I'm sorry you misunderstood the situation."

"Me too," said Lillian. "So how about we do something to take our minds off of all this. Would you be able to get away this evening? I can apologize to Tru, and then we can all go out for dinner together."

"That isn't the only thing I wanted to talk to you about, Lil."

Lillian frowned. "Then, what?"

"When Truman called, he asked me to tell you that he is leaving."

Lillian's pulse raced. "What? What do you mean, leaving?"

Paige shrugged. "I'm not sure for how long, but he's taking his dog, Cody, and will be gone for a little while. He likes to travel and find new places to paint. He said that he has been thinking about taking a trip to broaden his work beyond the florals he has been doing. He said you were his inspiration to do it."

"Then why leave me? And why can't he tell me himself?" Lillian's mind raced. "I just saw him and he didn't say anything."

"I think the decision was spontaneous," Paige explained. "I tried to talk him out of it, but he said he has caused you enough pain. When he saw how hurt you were at Kitty's today, he realized you might not be ready for a relationship yet. He said you both need time."

Lillian stood. She couldn't stop a tear from rolling down her cheek. "I just never thought he would be the one to leave."

Paige jumped up and placed her hand on Lillian's shoulder. "He's not leaving for good. He just needs time to think," she said, "like you did in Sacramento. And he wants to give you time to figure all this out. He said to tell you to forget about the painting and to forget about him if it helps you to move on."

"I can't forget about him. Not him or the painting. They both mean so much." Lillian choked back a sob.

"I know they mean a lot to you. The painting means a lot to Truman as well. He is sick that it was stolen, but he cares more about the woman in the painting. The rest is just a canvas with smears of paint."

She shook her head. "No, not smears. It was beautiful. It's what brought us together." She held her hands up in frustration. "It's more meaningful than I can explain. I know it sounds silly, but it's more than just a thing to Tru and me."

"No, it's not, Lil," Paige said. "It's just a painting. The only reason it matters at all is because you walked into his life that day in the gallery."

"Well, maybe if I find the painting, Tru will come back."

"That's not what will bring him back," Paige said. "Don't you know,

Lil? Your wanting him in your life with your full trust and faith is the only thing that will bring him back."

"I have to see him." Lillian grabbed her purse.

"He will be gone by the time you get there."

"Then I will call him," Lillian said, digging into her purse for her phone.

"He doesn't carry a cell phone, remember?"

Lillian grew more distraught. A sob escaped. "I don't want him to go."

She sunk into the settee, and Paige sat down beside her. Lillian buried her face in her hands. How could she have been so miserably wrong about things?

Paige engulfed Lillian in a hug, letting her bury her cries in her shoulder. She didn't say anything else, which was a blessing to Lillian, who couldn't bear to hear anyone say that everything would be okay.

~✆~

"Hi, Gracie."

Gracie's smile was wide and welcoming as she rocked back and forth in the painted rocker. She was excited because Kitty had said she could go anywhere she wanted around the Rose House, as long as she didn't go inside.

Charles sat down beside her in one of the adult rockers on the porch. "These chairs are neat," he said and began to rock, matching the rhythm of the smaller rocker.

"This one is just my size." Gracie giggled. "And that one is your size."

Charles smiled. "Yeah, it's like they were made for us, isn't it?" He glanced around the yard. "So where is Kitty?"

"Dunno. Daddy went to get our picnic lunch. She is making it."

Gracie kicked her feet up while she rocked. "Hey, Charlie. Can you come to our picnic too?"

Charles's face broke into a bright grin. "Yes!" he said, nodding his head. "Yes, I can."

They rocked in silence for a long time, the only sounds a bird calling nearby and the wind rustling through the tree branches.

"Gracie," Charles asked, "have you ever been inside the Rose House?"

She shook her head, her curls bobbing back and forth. "No," she said very seriously. "Kitty said I am not allowed."

"Too bad," he said. "I wonder what it looks like in there. Do you think it would be okay if we just looked through the windows?"

"Let's!" She jumped up.

The rockers, now abandoned, still rocked back and forth.

~◎)~

"Where did you leave her?" Mark asked, his voice bordering on frantic.

"On the porch in the rocking chair." Kitty frowned and placed the picnic basket on the porch. She planted her hands on her hips and looked around. "I got busy worrying about Truman and all." She stepped onto the porch and glanced around.

"Gracie!" Mark called out.

Kitty pushed a rose aside, shaded her eyes with her hand, and looked in the window. "Found them!"

"Them?" Mark jumped onto the porch and joined Kitty at the window.

Kitty was shaking her head, her hands still planted firmly on her hips. "Those two ornery kids. How did they get inside?"

She tried the doorknob, but it was locked. Pulling a key out of her pocket, she unlocked the door and swung it open. Both Charles and Gracie looked up from an old board game they had found in the house. Gracie's face wore an excited expression, Charles's wore alarm.

"Young man," Kitty said, "is your sister here?"

He shook his head, his face washed white. "No ma'am. Kara was busy at the gallery, so I took a walk."

Mark spoke up. "All the way out here, Charlie?"

He nodded, his lip quivering. "Am I in trouble again?" He suddenly didn't look so much like a grown man.

Kitty walked into the house, its interior still warmly decorated and spotless. "I will leave that between you and your sister, Charlie. Now come on out." Everyone walked out onto the porch, and Mark took a moment to chide Gracie about not minding grownups.

"You scared me half to death!" he said.

"But it took you a long time. I was bored!" Gracie exclaimed.

Mark leaned down and planted a kiss on her face. "Never mind. Now we're ready for our picnic."

Kitty looked sternly at both Gracie and Charles. "You are never allowed inside of the Rose House. Got it?"

They both nodded. "I'm sorry," Charles said. "I didn't mean to scare anybody."

Kitty nodded. "It's okay, Charles, but you need to be careful. These are the kinds of things that get you into trouble. Kara won't be happy."

He frowned. "No, she won't."

Mark, who had been standing silently the whole time, took Gracie's hand. "Just don't let it happen again. If you keep taking Gracie off without asking, people will not trust you."

Charles nodded, his frown deepening. "I'm sorry."

"I'm sorry too, Daddy." Gracie smiled at her daddy. "We were just playing a game."

Mark chucked her chin. "I know, sweetie."

Kitty turned the key in the lock and slipped it back in her pocket. "How did you all get in?"

Charles stared at the ground but didn't answer. Gracie, on the other hand, was eager to share. "The side door is easy to unlock. You just jiggle the knob, right, Charlie?"

Kitty and Mark shared a look and then turned their attention to Charles.

"Charles," Kitty said, "why don't we go back to the house and Blake will take you to your sister, okay?"

"Okay," he said. "I'm really sorry. I didn't mean any harm at all. We were just looking around." He looked at her, his eyes sad. "I would never take anything or anything like that."

She reached for his arm, allowing him to be the one to escort her back to the house. "I know," she said. She waved at Mark.

⁓◍〉

Mark turned back to Gracie. "Well, kiddo, I guess it's just you and me." He reached out to ruffle her curls. "How about that picnic?"

Gracie's lower lip protruded. "But I wanted Kitty and Charles to come too!"

"But they have to go."

Gracie looked up, her eyes misty. "Is Charlie in trouble?" Her lip quivered. "It was mostly my idea, Daddy."

"Yes, but Charles is older than you, Gracie. He needs to know how to follow the rules better than you."

She folded her hands over her chest. "But he didn't mean to make you and Kitty upset."

"I know that, sweetie. But do you remember when Charles got in trouble for having you go to Lillian's cottage without asking my permission? And then he gave you a doll?"

She nodded enthusiastically. "I like my doll."

"It's okay that he gave you a doll, but people misunderstood when he asked you to do something you didn't have permission to do. Do you understand?"

She shook her head. "Daddy, what are you talking about?"

Mark picked up the picnic basket and walked Gracie toward a picnic area. "Gracie, we need to help protect Charlie from getting in trouble too."

"Why?"

"Because people sometimes misunderstand him and think he is doing something wrong when he thinks he is doing something right."

"That's not fair," said Gracie.

"No, sweetie. It isn't fair. Just remember that when you know you don't have permission, then tell him this, okay?"

"Okay, Daddy," she said, but Mark wasn't sure she was listening as she let go of his hand and ran toward the picnic table.

41

Sounds of dishes clattering carried into the dining room of Carlos's Diner, and the aromas of garlic, grilled meats, and fresh baked bread made Lillian's mouth water. Paige unfolded the menu in front of her.

Lillian smiled and opened her own menu. "I'm having pancakes with strawberries," Lillian said. "They're my favorite."

"For lunch?"

"I always have breakfast for lunch when I come here with Tru."

"Have you heard from him yet?"

Lillian's heartbeat quickened. "From time to time."

Paige looked at Lillian, a question in her eyes. "You haven't mentioned it at all. And here I have been worried about you."

Lillian cherished each and every letter she got from Tru, as well as the few short phone calls she had received from him. The last time they had talked, he only wanted to talk about her, encouraging her not to be anxious about his being gone, but to try and figure out what she really wanted to do with her life.

"I just haven't wanted to talk about it," Lillian said. "Besides, I've been so confused, trying to decide what I should do with my life, and I'd rather talk about that with you."

"What's going on?"

Lillian remembered the most recent phone call she'd had from Chef George.

"George has been trying so hard to get me to go back to work for him. He has even mentioned my helping him start a new restaurant."

Paige looked impressed. "That sounds like an amazing opportunity."

"It is, but what if Tru comes back and I'm not in La Rosaleda?"

"Then he will go to you wherever you are." Paige flashed a silly grin. "Maybe he'll send you a secret message in another painting."

Lillian rolled her eyes. Paige was ever the romantic. "And if he doesn't?"

"Then it's not meant to be, but I can't imagine he won't come back, Lil. How often does he call you?"

"Occasionally," Lillian said. "And sometimes he sends a letter." Lillian carried each letter he had sent in an envelope in her purse. There were sketches of flowers, scenes by the ocean, small portraits of her, as well as drawings of the two of them in places she had never been before; places, she fantasized, he planned to take her someday. "He sent flowers the other day."

"See?" Paige said, her voice breathless. "It is so romantic, Lil. How many men go to all that trouble?"

Lillian exhaled a long breath. Paige was right. Tru was different from any of the men she had known, except, it seemed, in one way. "How many men leave the women they love?"

"I don't know," Paige said, "but how many men are really like Tru? Be honest with yourself. He didn't leave because he didn't want to be with you."

It was true. He had left because he wasn't sure Lillian wanted to be with him. He needed space and was giving her space.

"But maybe," Lillian said, her eyes misty, "he will realize it's not worth waiting for a woman with such heavy baggage."

"If he ever comes back, Lil, and he will, do you think you two would get married?"

Lillian remembered conversations she'd had with Tru about marriage, both lighthearted and serious. She looked up, the warmth she felt difficult to contain, but her face faded into a frown as she looked beyond Paige's shoulder.

"Geena."

"Hi, Lillian." Geena stopped beside their table. She wore an apron tied about her waist and held a pen and notebook in hand.

Lillian's mouth opened, then closed again.

"I heard you talking about Truman," Geena said. "Are you okay?"

Lillian wondered what Geena's motive was. Did she really care? Or was she trying to weasel out information to use against Tru for her personal vendetta?

"He hasn't come back yet?" She shook her head, placing one manicured hand on the slim curve of her hip. Her red nail polish punctuated the gesture. "What a jerk, Lily Bug. I tried to warn you. Are you okay?"

"I'm fine." Her voice was soft. "What are you doing here, anyway?"

"Working."

Lillian's eyes widened. She guessed it had been a while since she'd eaten at the diner. Not since Truman left. "How did you get Carlos to hire you? Doesn't he know how much you dislike Tru? They're good friends, you know.

"It wasn't actually Carlos who hired me. It was his assistant manager." Geena gestured toward the counter and waved at a young, handsome Hispanic man who obviously only had eyes for Geena.

"Mario put in a good word for me." She smiled in Mario's direction. Mario saluted.

Lillian sat silently, not sure what to say to Geena. It was impossible to trust her after all her shenanigans.

"Hey, sis," Geena said, "I wanted to talk to you about Aunt Bren and Pastor, but you won't return my calls. They are worried about us, and I promised them I'd try to make things right." She grabbed a cloth from the belt of her apron and began to wipe a spot on their table. "So I'm staying until everything is worked out between us."

Paige interjected. "Who do you think you are, coming and bothering Lillian this way? You ran off just when she needed you, and the rest of us had to pick up the pieces without—"

Geena shifted her weight to the other hip and pointed her pen at Paige. It was obvious there was no love lost between them. "What business is this of yours, you little—"

Lillian signaled for Paige and Geena to stop. They both stared at her, their faces pinched.

"I'm tired of fighting," Lillian said, her voice strained.

Paige looked as if she'd suddenly fallen out of her chair. "But how can you trust her?"

"I don't know if I can," Lillian said, "but I can't fight anymore." Lillian smoothed a strand of hair behind her ear. She knew it sounded crazy to Paige, but Paige had never had a sister.

Geena offered Paige a smug look.

"And," Lillian said, directing her gaze at Geena, "I would appreciate it if the two of you wouldn't start fighting either."

"Fine," Paige said, grabbing her menu.

Geena stood with her pen poised above her order pad, staring pointedly at Paige.

"Let's just get on with our lunch," Paige said. "I have things to do." She didn't look up at Geena as she rattled off her order. "I'd like the grilled turkey club, no mayo, no onions, but everything else."

Geena scribbled on her pad. "To drink?"

"Hot tea."

"We have Earl Grey, English Breakfast, lemon, and mint."

"Mint, please."

"And you?" she said to Lillian.

"Strawberry pancakes."

"And to drink?" She didn't look at Lillian. "Perhaps mint tea as well? Carlos grows the mint himself."

Lillian's mouth dropped open, and for the first time, she thought she might jump up and hit her sister. Was she toying with her? "You have got to be kidding me, Geena." Maybe Paige was right: Geena couldn't be trusted.

For a minute Geena looked genuinely confused, then she met Lillian's eyes. A look of recognition passed between them, and Geena's face paled. She remembered.

"Actually," Geena said. "How about Earl Grey? You look a little peaked, like you could use the caffeine."

Lillian sighed. "Let's just make it an orange juice."

After Geena collected the menus, Paige and Lillian leaned in to speak to each other. Lillian tried explaining to Paige that everything was okay. Unexpectedly, Lillian felt a hand on her shoulder.

"Actually"—Geena's voice was sweet as she directed it at Paige—"I'm so sorry that I can't bring you any mint tea. We must have used it all up. I can't seem to find it anywhere."

Paige looked at her suspiciously. Lillian felt sorry for her. Poor Paige had no idea why Lillian hated mint tea or that Geena was playing a game, this time a make-up game, with Lillian. However, Paige was still good at knowing how to spot a half truth.

"No mint at all? But you just said it was Carlos's special mint from his own garden."

Geena shrugged, sneaking a wink at Lillian. "It's gone. I can't find it."

Paige made a big show of looking at the menu that Geena handed her. "Then I guess it will have to be lemon." She thrust the menu back at Geena.

"That would be a better choice," Geena said. She flashed an apologetic smile. "We are just completely out of mint, and I don't know when we'll get more in." She spun around, her sneakers making little squeaky noises in her wake.

Paige shook her head as she unfolded her napkin and placed it in her lap. "Your sister is something else, Lillian. I just don't get her."

Lillian focused on straightening her napkin, a slight grin on her face. "More often than not, I don't get her either."

⌐◯

Seeing Geena working at the diner reminded Lillian of how empty her own days had become. Without Tru around to spend time with, taking each day at a leisurely pace was pointless, so she had asked Paige if she could work at the B&B.

"I'll do it for free," Lillian had said.

"There's no need to be desperate about it. You're hired."

After that, Lillian's days became filled with running breakfast at the B&B. Paige helped out when she could, but gladly handed management of everything from inventory to cooking to menu planning over to Lillian.

"We should have done this sooner," Paige said, wiping down a table after breakfast one day. "I don't mind cleaning up, but I have never been as good at breakfast as you."

"That's not true," Lillian said, counting her eggs for the next day. "You make a very mean omelet and you know it."

"I do," she admitted. "But most of the time Mark finds himself making them instead. I'm just too busy. It's so nice to wake up now and spend some time with Gracie in the mornings. She's getting to be quite a handful at her age. She needs my attention."

Lillian smiled, her heart doing a small flip-flop. Her own children would never grow to be the age Gracie was now.

"She starts kindergarten in the fall," Paige said. "I can hardly believe it's that time already." She walked to the sink and rinsed the washcloth before returning to wipe down the remaining tables. "I hear that some moms cry on the first day of kindergarten. I'm not looking forward to that."

Lillian turned back to the refrigerator, busying herself with taking inventory of the other ingredients she would need for tomorrow's orange french toast. It was a topic she wasn't familiar with since Sheyenne and Lee had never made it to kindergarten. When she turned back to face the dining area, Paige stood there, the cloth lying useless on the table beside her.

"I'm sorry," Paige said. "For a minute I forgot. I just— I didn't mean to be insensitive."

"It's okay," Lillian said. "I don't expect you to tiptoe around me all the time."

Paige picked up the cloth and walked into the kitchen, moving from area to area, wiping down things that didn't need to be cleaned. She coughed and finally stood in the center of the kitchen, staring at Lillian like she was waiting to be flogged.

Lillian put down the pad and pencil she was using to make her grocery list. She motioned to Paige to come and sit as she poured two cups of coffee. "Sit," she said. "And stop worrying about it."

Paige sat on the barstool, crossing her long legs and swiveling around to set her cup on the countertop. "Lillian, I just realized that I run around gabbing and bragging about my little girl every minute of every day."

"Not every minute," Lillian corrected. "Just most of the time."

A look of guilt passed over Paige's face.

"I'm just teasing," Lillian said. "To be honest, I don't mind. I like hearing about Gracie." She added a dollop of cream to her coffee, and the spoon tinkled in the cup as she gave it a quick stir. "In some ways, being around Gracie helps me."

Paige sipped her coffee. "It must be hard. Is there a moment that goes by when you don't think about them?"

Lillian put the spoon on a napkin and picked up her cup. "Not often," she said. "It takes really getting thoroughly lost in something to not think about them. And even then, they are hovering in the background somewhere."

"What's it like?" Paige said.

Lillian reflected on the best way to explain her feelings. "It's hard," Lillian said. "It's hard not to—" Her voice cracked and she cleared her throat. "It's hard knowing I can't hold them or kiss them anymore."

Lillian held out her arms, as if she would embrace somebody, and then folded them across her chest. "My arms are always empty." Her breath came out in a shudder. "But holding Gracie helps." She sniffed. "I hope that doesn't sound weird to you. I know Gracie is your little girl, not mine."

Paige sniffed loudly, having given up on trying to keep her own emotions in check. She placed her arm around Lillian. "It would only sound weird to a mother who can't imagine what it would be like to lose a child." Paige gave her a little hug. "You can hold Gracie all you want to."

Paige gave her another squeeze and stood to heat her coffee in the microwave. "The coffee is cold now. Want me to heat yours too?" she asked.

Lillian handed her mug to Paige.

Paige gave her a regretful look. "I'm so sorry, Lillian. It's something I could never go through myself. God forbid it should happen to Gracie. She jabbed some buttons on the microwave.

God forbid, indeed, thought Lillian. "It won't happen to Gracie," Lillian said. "But I would be there for you, just like you are here for me."

"But I wasn't there when it happened," Paige said, opening the microwave door. She handed Lillian's mug back to her. "Did you have anybody at all to go through it with you?"

"Aunt Bren came for the funeral and then we talked on the phone quite a lot. We still do."

"But no friends?"

"For a while, yes."

Paige leaned against a countertop, facing Lillian. "I wish I'd been there for you, Lil."

"But you are now." She gave her friend a grateful squeeze and they sipped their coffee in silence. Every now and then, Lillian heard Paige sniff and could easily imagine what was going through her mind: every mother's fear.

⁓◍⁓

By the time Lillian put her apron away and headed for the cottage, she felt she had accomplished a great deal.

"Lily! A letter for you." Gracie smiled proudly and held out an envelope to Lillian.

Lillian spun around. "Thank you, Gracie! How nice of you to bring it to me."

"My mom says it's from Truman."

Lillian glanced at the letter, her heartbeat quickening. It was postmarked from Maine, with a return post office box address. Her heart soared. She had wanted so badly to write him a letter, and now she'd be able to.

"Thank you, Gracie." She chucked the girl under her chin. "You have a good day now, okay?"

In the cottage, she slit the letter open and began reading it even before she made it into her bedroom to kick off her shoes and lie across the bed on her back.

Hello, Lil,

I wonder when you will get this. If you decided to take Chef George's offer, maybe Paige will have to send this to you. It makes me wonder, did you take the job? You should be using your own talents, Lil. The longer I am away, the more I reflect on how eagerly you set aside your own life to spend time with me while I never stopped painting. I regret that. It should go both ways, and if you once had a dream of being a real chef, then maybe now is the time to pursue that. Just think about it.

Lillian turned over on her stomach. She wondered what Tru meant. Did he mean she should move on without him?

Yesterday Cody and I visited three different lighthouses. They are so breathtaking the way they are built. Being inside one is truly amazing. I saw a whale from one lighthouse today and tried to imagine painting it. As remarkable as it was, I wasn't inspired by the whale itself, but the lighthouses are another story.

I have never thought about the importance of lighthouses. One can really sense the gravity of their importance when gazing from the lighthouse into the ocean, imagining a storm shaking the waters. I am enclosing a sketch I drew of one of them.

She shuffled through the papers and found the sketch. Like the others, he'd trimmed it down to about five by five. The lighthouse stood tall and strong against a torrent of rain and waves. The sky was dark in the background and the sea turbulent. The yellowed light shining from the lighthouse and illuminating the windows was the only color on the otherwise penciled sketch.

If she hadn't grown used to seeing hidden images in Tru's work, it would have been easy to miss this one. She carefully smoothed out the crease in the center to better see the shadowed image in the lighthouse window. It was hard to tell what Tru's motive was this time, but to Lillian, the figure looked relaxed, safe from the storm. She peered closer, but the figure looked more like a man than herself.

Wishing you were here…
   Tru

42

"YOU'RE IN LOVE WITH this Truman Clark?" Aunt Bren's voice was a little loud in Lillian's ear, her Southern accent punctuating her words. "Are you sure that's a wise decision, honey?"

Lillian smiled at Aunt Bren's blunt response.

"Yes, Aunt Bren. Truman is like a gift from heaven, except that I scared him away by being so insecure."

"Thanks to Robert," Aunt Bren offered.

"Thanks to him," Lillian agreed.

Lillian walked as she talked to Aunt Bren. Turning at the end of the drive, she headed toward the main square of La Rosaleda.

"I don't know if it's wise for you to just up and decide to trust him," Aunt Bren said. "Are you still being followed?"

"I don't think so," Lillian reassured her. "It seems to have stopped. Maybe whoever was stalking us, if they even were, got their kicks and moved on."

"I hope so," said Aunt Bren. "But Geena says—"

Lillian tried to hold in her frustration at the stories Geena seemed to be worrying Aunt Bren and Pastor with. "Don't listen to her so much, Aunt Bren. She is a little bit overdramatic."

"Yes, but it's because she is worried about you. She came there to work things out, you know."

"Geena and I are fine, Aunt Bren." Lillian sighed into the phone. "Sure, my heart tells me to proceed with caution, but I think that's just because I've been burned by her so many times."

Lillian dodged around a stroller and cut across to the plaza, where she found a bench in front of the duck pond.

"Geena is not your enemy, Lillian. That girl has been working very hard to make things right."

"I know," Lillian said, "but maybe it's too late to make things right, Aunt Bren. I just need to let it go."

"No, I suppose she can't ever make up for it, especially when she is the fall guy for a dead man."

Lillian stared at the phone. That wasn't something Aunt Bren would normally say.

Aunt Bren continued. "It's just that— I tell you what, Lillian. I think Robert Hastings sure did leave a wake in his path, didn't he? I grow angrier at him the longer he's gone."

"Me too," Lillian said.

"Now, tell me," she said. "Is there any word on that stolen painting?"

"I told Kitty I would raise Truman's offer of a reward up to five thousand dollars."

"Honey, you don't need to do that. Is it even worth that much?"

"To me it is worth even more."

"Well, that's probably exactly what whoever stole it wants out of this whole thing—your money!"

"It's just money, Aunt Bren. And I have no idea why somebody would steal the painting, but surely not for the money." She could see the gallery from where she sat and wondered how the culprit had gotten in and why he had done it.

As she listened to Aunt Bren turn the conversation to the craft class she taught to the young mothers at church, Lillian watched people walk in and out of the gallery. She was surprised to see how many people visited the gallery and wondered if it was that busy every day.

Charles walked out of the gallery with Kara close behind him. He put out his arm for her to take. *He seems so sweet,* thought Lillian. She wished Geena could see it.

Turning her mind back to Aunt Bren, she listened to her tell about the various women who were part of the group. When Lillian looked up, she thought she saw Tru coming out of the gallery. She looked closer. The man's head was shaved close, and he was donning a fedora that looked just like Tru's. Lillian jumped up as he seemed to be leaving.

"Aunt Bren, I have to go. I'll call you back." She left Aunt Bren hanging somewhere between the yarn and the brownies as she walked quickly across the square to catch him.

"Tru!" she called, but her voice was drowned out by an ice cream truck coming around the corner. She picked up her speed to a jog.

"Tru!" she called, sure that it was him, but he hadn't heard her. When he ducked into an alleyway, she paused for a minute to catch her breath. She shook her head, wondering who it had been. "How strange."

~◦~

The bell on the gallery door chimed as she breezed in. She expected to see Louise, but the counter was empty.

"Jake!"

He looked as surprised to see her as she was to see him.

"Mrs. Hastings."

"Miss Diamon," she corrected, trying to find her smile, but it didn't quite make it to her face.

"Of course." He smiled widely. "Miss Diamon. My apologies. Old habits die hard. I suppose you wonder what I am doing here?"

She glanced at her phone, pretending to look at the time. "Not really. I am just surprised to see you, is all."

"I drove somebody here today. She is shopping now. I just thought I would have a look around, but it seems nobody is on duty, doesn't it?"

Lillian, still slightly confused, nodded in agreement. "But Louise would never leave the gallery empty. I'll bet she's here. Just let me check."

Lillian ducked into the storage room and found Louise digging in a closet. She wheeled around. "Lillian!" Louise placed her hand over her chest. "You scared me to death!"

"I'm sorry, but did you know Kara left and that there is a customer waiting out there?"

"No, of course not." She bustled past Lillian and out to the front of the gallery. Jake was still standing where Lillian had left him. "May I help you?" she asked.

"Uh, yes. I'd heard you had a painting I am interested in buying."

"By which artist?" she asked.

"Truman Clark."

Lillian gawked at him until she realized that she was being rude. Why wouldn't Jake be as interested as the next person in Truman's work? Lillian knew that his work as a driver paid him well and that he received tips from his customers. Why wouldn't he be interested in spending his money on fine art?

Jake glanced at Lillian, as if waiting for her to leave. That's when she realized he might be uncomfortable making a purchase in front of somebody who was his customer.

She pointed toward the door behind her. "I think I'll just go now. I only came over here because I thought I saw somebody I knew."

"Who?" Louise asked.

"I thought I saw Truman leaving the gallery," Lillian said.

Louise's eyes widened. "He hasn't been in here," she said. "He's still out of town, isn't he?"

Lillian nodded. "Yes. How silly of me. I just thought I saw him. I'll go now," she said as she backed toward the door, but at that moment, Jake walked toward her and grasped her hand.

"It was good to see you again, Miss Diamon. I hope all is well with you."

Her heart melted as she remembered all the times Jake had sat in the car, waiting patiently for her at the cemetery, pretending not to see her cry. He had always been so reliable.

"I've missed you," he said. "Please feel free to call any time you need me. I'd be happy to drive you again."

She suddenly smiled. In a way, she had actually missed his unassuming, reliable presence. "Thank you, Jake." She squeezed his hand in return. "I want you to know that I didn't stop using you because I was unhappy. I've been trying to do more things for myself."

"I'm glad, Miss Diamon. Very glad. And it makes me happy to know it isn't because of me that you haven't called for a driver in a while."

"No, Jake." She smiled reassuringly, sad that he would wonder. "Not at all."

He nodded and for a second she thought his eyes misted over. She said good-bye and walked out into the sunlight. What a strange thing to run into her old driver in La Rosaleda. And he was driving for someone else? She laughed at the thought.

"I've been replaced!" she said out loud with a chuckle. It was just one more sign that she had moved on with her life. Another step away from the nasty wake Robert had left for her to drown in.

~⚬)~

"How is old Jake doing?" Geena asked. She sat cross-legged on the counter that evening as Lillian whipped up the ingredients for the following day's recipe.

"Geena, would you please get off the counter? As a waitress, you should know better."

Geena hopped down as if she hadn't just been chided by Lillian at all. "What was he doing all the way over here?"

"He seemed to be doing great," Lillian said. "He was driving some-one here to shop." Lillian broke several eggs into a glass bowl and began to beat them. "It was really nice to see him. I'm glad he is doing well."

"Me too," Geena said. "He was always a nice guy. There were a few times that Robert and I had him join us for drinks and—" She stopped cold.

Lillian kept beating the eggs, as if she hadn't heard Geena at all, but she *had* heard. Maybe that was why Jake had always been so especially nice to her. He knew more about Robert's wrongdoings than she did.

"I'm sorry," Geena said.

Lillian shook her head. "Forget about it. We have to get past all that." She looked at Geena pointedly, careful to hold her face in a neutral expres-sion. "But you can't bring it up all the time, Geena. I've changed my mind. I know as much as I need to know. I don't want to know any more."

Geena walked over and took the bowl from her. "Tell me what to do. I want to help."

"No, thank you," Lillian said, pulling the bowl back.

"But I want to," Geena said. "I've been awful; now let me pay you back by helping. I want to help you more." She reached for the bowl just as Lillian pulled on it, sending the whole thing tumbling onto the floor. Thick, slimy eggs covered the kitchen tile.

They both stood staring down at the floor just as Paige walked in.

"I guess this would be a bad time for me to ask if the two of you are getting along well enough to do some catering for me on the side," Paige said.

They both stared at her as if she'd gone mad.

"Are you kidding?" Lillian asked. "You want me to cater with her?"

"She's a good waitress," Paige said. "Besides, I'm not the one who suggested you get cozy with her again. That was your idea."

"Hey!" Geena exclaimed. "I don't think we need your commentary right now, Paige. Can't you see we're in a little bit of a mess here?"

Paige walked into the supply closet and came out pushing a mop bucket. She handed the mop to Geena. "You mess up my kitchen, you clean up my kitchen."

Geena huffed and pointed at Lillian. "But she did it too!"

Lillian threw her hands out from her sides, palms up. "Sorry," she said. "It's my kitchen too. And besides, I'm her favorite." At that, Paige retrieved another mop from the supply closet and handed it to Lillian.

It was Lillian's turn to huff, which caused Paige to laugh. "I don't understand you two, but you had better get your acts together. I have a last-minute wedding to cater this weekend, and I don't want a mess like this. The mother and the mother-in-law are on the feisty side. We want to make them happy." With that, she spun around and walked out of the kitchen, leaving Geena and Lillian shaking their heads.

For a few minutes, neither one of them moved to clean up the mess. Finally, Geena began to mop through the egg mixture. "I've actually cleaned up more disgusting things than raw eggs in my line of work. This is nothing."

Lillian began to move her mop as well. "Yeah, me too."

"I bet I've cleaned up grosser things."

Lillian held a smile in check. "Oh, yeah? I've cleaned up fish guts that fell on the floor and splattered all over the kitchen."

"Really?" asked Geena, sounding unperturbed. "You should try cleaning up the dance floor after the dancers have had too much to drink. The mop gets—"

Lillian stopped mopping and held her hand up. "Okay," she said, "you win."

They both went back to mopping, until Geena expelled a small laugh. "I win."

Lillian rolled her eyes, trying to ignore her as she wrung out her own mop.

"I win," Geena said, snorting. "I never get to win."

Lillian looked shocked. "Are you kidding? You always win!"

"No, you do."

"No," Lillian said, "I don't. You do!"

Geena giggled and this time it was contagious. Lillian joined her.

"So," Lillian said, "are we really going to cater a wedding with Paige?"

"Sure," Geena said, "count me in, as long as you won't spend the whole time arguing."

Lillian gave her a warning look. "We won't argue as long as you drop this crazy notion that Tru and Charles are somehow trying to harm me."

Geena shrugged. "Okay, but somebody could be."

"Was," Lillian said. "Let's just forget about it since nothing else has happened in months."

"Okay," Geena said, "I'll drop it if you will give me a break once in a while. You are very judgmental, sis. I am trying to change. I haven't had a drink of alcohol or wine in a long time, and being in the wine country, that's no easy feat."

"Fair enough," Lillian said. "I will give you an occasional break."

Geena smirked at her. "And," Geena added, "you could loan me some money to buy something nice to wear when I serve."

Lillian couldn't hold back her chuckle. "Some things never change." She pulled several twenties from her purse and handed them to Geena.

Geena stuffed the money in her pocket. "Thanks, sis. I'll pay you back."

"No, you won't," Lillian said. "You never pay me back."

"I will this time," Geena said.

"I don't want you to," Lillian said as she ran the mop back over the floor one last time.

"But I want to this time."

"Wanting to do something and doing it are two different things. I have extra money and I know you don't. Just keep it, okay?"

"Thanks, sis."

"Don't mention it." Lillian helped Geena put the mops away.

~֍~

Geena lay down in her bed. With Mario's help, she had finally found a decent apartment in La Rosaleda. Mario would have been more than glad to have her move in with him, but at the last minute, Geena had decided that saving money wasn't as important as starting off right with Mario.

Moving in was what she'd always done when she found herself in a new relationship, but this time she had a mind to make the guy work a little bit harder. She was tired of the way men treated her. It was something she had started to think about at Safe Circle when someone asked her why she kept putting herself in situations that allowed men to use and abuse her.

The idea had haunted her ever since, and she had finally decided that moving in with a man she didn't know had never really gotten her very far. Why not try another way? Lillian's way. Rolling over in bed, she snuggled into her pillow. She'd always accused Lillian of being so uptight, and she had even told herself it was the reason Robert had chosen her over Lillian.

Geena sniveled, thinking about Robert. Had he used her too? Or had he loved her? Had he still loved Lillian? She supposed she would never know. She wondered if her thoughts were similar to the questions

Lillian had about Robert. It didn't make Geena feel better to realize that she would never have answers either. But now Lillian had found someone else to love.

Geena had stopped her petty comments against Truman. She now wondered if she disliked him so much because she was jealous. It seemed unfair that Lillian had been Robert's wife and then found Truman too. How was it fair that one woman could have two remarkable men in one lifetime?

43

To LILLIAN'S SURPRISE, catering the wedding went flawlessly. The wedding was held at a local vineyard very similar in size to Frances-DiCamillo but, in Lillian's opinion, not nearly as lovely.

The cake, made very quickly by Lillian herself, was noted as stunning by the mothers of the happy couple, and the sugarcoated rose petals that were set in small bowls at every table were delectable. The guests adored the platters of shrimp and special cocktail sauce made from scratch that Geena kept sneaking when nobody was looking. The home-baked breads had been cut into squares to be dipped into all different flavors of infused olive oils, and the teriyaki beef medallions were popular with the groom and his friends.

Lillian shared how successful the catering was going one Sunday with Kitty after church. Lillian had helped Kitty do all the dishes after everyone had gone home, then followed Kitty out to the Rose House. Kitty handed her some gardening shears, and this time Lillian knew exactly what to do.

As she snipped off the dead heads and placed them in Kitty's basket, she found herself rambling on about the latest wedding.

"And you should have seen the groom with the cake at our last wedding!" she exclaimed. "I felt so sorry for that poor bride." Lillian shook her head. "I think we need to make some kind of rule about not using our frosting to ruin the bride's makeup."

Kitty paused, stood, and pulled an embroidered handkerchief from her pocket. As she wiped it across her forehead, she glanced over at Lillian.

"You girls have developed quite a reputation in a very short time for how you cater weddings."

"Thank you," Lillian said. "We are enjoying ourselves. I would still like to have my own restaurant someday, but for now it seems I have found a niche."

"Kara is getting married in a few months, and I'm donating the use of the vineyard for the occasion. Her caterer just went out of business, though, and she's very upset about it."

"That's terrible!" Lillian said, wondering what could have happened to make a caterer go out of business in the middle of a project. She made a mental note to go over her books and make sure things were foolproof for herself, Geena, and Paige.

"Why don't you girls cater it for her? I can recommend you. Paige already knows her way around my kitchen, and you are starting to as well."

Lillian couldn't keep the smile from spreading across her face. This would be a huge opportunity. For all their efforts to avoid being pretentious, Kitty and Blake were the premier family in the world of vineyards and wineries, as well as the social circles in the region. If they impressed Kitty at Kara's wedding, they were liable to become so busy they might have to hire help.

"Of course," she told Kitty. "I'm sure I can speak for Paige and Geena. We would love to do Kara's wedding."

Kitty smiled. "Wonderful! Then it's all set." She went back to work as if she hadn't just bolstered Lillian's spirits as high as the moon. Lillian tried to go back to pruning but was having a difficult time thinking about anything except the wedding.

She quickly worked her way along the porch, collecting, with Kitty's permission, a bouquet of roses, their petals perfect for the cake decorations she was working on.

It occurred to her that she could market and sell the cakes as lucky, if she decorated them with petals from the Rose House. They would be able to sell them all over the area and maybe beyond. But somehow she knew Kitty probably wouldn't go for it. But what she would go for, thought Lillian, was using them on Kara's cake.

Lillian thought how extraordinary it was that she was picking a bouquet of roses from the Rose House when four years ago, now almost five, she had been standing in this same place, filled with fresh grief. And truth be told, if she rewound all the way back to when she had lost her parents and brothers in the fire, she had come even further. She had picked roses in the same manner with her mother when she was only a little girl, not ever imagining the rose bush would wither and burn with the house.

"Did I ever tell you about the rose bush my mother had?" she asked Kitty.

"I don't believe you ever did. Was it beautiful?"

"Not as remarkable as these roses," Lillian explained, "but yes, it was lovely. The rose bush was not as big, but it did climb halfway up one side of our little house."

"What color were the roses?"

"Red," Lillian said. "Almost a wine color. It burned with the fire, but a few years later when I was visiting the place where the house had been, I noticed that the rose bush had grown back. It was only a small bramble, but it was still trying to grow back. How is that possible?"

Kitty set her basket down on the porch and sat in one of the rockers. She fanned her face with her hand. The temperature had grown warm and Lillian was hot too. She joined Kitty.

"It's possible," Kitty said. "It just depends on how much of the plant actually burned. It's rare, but I've heard of it happening once. My mother told me about a rose that burned down with a shed here at Frances-DiCamillo. She said it eventually came back stronger. Do you want to see it?"

"I would love to."

"But first, let's get a drink. I'm parched."

To Lillian's surprise, Kitty pulled a key out of her pocket and inserted it into the front door of the Rose House. She walked in, obviously expecting Lillian to follow. Lillian stood on the porch, staring after her. It was one thing for Charles and Gracie to so innocently trespass on Kitty's special place, but Lillian felt like an invader.

"Aren't you coming, dear?"

She cleared her throat. "Okay."

She followed Kitty tentatively into the house, surprised when Kitty walked into the small kitchen, opened the old-fashioned fridge door, and pulled out a pitcher of lemonade. She held a glass out to Lillian.

"What's wrong, dear? You look like you've seen a ghost. I already told you there aren't any."

"It's nothing, really. I just wasn't expecting everything inside to be so—" She reached for the right word.

"You expected it to be all musty, dark, and everything to be covered with sheets?"

"Yes!" Lillian said before taking a gulp of the cold drink.

"Well," Kitty said, as she led the way into the living room, "If it were like that, I would never want to come in here."

She sat down on a sofa that was covered with a quilted coverlet. Lillian sat across from her in a small rocking chair.

"Do you come in here often?"

"Just when I need a drink or when Blake and I want to get out of that big old house and be able to find each other," she said, chuckling. "Some folks have RVs. We just spend a few days in the Rose House. Of course, we have to time it when there aren't visitors."

"It's lovely in here," Lillian said. "Very simple."

"We lived simply back when we were young. We try to do the same over in the big house, but for us, it's just not the same as it was here when we were trying to do things on our own. Blake built every bit of this, with my dad's help."

Lillian glanced around. Quilts, presumably made by Kitty, were draped on the furniture. Lillian was surprised at how many paintings covered the walls. They all looked like portraits of the same person.

"Most of those are of my daughter Ruby," Kitty said. "My granddaughter, Lucy, painted them. Some of the others were painted by Ruby herself."

"I didn't know there were artists in your family."

"Oh yes," she said. "I painted when I was young too, but I was always more interested in quilting than anything else."

Lillian tried to take in the fact that she was sitting inside the famed Rose House enjoying Kitty's company and the simple beauty around her.

"Kitty, why do you think somebody took the painting?"

"Who knows, dear? Money, attention, or maybe even some kind of crazy infatuation with Truman or you."

Lillian tried to laugh, but the sound came out hollow.

"If you are afraid, dear, you can stay in the big house with me and Blake. Or I'm sure Paige would let you stay inside the B&B instead of the cottage. Would that help?"

"Oh, I'm not," Lillian said. "I haven't seen signs of someone following me for a long time now. The painting being stolen is the only odd thing that has happened in a while. And it's probably unrelated."

"Well, I'm glad. And how is everything else, dear? Do you miss Truman?"

Lillian's eyes misted. "Terribly," she said. "Sometimes I wonder if he'll ever be back."

"Dear, everything will work out fine. You just have to see it through. If I ever have enough time to tell you my whole story, you will see how seemingly bad things can take a turn for the better." She gestured around the room. "Just look at where I am now. I was always so sure my story would have a different ending."

"It's more unassuming inside than I had expected," Lillian said. "I thought the Rose House was beautiful the first time I saw it from the outside. I was captured by a feeling that there might still be something lovely left for me even after God took my children. I don't know if it was the beauty of the roses or if it was just because the vines seemed so persistent in the way they rambled all over the house." Lillian thought about it for a moment and realized that was it. "They have weathered time, haven't they? How old are those bushes anyway?"

Kitty sighed and stared at one of the paintings on the wall, as if she were trying to count the years. "It's hard to say, dear, but I think they are about thirty-five or forty years old. Blake has kept up with them for years, and now I help him.

"Blake started out with three vines, and when he saw that they were good climbers, he started putting latticework up on the side of the house. When he noticed they were healthy, he had the gardener from whom he had bought the first three order more vines. He planted them all around, and over the years has babied them something fierce. He even put lattice on the roof so the roses could ramble right over the top."

"He did that just for you?"

"For me. And for our daughter Ruby. I suppose we keep them going for Lucy as well. Sometimes when she visits, she even sleeps here in the Rose House in her mother's old room."

"I wondered if anyone ever stayed in the house anymore," Lillian said, testing her rocker, which caused a few boards beneath her to creak.

"Oh, the house will always be livable and cared for, at least I hope so," Kitty said. "Its creator would never willingly let it go. It has become sentimental to Blake; a symbol or some kind of tribute, really. I suppose when we are gone, Lucy will keep the roses up, now that she knows the secret."

"There's a secret?"

Kitty laughed, as if holding the secret in her eyes. "Oh yes, dear. There is a secret, but it's not only how to grow the roses. There's more to it, and you discovered a little bit of it back when you were captured in paint by our Truman. There's a secret in this house for everyone. We each have our own truth in it."

Lillian smiled. So there was something a person was supposed to take away from it. For some it was just a pretty house, perhaps the result of good gardening. For others it was a symbol that spoke deeper. Like the painting did for Lillian. It represented the tragedies hidden away in her mind, but it also told her story of hope and survival; it spoke of her dreams.

"I wish we could find the painting," Lillian said.

"Don't worry, Lillian. We'll find it someday. For now, just be happy that we have the best parts of it. You and the house."

Lillian thought of the lone figure in the lighthouse sketch. "But we don't have Tru," she said, continuing to rock. Kitty watched her, a sad look on her face, but she didn't respond with her usual wise words of advice or encouragement. She closed her eyes, as if taking a nap. Lillian did the same, the creaking boards beneath the rocking chair the only noise around them.

44

PREPARING FOR KARA'S WEDDING kept Lillian busy for the next several weeks. Even Saturdays were taken up with preparations and they had to be strict about their policy of no new weddings on short notice. On one particular Saturday, Lillian was poring over lists that she kept having to reread. She couldn't figure out why she felt so horrible. She'd woken up in a sour mood. It wasn't just a bad mood, but bordered on despair. She hadn't felt that way for a long time.

"Good morning, sis." Geena walked into the kitchen, followed closely by Paige. Geena handed her a card. "It's from us."

"What's this?" Lillian picked up the pink envelope. The card was covered with cheery pansies in purple and gold. Inside they had both inscribed their names beneath what appeared to be a sympathy note. Then Lillian peered closer at what Geena had written.

They will never be forgotten.

Lillian burst into tears. Images of Sheyenne and Lee danced around her. When she regained control, she looked at Geena and Paige. "I forgot," she said. "How could I have forgotten?" She had been so busy that the anniversary of the accident had come and she had not even remembered.

Paige moved to her side. "Oh, sweetie." She placed her arm around Lillian as Geena did the same on the other side. "Obviously you didn't forget or you wouldn't be feeling so bad."

Lillian sniffed. "You're right! I was wondering why I felt so awful today. You're both sweet. Thank you."

"Why don't you go to the cemetery today?" Geena asked. "We can handle things here while you're gone. It won't take you long."

"But do take your time," Paige said. "Take all day if you need it."

Geena agreed, and within the next half hour, Lillian was in the car on her way to Sacramento. With Tru gone, Lillian had nothing in particular to do on Saturdays, so she was happy to spend her weekends working except for when she attended services at the vineyard.

She accelerated as she left La Rosaleda and smiled at the vineyards rolling past. It had been a while since she had been to the cemetery, the longest she had ever gone without seeing the children. Her heartbeat intensified the closer she got. It would do her good to just be able to touch the stones. She needed to be reminded that she had once been a mother, and even if she never had another child, in her heart, she would always be the mom of Sheyenne and Lee.

⌀

Chills crept along her arms, giving the cemetery a cold, dismal feeling. The flowers she had so lovingly planted around the graves recently now lay scattered around the markers, their roots bare. Clumps of dirt seemed to have been scattered purposely across Robert's grave, but Sheyenne's and Lee's were the worst. Colorful petals, some of them shredded, were crushed and strewn upon the ground. The upturned earth looked fresh.

For a moment, Lillian just stood there, staring at the disaster, trying to imagine who would do such a thing. *The caller.* The thought made her shiver. Had Geena been right all along? She glanced around nervously, her hands covering her mouth. Her hands moved to her head, pressing against her temples. "Leave me alone," she whispered. Then louder, her voice echoing across the cemetery. "Leave me alone!" she cried, praying silently that the vandalism was something random. Then she dropped to her knees, crying openly as she crawled back and forth from one stone to the next, gathering the flowers and placing them in a pile beside her.

Once she had gathered the limp plants, she retrieved several bottles of water from the trunk of her car and hurried back to the gravesites. She vehemently worked the soil with her fingers, replanting each plant, plucking and discarding dead blooms, and then sprinkling water over the newly turned soil.

When she was finished, she sat back on her heels and surveyed her work. It looked like a mini tornado had hit the three plots, but some of the plants seemed to be perking up. She was still furious, but she felt a little bit better. Crawling over to the markers of Sheyenne and Lee, she kissed them each, the feel of the cold marble on her lips providing a little solace to her heart.

She touched Robert's stone but felt no reassurance there. While she would have given anything to have him back on earth again, she would never know if he had really loved her, would never know his secrets.

Running her hand back and forth across the smooth stone, she whispered soft words. "I'm sorry for the pain you must have felt in your life, sweetheart. I'm sorry for any of it that was my fault."

Before she realized what she was doing, she found herself spontaneously pulling up the flowers she'd just planted around Robert's headstone. She shuffled to each of the children's stones and tucked the flowers around theirs. She pressed the loose soil back around Robert's stone and dusted her hands off.

Ignoring Robert's stone for the moment, she placed the fresh-cut flowers she had brought from La Rosaleda in the vases on Sheyenne's and Lee's headstones. When she turned back to his grave, she placed the remaining flower, a yellow rose, neatly on the grass below his stone. It would be the last time she would leave flowers for him.

After kissing her palm, she pressed it into his stone. The rhythm of her heart slowed until it was even and calm. She had so many questions that could never be answered, but Geena had answered enough of them for her to know that if Robert had lived, their marriage would have needed more than a miracle to survive. Robert might even have gone to jail.

"Good-bye, Robert," she whispered. That was the miracle, she realized, that she could move on.

She could forgive Geena, which had become easier with every new day, and she had new friends in Paige and Kitty. She'd never lost Aunt Bren or the pastor who raised her, and even Chef George had become a real friend to her. But the biggest part of her miracle was finding Tru.

Even Tru couldn't have painted a more telling picture of how her life might have gone; but if she was at all lucky, or blessed, as Aunt Bren would say, he would have the chance to try. As soon as she got back to the cottage, she would write him a long letter.

~✆

On her way out of the cemetery, Lillian slowed her car to drive quietly past a funeral. She ached for the woman in a black dress and dark sunglasses. She had been in that position. She reached over to roll her window up when she noticed Jake, her old driver, standing soberly beside one of the black sedans.

He was dressed in his uniform and when he turned in her direction, she gave him a small wave. He paused, as if he didn't recognize her at first, and then he sent her a small, surprised smile. For a moment he looked like he might approach the car, but then, stepping back into his place, he tossed her just the slightest wave of acknowledgment.

How strange life could be, Lillian mused. She couldn't have been happier to be the one behind the wheel.

45

HALFWAY TO LA ROSALEDA, Lillian's hand flew to her neck. Her pendant. She patted all around her neck and then the seat around her. Nearly swerving off the road, she pulled over and placed the car in park. Leaving it running, she stepped outside to examine her clothing, but the pendant was nowhere to be found.

She climbed back into the car and looked on the floors and between the seats. She even popped the trunk and looked inside, thinking the pendant might have fallen off as she was getting the water bottles. Still no pendant.

She felt the place just below her neck where the pendant always rested.

A puff of air escaped her lips. Where was it? She walked back to the driver's side and sat motionless behind the wheel. Tears traced a path down her cheeks, falling down her neck to wet the spot where the pendant used to be.

She wondered if it had fallen at the grave sites, so she turned the car around. The fifty miles seemed like five hundred as she imagined someone else finding her pendant. Her heart thundered. Maybe someone would find it and turn it in. She shuddered at the thought of an employee collecting it and possibly throwing it away.

Back at the cemetery, she drove toward the area where her children lay. The funeral she had passed was over, the fresh grave seemingly abandoned except for the woman in black kneeling beside the grave with a handkerchief to her face. Lillian wished she could go to her and tell her how much time it can sometimes take to even feel like surviving—and to never give up hope.

Her own sad memories of a funeral fresh again in her mind, she parked and stumbled to the grave site. She looked all around, even digging down into the dirt, hoping to find the pendant, but no luck. After an hour of looking, she sat back on her heels and cried.

She had promised to let go of Robert, pledging to move on and open her heart to Truman, but letting go of Sheyenne and Lee had been nowhere in her thoughts. She needed her pendant.

She looked skyward, her weeping silent. *This is too much, Lord.* She placed her hands over her face, wiping the wetness from her cheeks. Why was this happening? First the painting, then Truman, and now the pendant; all things that represented her most treasured feelings and hopes.

She raised her damp face and stared at the tops of the trees dotting the cemetery. *Please, give them back.*

46

THE MISSION BELL GONGED repeatedly, its echo reverberating across Frances-DiCamillo. The jubilant ringing was pleasantly reminiscent of weddings gone by and could be heard all the way into La Rosaleda.

Lillian had once asked Kitty about the bell. In the past, it had been used to alert the vineyard workers that it was lunchtime, but more importantly to announce special occasions to the community. If someone in La Rosaleda heard the bells ringing, they knew it announced something special, most often a wedding or a birth.

Once again its sound signaled an event that promised to be a festive celebration. Lillian couldn't be more excited. She was so nervous that things wouldn't work well, but she had planned each and every part of it with Paige and Geena. They were as ready as ever.

She busily inspected the catering area to make sure everything was perfect. Tents were set up to shelter a dozen or so tables spread with delectable hors d'oeuvres and a cinnamon-vanilla wedding cake decorated with delicate sugarcoated roses from the Rose House. Lillian had spent hours working on the cake, down to personally coating each and every rose petal, and was thrilled at the bride's reaction.

"Are those petals from *Kitty's* Rose House?" she exclaimed. When Lillian said yes, Kara broke into happy tears, which was just the reaction Lillian had been hoping for. She didn't tell anyone that she had consulted with Chef George to find just the perfect recipe for the cinnamon-vanilla cake and frosting. It had been tricky to get it to look like a wedding cake and still taste like cinnamon and vanilla, but they had figured it out.

She glanced around, spotting Chef George and his wife, Barbara, chatting with Blake Birkirt. He had come at her request to evaluate what might need improving before she considered taking the business with Geena and Paige to the next level. George, of course, was really there to lure Lillian to go into business with him, either by coming back to his own restaurant or opening a new one in another part of Sacramento.

Turning back toward the tables, she bustled over to Geena, who was flitting about, dressed in a chic black dress that only a waitress with her level of experience could pull off. Geena had tied an elegant apron over it and wore a white hat. Lillian herself had opted for a blue sleeveless silk dress that was more evocative of a garden setting, but she also wore a white hat, as did Paige. Kitty had said specifically that Kara requested that all the women and girls among her guests would wear hats.

"Then let's all wear white hats to distinguish us from the rest of the crowd," Paige had suggested. Lillian thought Paige looked pretty in her hat and her soft yellow dress. Lillian noted the gold cross Paige wore on a chain around her neck, a Mother's Day present she'd received from Mark and Gracie.

Lillian's hand automatically touched her chest, bare of the silver pendant that had been worn by Sheyenne until the accident. She had never found it. It had just disappeared, as if it had never existed, almost like Sheyenne herself. Luckily she still had Lee's toy car, which stayed nestled in her purse along with the sketches from Tru, including the most recent one; a simple miniature sketch of the Rose House that resembled the photograph she had once tucked in the visor of his truck.

"How are the warmers?" she asked Paige.

"Everything is holding up great." Paige smiled broadly. "Doesn't it smell delicious? You are magnificent, Lil. Chef George better cough up a good deal for you if he wants to deserve having you come back."

Lillian waved the comment away with her pink-polished nails. "It's not about that. It's about doing something I love."

"Truman would be proud of your efforts," Paige said.

Lillian offered a half smile. She didn't mention to Paige that she hadn't heard from Tru for at least a week. She was pretty sure that if Tru was coming back, he wouldn't want her to go to work for Chef George in Sacramento, but it was starting to look like he never was coming back. Months had passed. Even the leaves on the vines were starting to turn, despite the warm temperatures in La Rosaleda.

Lillian had tried to reflect some of the turning leaves in her cooking through colors and presentation. Kara wanted things to be elegant but also relaxed, so she'd chosen a large variety of dishes. Heaps of sweet garlic and goat cheese penne pasta, Mongolian ginger beef, and coconut shrimp with red curry sauce were among the dishes prepared for the big day. Kara had specifically requested Mexican wedding cakes and mantecadas to go along with the key lime tarts and mini baked Alaskas. Already, guests were hovering around the dessert table, exclaiming over how scrumptious they looked.

As more guests arrived, Lillian and Geena had fun admiring the various hats the guests were wearing. It looked as if they were going to live up to Kara's expectations. As Lillian moved among the guests, she overheard some of them saying that they had special-ordered their hats from England, while others had found theirs in the dress shops downtown. They all looked adorable, especially the ones on the little girls.

"Do you like my hat?" Gracie cried. It was a straw hat with a red rose as big as Gracie's face, but it looked adorable with her little pink sundress. Gracie slipped her hand into Mark's. "We're going to find Charlie!" she called back.

"Too cute," Lillian said, turning back to her work. She checked with Geena and Paige to ensure the food stayed warm in anticipation of the reception.

"We're going to have a full house!" Geena cried, glancing around the grounds. "Will there be enough food?"

She was right, Lillian observed. In addition to family and friends, vineyard workers and their families were in attendance, as well as a few tourists lucky enough to run into Kitty on the street. They had shown up in their touristy best and were pleasantly offered their choice of hats from a stack of decorative hatboxes Kitty had arranged around the gift table.

The wedding itself was a garden fantasy. Kara looked like a garden fairy in an iridescent ivory silk strapless gown adorned with a spray of wine-colored roses at the side of the waist. Lillian smiled at the proud look on Charles's face when he saw his sister walking from the gardens, following a pebbled path to the Rose House created for the sole purpose of the wedding.

Lillian smiled as the crowd shouted encouragement during the bride and groom's kiss. It had been a beautiful day. The only part missing for Lillian was Tru. She thought he would be proud of her catering business, but she would just have to accept that, like the missing painting, gone without a trace, Tru might never be part of her future.

Turning back to the catering tents before the crowd could beat her to them, she spotted Chef George. Before the wedding was over, she would tell him she accepted his offer, with just a small change in his plan.

⁓₯⁓

"Next time we're going to need more food!" exclaimed Geena during a brief lull in the reception.

"No need," said Paige, filling cups with strawberry champagne punch. "There won't be another wedding this big for centuries." She paused and stared off toward the path. "Or maybe there will be," she muttered, then broke into a smile, dried her hands on a cloth, and ducked out of the tent.

"Where's she going?" Lillian asked, spinning around. She dropped a serving spoon onto the grass and her hands flew to her mouth. She couldn't breathe.

Geena looked at Lillian. "Oh, my word, Lily Bug. You are as white as a ghost. Are you okay?"

Lillian opened her mouth, but words failed her. She turned away from Geena, busying herself with checking the warming dishes. Guests lingered around her, waiting for their favorite dishes to be refilled, and she worked quickly, glad to have an excuse to put off turning around.

She felt a hand on her shoulder but refused to turn away from her task.

"Lillian, turn around."

At the sound of Paige's voice, Lillian spun to see her friend drawing closer to her.

"It's okay," Paige said. "I thought it was Truman, but it was only someone who looked like him."

Lillian raised herself to her tiptoes, looking over Geena's and Paige's shoulders.

Geena wrinkled her nose. "He even has a hat very similar to Truman's, and he is bald!"

"Geena!" Paige chided. "Tru is not bald; he just shaves his head."

Lillian shook her head and motioned for them both to be quiet. "I've seen him before." She told them about the day she'd thought she saw Tru, but it had been that man coming out of the gallery. "He disappeared down an alley. I didn't see him again."

"Truman would never wear a black leather jacket. That's too fancy for him," Paige said.

"That man is definitely not dressed the right way for a wedding," Geena said.

"I wonder who he is?"

"Let's ask Kitty." Paige turned and pointed to Kitty as she walked toward them.

"Ladies, you have outdone yourselves!" She spent the next few minutes gushing over the reception, and in return, they all gushed over the wedding, telling her how lovely she looked and how sweet the ceremony had been.

"Kitty," Paige said, "who is that man?"

Kitty turned to look where all three of the women were pointing. At that exact moment, he walked toward them. They all slapped their hands down to their sides as Kitty gave him a welcoming smile.

"Why, Tom Bentley, what are you doing here?" She reached out her hands, and he squeezed them warmly.

"Hello, Kitty. It's so good to see you." His voice was nasally. Lillian immediately disliked him. Maybe it was simply because both times she had seen him, he had made her think of Tru, but of course, he could never live up to Tru. She glanced at Geena, who, from the frown on her face, didn't like him either. Of course, Geena didn't like most people at first impression, so her opinion couldn't be fully trusted.

Kitty turned to the three women. "This is Tom Bentley, one of my favorite buyers. He almost keeps the gallery running with his purchases."

"With those she will sell," Bentley said, winking.

Paige reached out to shake his hand, while Geena and Lillian just smiled. He looked at the two of them quizzically, his eyes resting a little too long on Lillian for her taste. She wanted to tuck her hand into her pocket, to hide that she was single. "You are a collector?" she asked.

"I am. Are you?" He smiled at Paige.

"Of sorts," she said. "I haven't seen you around. Where are you from?"

"Sacramento," he said. "I learned about Kitty's gallery from Louise."

When Lillian realized he was a friend of Kitty's and Louise's, she relaxed, but she still wished she had a ring on. The glances of interest he kept shooting her way unnerved her.

Mr. Bentley turned back to Kitty. "I didn't mean to crash the wedding. I was just in town and thought I'd drop by and talk to you about some of the paintings we discussed last time I was in town."

"It's no problem," Kitty said, gesturing toward the food. "Have a bite to eat." She lifted her skirt slightly so she could walk across the lawn without tripping. "When I have a spare moment, we can talk in my office."

He nodded.

At that moment, Gracie and Charles hurried across the lawn and stopped in front of Paige.

"Look!" Gracie cried. "Charlie caught a butterfly!"

They turned to look at Charles, including Mr. Bentley, as Charles, slightly hunched over, a look of wonder on his face, opened his hands and let the bluish-green butterfly flit away. Everyone watched it until it disappeared into a nearby tree.

"That was amazing!" Paige said, placing her arm around Charles.

"Wow," Lillian said, "I've never seen a butterfly so beautiful as that one." Lillian noted that Geena avoided speaking to Charles, as she always did. It embarrassed Lillian to think her sister was slightly prejudiced toward someone like Charles, but she had hoped that in time, Geena might grow to like Charles, who was a close family friend of the Tenneys.

"Well," Mr. Bentley said, "that is something. How did you do it?"

Gracie and Charles both began talking to him a mile a minute. "We found it at the Rose House," cried Gracie. "Wanna see?"

Paige called out a warning before turning back to check on the food. "Mr. Bentley would have his hands full if they were to sneak into the Rose House again."

"He seems nice enough," Paige whispered, "but it did surprise me when I got close enough to see his face and it wasn't Truman." She glanced over at Lillian. "Did you know that your old driver, Jake, is here? I think he drove Mr. Bentley."

Lillian glanced up, partially surprised; however, she had noticed him driving other new clients the last couple of times she had seen him.

"Geena and I will have to say hello to him. Where is he?"

Paige looked up from her task and pointed toward the parking lot. "We're wrapping up," she said. "You two go ahead."

Lillian smiled at Mr. Bentley, who held Charles and Gracie captive with his own butterfly stories. They both stared at him in rapt attention.

Jake was standing by a large black sedan. "Jake!" Geena called.

He broke into a smile and stepped forward. "Miss Diamon!" He glanced at Lillian. "And Miss Diamon!"

They exchanged greetings and small talk for a while, before Jake raised his finger, suddenly seeming to remember something important. "Miss Diamon," he looked at Lillian, "I have something of yours."

He dug deep into his pocket and pulled his hand out. The silver chain sparkled as he let the red-jeweled cross drop. The red jewel glinted in the sun as she stared at the dangling cross, her eyes wide.

"I think this is yours."

Lillian's face broke into a smile as she stared at the pendant.

"On the day I saw you at the cemetery, I took a long walk after the funeral. The widow took a long time to say good-bye. I happened to walk past your family's graves and saw this sparkling on the grass. I recognized it as yours."

With one hand, she took the cross and brought it to her lips. Laughing, she glanced up at the clear blue sky.

Thank You.

She brought the cross back to her lips.

Thank You.

—◌

Geena held Lillian's hand as they walked up the path. She smiled at how Lillian toyed with her pendant, obviously still elated to have it back.

"It's almost time to cut the cake," Lillian said. "Are you okay?"

Geena looked at Lillian, surprised that she had gotten so lost in her thinking. "Yeah, sure. I'm just tired."

"We've been moving full speed all day," Lillian said. "Take a few minutes to catch your breath. Paige and I can handle things."

"Thanks," Geena said. "I'll be up in a minute."

After Lillian left, Geena sat down on a stump that was surrounded by clusters of pansies and violas. She watched guests decorate the limo, wondering what it would be like to actually be in love with someone who would want to marry you and have a real wedding.

She leaned over to pluck a tiny viola. She'd always thought they looked like flowers with beards. She smiled at the blossom and glanced back down the driveway, noticing a blue Jeep pulling through the gates.

Blocking the sun from her eyes with one hand, Geena tried to see who it was. The Jeep stopped in the parking lot and the passenger door swung open.

"Mario!" she cried and rushed over to him. "What are you doing here?"

"Mi corazón!" He opened his arms in welcome. "I came with him."

She turned to see Truman Clark leaning over the Jeep. Geena noticed he had only gotten better looking since she'd seen him last. His eyes looked vibrant against his tanned skin, and she didn't think he got those muscles from painting.

Plunking his hat on his head, he grinned at her. She wondered how anyone had ever gotten Mr. Bentley's hat mixed up with Truman's. It was completely different.

"Miss Diamon," Truman said.

She felt her face grow pale and waited for him to tear her to shreds. She deserved it for all she had accused him of in the past.

He walked over and took her hand, bringing it briefly to his lips.

"When Mario told me he had met the woman of his dreams, I had no idea he meant you." He gazed into her eyes. "I declare, it always surprises me how little we know of a person until the passage of time shows us."

Geena smiled, returning his humor. "Indeed, Mr. Clark." Winking at him, she linked arms with Mario.

Halfway down the path she turned back to see if Truman was following. He stood between the parking lot and the path, appearing unsure of what to do.

"Truman Clark," she called. "Come on. You have a lot of time to make up for."

He looked at Mario and Geena, his self-doubt suddenly apparent in his tall frame. He glanced sideways and said, so that Geena could barely hear him, "What do I say to her?"

She shook her head. "I don't know, Truman, but when the time comes, you'll know." She smiled up at Mario, one of only a handful of men she had dated who was taller than she was. "Right, Mario?"

"Right." Happy to be with Geena, Mario flashed an encouraging smile at Truman. "Let's go."

Lillian was gathering empty dessert plates when she turned to see Geena and Mario.

"Sure," she teased, "show up when all the work is done, sis!"

Geena had a huge smile pasted on her face that seemed a little strange. When they got closer, Geena and Mario separated and turned away from Lillian. She followed their gaze.

She saw him walking toward her, but surely she was mistaken. Maybe it was Mr. Bentley. When she looked around for him, he was nowhere to be seen. She watched the man get closer, his gait more and more familiar. Before she could catch her breath, he strode right up to her and reached for her hand.

Halfway in shock, she extended it, watching him plant his lips in a kiss that she was too anxious to feel.

"Lillian," he said, his voice strong and familiar, yet strange. She let it wash over her.

"Tru?" she whispered. She swallowed and then cleared her throat. "Tru—I didn't think you would come back." Tears gathered in her eyes.

His thumbs caressed the palms of her hands, his eyes staring intently into hers. "I got your letter."

She smiled. She had tried hard to explain her day at the cemetery, hoping Truman would understand. It had been so hard to put her feelings on paper, but she'd hoped he could read between the lines enough to understand what she herself barely understood. That she was free. Her heart was free of all the things that had been blocking his way.

He was close enough that she could hear his deep breaths, and when she saw the flush of his cheeks, she realized he was nervous. Just the idea gave her strength.

"Are you going to just stand there?" she said, deciding that teasing might be a way to ease the tension.

He didn't move, but his eyes mirrored her own desire to touch.

"Tru?"

He flashed a crooked smile as he held his arms out wide. When she got close enough, he swooped her into his arms. She buried her face in his shoulder, unable to believe that Truman was standing right there, his arms wrapped around her. She inhaled, enjoying the familiar smells of cologne, soap, and the always lingering whiff of paint.

He hugged her tightly, lifting her off her feet. After he seemed sure she was real, he set her gently down. Leaning down to plant a light kiss on her lips, he said, "And there's more where that came from."

Paige magically appeared and teased both of them. "Hello, Truman."

He turned away from Lillian to engulf Paige in a bear hug. Soon the word got around that he was back and everyone crowded around.

"Sorry I'm late," he said sheepishly when Kitty approached.

"You'd better be!" she said, leaning on her cane, but everyone knew she didn't mean a word of it.

Lillian's heart pounded as she watched Truman, beloved by so many, make his rounds.

"Have you seen Gracie?"

Lillian turned to Paige. "No, I haven't, but she was with Charles."

"Well, I'm going to look for her," Paige said. "She will be thrilled to see *Uncle* Truman." She patted Lillian on the shoulder. "I'm happy for you, Lillian." They shared a hug and then Paige set off to find Gracie.

"You look beautiful." Truman put his hand on her elbow and steered her away from the wedding toward an entrance into the vineyards. Pausing just outside a row, he turned to her.

"Take off your shoes."

Laughing, she took them off. She glanced down at her pink-petal toes and bemoaned the loss of her pedicure. Reveling in the cool earth beneath her feet, memories of their picnic when they had first met encircled her thoughts. Accepting the offer of his hand, they walked along the rows of grapes that were almost ready for harvest.

As they wound deeper into the vines, Truman released her hand and placed his on her waist. He pulled her tight beside him. They made their way, meandering slowly through the vines.

"I missed you, Lil."

He gently turned her shoulders to face him. He leaned in, brushing her lips, but she gently pushed back.

His eyes wore a mixture of regret. He turned away to look out over the rolling hills of the vineyards. "I'm sorry, Lillian. I tried to force my way into your heart." His chest rose and fell with a heavy sigh. "After painting you, your grief was evident to me. I should not have intruded further by allowing myself to fall in love with you."

Truman began to walk again. Lillian followed behind, studying the tightness in his shoulders, the sadness in his gait.

"You didn't even explain things to me before you left," she said.

He paused, started to turn, but then commenced walking. "I'm sorry, Lillian."

"It hurt. You could have given me a chance to work out my feelings without leaving me," she called after him.

"I was giving you a chance by leaving," he explained.

She hurried to keep up with his pace. She had to admit it was true that with him gone, she had been forced to really think about what she wanted in life without Robert and her children.

"Truman, stop!" she called out.

He froze.

"Would you please look at me?" she implored.

He turned slowly, the pain on his face ripping her heart.

"If you had told me what you were thinking, then maybe we could have figured it out a different way instead of this"—she reached her hands into the air—"this crazy loneliness." Her voice cracked.

He didn't say anything. She wondered if he disagreed with her.

"I left for you," he said, his voice hoarse. "I wanted to give you the time you needed. I hated the fact that I pushed my way into your life with barely a thought about whether you were ready to move on from your grief."

"But I will always grieve," she said softly. The compassion in his blue eyes melted her. She wanted him to engulf her in a hug, but he stood stock-still.

"And," she said, "if you had warned me that you were coming back, I wouldn't have told Chef George that I was going to go into business with him. It might be a little bit complicated now that you are back. You might not like my plan."

His eyes met hers, his face a façade of calm. "I'm so proud of you, Lillian. You deserve to have your own place."

"But it would have been wonderful to share the decision with you."

He buried his hands in his pockets and shook his head. "Lil, I don't pretend to understand every little thing about how you are feeling. You are losing me in the details, but whatever you have decided, we can work it out. Unless—" His face clouded. "Unless you don't want to work it out."

She smiled. "Oh, Tru, I'm sorry." She put her hand in his. "I'm so glad you are back. I didn't think you were coming. It's been so long."

He did pull her into his arms then and they embraced for a long time.

"Where have you been?" she asked into his shoulder.

"Lots of places, doing lots of thinking. I hope we are going to have a lot of time to talk about all the places I've been. Me and Cody."

"Where is Cody?"

"He's at home, but we got you something."

He dug his hand in his pocket. "I've heard that women like to pick out their own rings, so I got this for you instead." He reached into his pocket and pulled out a silver necklace with a small, shining lighthouse charm dangling from the end. "Maybe it will help you find your way into the future."

Lillian's eyes misted as she turned and lifted her hair. He fastened the necklace at a snail's pace.

"These things are tricky for big hands," he complained. Taken by surprise, she shivered at the feel of his lips at the nape of her neck. She leaned her head back so he could trail kisses up to her cheek. Then, spinning her slowly around, he grazed his lips across hers. It was soft and unsure at first, and then as the longing in each of their hearts increased, so did the kiss. They were pulling themselves away when the first sounds of screams carried across the wind.

"What's that?" Lillian asked.

"I don't know."

"It sounds like people calling for Gracie."

Truman's face paled. "Do you think she's lost?" Lillian was too busy listening to answer. "Let's go," he said. He took her hand and they ran all the way back.

When they approached the yard, people were gathered at the end of the vines, arguing.

"Charles is missing too," Geena said. "Maybe—maybe he has Gracie."

Kara's voice was shrill as she squawked angrily at Geena. "What are you trying to say? He's my brother!" She was still wearing her wedding dress and tears trailed mascara down her cheeks.

"Maybe he took her," Geena said.

People around them began to mumble, most of them agreeing that Geena might be right.

Kara grasped her husband's hand tightly. Her voice was wobbly as she implored the crowd, "Please, he wouldn't do anything to her. He is not some kind of"—she spat the words out—"creepy predator."

Truman approached Geena. "Whoa, everybody. Now hold on. Why are we already blaming Charles when we have no idea what has happened? Let's stop wasting time and find them both." He placed his hand on Kara's shoulder. Lillian moved in and gave her a little hug.

"Once both of them are found, we'll settle this."

In the midst of the arguing, Blake showed up. "Let's start in the vine-yards." He began to divide people up into teams, telling them what parts of Frances-DiCamillo might be hiding curious kids.

"He's not a kid," Geena argued.

"Let's stop this," Lillian said to Geena, although at the moment, anything was possible. She hated to think that Charles could be responsible for Gracie's being lost. She glanced around and saw Mark Tenney, his face pinched tight. "Where's Paige?" She turned toward Geena.

"With Kitty," Geena said, "in the house. She is hysterical, naturally, so Kitty decided it was best to keep her in there."

"Has anyone called the police?" Truman asked.

"Not yet," Blake said. He nodded to someone in the crowd, who pulled out a cell phone.

"Let's get going!" Truman yelled.

~⌒)

Lillian followed Truman, torn between going to Paige and wanting to help find Gracie and Charles too. Tears stung her eyes as she considered the possibilities. After the accident that took her own children, she no longer wore blinders as to what can happen to children. She could no longer pretend that life was guaranteed to be innocent for every child she loved.

And she loved Gracie. She realized with a start that the little girl had become so much a part of her life that she seemed to be like a niece. Her throat constricted. She remembered the conversation she'd had with Paige months earlier. Paige had related to Lillian's loss, revealing her own fear, every mother's fear, of losing her child. She couldn't lose Gracie.

Lillian, swiping tears away, nodded to Geena, who was headed for the area around the Rose House. Lillian quickened her steps toward the gardens.

She wanted to help find Gracie. That's where she wanted to be. That's where she should be.

~⌒)

Geena headed toward the Rose House where Blake had sent her.

"Look in the windows again," he'd said. "Maybe we missed something the first time." He'd tossed her a key. "On second thought, just go inside."

Truman shouted for somebody to look in the parking lot. Geena whirled around. "Talk to the driver of a black sedan."

Truman gave her a rueful look. That would be a quarter of the cars left in the parking lot. She stifled the urge to roll her eyes at him. Apparently, they still had a little ways to go to be tolerant of each other.

"Specifically talk to the one named Jake. He's here from Sacramento, if he's still here. Ask him to do the parking lot search."

Truman nodded to Mario, who sprinted toward the parking lot.

Geena trudged down the path, scanning the brambles and flower beds to see if a little girl could be hiding behind them. She couldn't believe Kara and Truman were so hardheaded about the possibility that Charles might have done something to Gracie.

It was so logical. And if he had done that, then maybe the photos weren't as innocent as previously thought. Maybe Charles even had something to do with the missing painting. Greed? Obsession with Lillian?

Geena's mind raced with the possibilities of how Charles might be harmful. Maybe he was being manipulated by the person who had terrorized Lillian right after Robert's death.

She stopped at the foot of the steps and turned her head to look toward the parking lot. A chill unfolded across her arms.

Jake. Jake had spent a lot of time driving Lillian around in the past four or five years.

She shook her head, remembering how angry Kara had been at her accusations of Charles. The idea that the driver who had safely driven Lillian around for years might have been stalking her seemed ludicrous. Her heart railed against it, thinking about the times he had driven her and Robert to places without ever asking a question.

She tramped up the steps and carefully peeked into the house, going from window to window. Jake had certainly kept secrets, she realized. And they weren't exactly noble. But still, she couldn't imagine—

She gasped when she saw movement in the house.

She wriggled her nose. "What is that odor?" She sniffed. "Gasoline?" Her heart boomed in her ears.

As she peered closer, Geena's heart lurched. Gracie sat crumpled on the floor, her usually olive face drained of color. Her cheeks were wet, and she leaned on Charles's knee.

Geena turned and yelled to the others. "They're in here!"

She quickly dug for the key and rattled it in the lock. It seemed to stick at first. Geena jiggled the key again. That gas smell could only mean bad news. She felt the lock give and pushed open the door. The eyes that met hers were like steel.

She felt a jerk on her arm and suddenly she was in the house.

What's that? She felt a thud on the back of her head.

Gracie.

Geena attempted to call her name, trying hard to keep her knees from buckling, but they folded against her will.

-◌)-

Having heard the shouts, Truman hurried to the Rose House, followed closely by Mark and Lillian. He pressed a rose bramble away and peered inside. He turned toward Lillian, his tanned face ashen.

"Where's Mario?"

"I don't know," she said. "He hasn't come back from the parking lot."

Truman's voice was rough. "Call the police."

"They're already on the way," she reminded him.

"Call them again!"

She relayed the message to the crowd of people who, still in their wedding clothes, were part of the search.

Shouts rang out across the gardens, and Blake joined Truman on the porch.

Kitty, with Paige on her arm, limped with her cane toward them. Lillian's eyes rested on Kara for a moment, face distraught, strands of hair plastered to her face from wet tears. Lillian wished she could go comfort her.

Blake dug in his pocket for keys to the Rose House. He rattled the doorknob and his face looked perplexed.

"Door's blocked. Let's try the back."

Lillian peeked inside. Her blood ran cold when she saw Gracie.

Charles stroked Gracie's hair, appearing to reassure her. Lillian's heart fell. When she turned to relay what she saw, Paige was standing at the foot of the porch. Lillian met her gaze.

Paige sobbed and began screaming. Lillian stepped off the porch and grabbed her shoulders. "Shh."

She forced Paige to look in her eyes. "You can do this, Paige. You can't lose it. Gracie is right inside. She might hear you!"

Paige's fingertips flew to her lips. "Oh, my God. You're right."

"Take a deep breath," Lillian said. "Be calm. If you can't, then go over with Kitty and her church friends to pray."

Paige nodded, as if it were decided. "I'm not budging from this spot."

Full understanding spread through Lillian. "I know."

Tears welled in Paige's eyes. "And I couldn't pray if I wanted to. I can't think."

"I know," Lillian said. "So let the rest of us pray for you."

During the hardest parts of Lillian's journey, she hadn't the energy or focus to pray. Sometimes not even the desire. If it hadn't been for Aunt Bren—

A scream that could only be Gracie's pierced the air.

Lillian whirled and ran to the window, leaving Paige to sink to her knees. Gracie was no longer sitting at Charles's feet. Lillian could see to the other side of the house where Blake and Tru hovered in the window.

Why was Charles just sitting there? Something glimmered in his hand. She scanned the room for Gracie. She was nowhere to be seen. Lillian's eyes fell on a large painting propped up against the chair beside Charles.

She gasped. *Beauty and the Beast Within.* Where had it come from? Had Charles taken it as a prank?

Lillian motioned to Truman in the opposite window. His eyes fell on the portrait. He looked taken aback. He shook his head only for a moment as he turned his gaze to an area Lillian couldn't see.

Could he see Gracie? Clearly, the magical appearance of the painting barely made a mark on Truman. Only the day before, Lillian had been hoping the painting would reappear. Compared to Gracie's safety, its value to her abruptly plummeted.

She saw Truman and Blake suddenly jump back. Tru gave Blake a warning look.

Truman started banging on the window. Lillian grew sick as she watched him jam his elbow through the glass. He had just stuck his hand through to turn the knob when a figure approached and clubbed Truman's arm. Truman jerked it back and disappeared.

Soon he appeared at the front of the house. "The doors are blocked!" he yelled. Angry words roared through his teeth. "Someone is in there with them," he called. "I can't tell who it is."

Kara shot the crowd a withering look as if to say, "I told you so." Then as the realization set in that Charles was in harm's way, her hand flew to her mouth.

"Where are the police?" Blake yelled, his weathered, lined cheeks flushed red. "You're all they sent?" he yelled at the single officer, Peter, lumbering up the path.

Blake met Peter halfway. The two consulted quickly. Simultaneously, Peter turned and said something into his radio.

Truman caught Lillian's eye and motioned for her to get off the porch. Lillian was taken aback by his bossiness but stepped down. She grasped Paige's hand.

"Gracie," was all Paige could manage to say. Lillian wanted to tell her it would be okay, but she was the last person to believe that was always true.

"Why don't you find Geena and wait with her?" suggested Lillian. "Have you seen her?"

Paige shook her head. "I'm okay. I'm not moving."

All the while Lillian kept an eye on Truman. He was yelling at someone inside. She knew that if she went back onto the porch, Truman would just push her away.

She hurried to the back of the house. An ominous sense of how grave things might be for Gracie and Charles filled her mind.

As she approached the back door, the smell of gasoline burned her nostrils. She tried to see the angle that had been out of view from the other side, but she didn't want to get too close to the broken window.

Who is the other person in the room?

She saw Charles still in the chair, his face white as snow. For a second, he seemed to be asleep, but then she noticed the scowl on his face.

A heavy bang ripped through the air. Lillian jumped back. She saw the front door splinter and fly off. It rocked in a squeaking, back-and-forth motion, hanging from one hinge.

A figure rushed toward the front door, and Lillian took the chance to peek around the corner. Nausea hit her full force. Geena was seated and tied to a red and blue carved chair, a pink floral print scarf that Lillian recognized as her own shoved into Geena's mouth.

Lillian gasped. Gracie was now sitting beside Geena's chair, grasping Geena's leg. She looked fine, except for a bruise on her cheek.

Geena's eyes flashed when she made eye contact with Lillian. She strained against the bindings. She looked down at Gracie and tried to say something, but the gag did its job. She grunted and moaned until Gracie slowly looked up. She stared at Geena for a long time.

Lillian's heart hammered in her ears. She dared not call Gracie's name lest the other person in the house hear her. *Stand up, Gracie!*

At a snail's pace, Gracie stood and laid her hand on Geena's shoulder. Geena strained toward her. Gracie's eyes were round. Lillian longed to hug the fear out of the little girl.

Finally, Gracie pulled the gag out of Geena's mouth. Geena rewarded Gracie with a forced smile and said something to her. Gracie nodded. She reached back up and put the gag back in Geena's mouth. She turned to face the door.

The terror in her eyes tore at Lillian. Lillian held her hands out and smiled encouragement.

Gracie took a few steps. Lillian glanced furtively toward the front door. Truman and Peter seemed to be arguing with the man. Her eyes connected with Truman's. He saw Gracie.

Just as the man seemed to be turning back toward Gracie, Truman tried to further engage him.

Lillian released a breath.

Gracie was a few steps from Lillian when she suddenly stopped. She turned to look at Charles. Lillian began to panic. She understood Charles was her friend, but she needed Gracie to come directly to her.

Lillian cautiously shook her head and motioned for Gracie to come. Charles, who had finally looked up and noticed Lillian in the door, waved Gracie toward her.

Gracie's eyes welled with tears, but she obeyed. Lillian reached in to turn the knob. Slowly she opened the door. It squeaked. Lillian froze.

The man whirled around. His face broiled with anger as he stormed their way. Lillian rushed in, grabbed Gracie around the waist and dove for the door. She felt something grab her foot. She began to kick, holding tight to Gracie.

Oh, God, she cried, silently. Oh, God, oh, God, oh, God.

She heard a clunk and a groan and her ankle was free. She scrambled out the back door into the waiting arms of Truman. As he pulled Gracie from her arms, Lillian turned back. She was just in time to see a man pummeling Charles in the face.

It had never been Charles. Her heart rejoiced. She wanted to run around to tell Kara who the real stalker was, but she had to focus on Charles and Geena.

Lillian rushed recklessly forward, but Truman grabbed her arm.

"How did Geena get in there with them?" she cried.

He threw her backward, where she landed in a tangle of arms and legs. Truman's voice rang out as he ducked down beside her. "He's got a gun!"

Lillian's breath came in gasps.

More police had still not arrived. She couldn't believe the town was so small that they couldn't even respond to a kidnapping. Peter came around the side of the house and gave her a look.

Get away.

She backed close to a tree away from the house, but she had already seen the tears coursing down Charles's cheeks. She ached for him and thought of Kara. They both had siblings trapped in the house with a dangerous man.

Peter looked down and said something into the radio attached to his shirt. He motioned for Truman to come closer. He wasn't waiting for backup.

From where she stood, Lillian thought the gasoline smell had grown stronger.

She crept forward. Peter and Truman had been joined again by Mario.

Lillian was close enough that when she rose up on her tiptoes, she could see inside. Geena sat very still, though her eyes were wide. Charles was crying. Lillian followed his troubled gaze to the spilled gas can beneath Geena's chair. He held a lighter in his other hand. He clicked it open and shut. With each click, his tears increased.

Lillian narrowed her eyes. Somebody was trying to make him light the lighter. Charles might not be like other men, but he wasn't stupid. One flick from the lighter would send himself and Geena up in flames.

"Lillian!" The man's nasally voice carried out into the yard.

Truman and Peter gave each other a foreboding look.

"Lillian! Come talk to me, Lillian."

Charles turned toward the group of men, and his eyes riveted on them. He cocked his head and started to say something, but Truman placed a finger over his lips.

Lillian hurried ahead. Maybe she could distract the man while the others freed Geena and Charles.

Truman's arm shot out. He tried to jerk her back. She pushed against him, but it was no use.

"I'm here!" she shouted.

Truman's mouth flew open. He shook his head, vigorously. She had to ignore him. It was her sister in there. And someone's brother.

"I'm here!" she shouted again. This time he came to the door.

Bentley's eyes raked over her. "Why do you keep running from me, Lillian?" His eyes were glassy and the smile that spread across his face seemed to chill the air around them.

All the strange events that had happened in Sacramento reeled through her mind like a film, but it didn't make sense that *he* was the one who had been stalking her.

"If you had just stayed in Sacramento, this would have been so much easier." He motioned around. "A painting, a retarded boy, you going back and forth."

Charles raised his chin, his face red with shame.

For a moment Lillian's eyes teared up. She put herself in Charles's shoes. She glanced at Geena, who was staring at Charles with deep compassion.

"Don't call him that!" Lillian raised her voice.

"Don't call him what?"

"You know what you said." She raised her voice louder. "Don't call him that!"

"Why not, Lillian? He's nothing in the larger scheme of things."

Truman enclosed her hand in his fist. He kept his grip tight.

"Yes, he is, and I want you to let him go."

"And what, Lillian?"

"And—" She glanced at Truman. "And I'll come in there."

A grin spread across Bentley's face.

Truman held her hand even tighter.

"What the heck, Lillian? You don't know what you're—" Peter was shaking his head vigorously. "Absolutely not. We don't bargain."

The man held out his hand and Lillian stepped forward. Truman jerked her back.

"Let her come!" the man yelled.

Lillian wasn't sure what to do. *Oh, God, oh, God.* She stood still and took a deep breath.

"I won't come in unless you let Charles come out."

Bentley studied her, considering it. After a long moment, he grabbed Charles by the arm. Charles staggered toward Lillian, and the man stopped a few feet short of the door.

"Come inside," he said.

"At the same time that Charles comes out," she countered.

He nodded. Wrenching free from Truman, she stepped forward across the threshold, while at the same time he shoved Charles out the door and jerked her inside.

He held her arm, pulling her close until she stood toe to toe with him. He smelled like alcohol, which she hadn't noticed earlier during the reception. She stared boldly into his eyes, even though her knees felt feeble.

When had she seen him before today? Before the gallery?

Her mind desperately searched for an answer, even as the smell of the gasoline added to her nausea and threatened to send her to the floor.

She glanced at her sister, who also looked green beneath her gag.

"Whatever is the matter?" Kitty's voice filtered through her memory. "What are you running from, dear?"

Almost five years ago. Recognition dawned. The man in the hat and leather jacket on his cell phone. He had been the one following her. She glanced at Geena, her mind trying to process the memories of that day. Charles must have been the man with the camera taking pictures of her, but Bentley had been there too.

The hazy memory emerged clearly, and in her mind she saw the man about fifty feet beyond Charles at the Rose House that day four years earlier. She couldn't make out his face, but when he had moved toward her, she ran. That's when she had met Kitty for the first time.

She recognized him now. Her face turned from white to blazing with anger. So Tom Bentley was the man who had tormented her after Robert's death: the letters, letting the air out of her tires, moving her newspaper, following her.

Bentley pushed her into Charles's chair. He turned to kick at the painting, then turned back to Lillian.

"Let's burn it." His face broke into the cruel grin of a lunatic and not an art collector.

Sensing he meant to use the painting to manipulate her, Lillian tried to look nonchalant as she shrugged. Her heart broke to think of the painting turned to ashes, but she would trade it for the lives of people she loved. She glanced at Geena and her heart swelled.

"I don't care," Lillian said. "Burn it."

Surprise registered on Bentley's sweaty face. "I thought you wanted the painting. It wasn't easy getting it in here, even with those kids helping. Told them it was a surprise!" The malice on his face deepened into a sort of grimace as his eyes sliced at Geena.

"You," he spat at Geena, "it's your fault. You were supposed to die in the accident with him. When you came back, you got nosy." He glared at Geena. "I left you that phone message so you would stop digging." His face twitched and his eyes danced around before falling back on Geena. "Why didn't you stop?" he roared.

Geena was rigid. She tried to say something under her gag. He walked over and yanked the gag out of her mouth. She leaned over, choking and spitting.

Lillian glanced surreptitiously toward the door. Truman, Peter, and the other men stood ready to pounce.

Out of nowhere, Bentley produced a new lighter, exactly like the one Charles had held. Bentley began flicking it. Peter motioned the men back.

Lillian ignored the fingers of ice that crawled up her back. She tried to bide her time by continuing in a halfway friendly voice.

"Did you know my husband, Mr. Bentley?" Sadly, she already knew the answer.

Bentley stared at her, as if considering whether to answer her or not.

"Did I know your husband? Of course I knew him! We were in business together." Bentley walked over to the wall and leaned against it. "Until he tried to cheat me."

"He didn't do that," Geena said, yanking at her bindings. "Your people set him up." But Lillian knew Geena was wrong. Robert had lived some kind of double life.

He shook his head, walking over to Geena and running one hand down the side of her face. Geena tried to lean away from his touch. "No, not me, sweetheart. Nobody would listen to me, but even though I tried to get a good deal for Robert, he cut me out."

Geena stared hard at him. "How come I never saw you?"

"I wasn't supposed to be seen."

He walked over to Lillian. Her eyes grew wide as he reached for the gas can. "I liked you, though. I thought I might have you myself."

Lillian wondered if she would be sick. Moisture beaded on Bentley's upper lip. He had removed his jacket, and now sweat gathered in large circles under his armpits.

"I watched you," he said, "to make sure you were okay."

"Did Robert ask you to," she asked, "when he was alive?"

He smiled sadly, his eyes taking on a glazed look. She wondered how she had ever mistaken him for Truman.

"He didn't have to," Bentley said. "I just wanted to. And it was easy to find you because of your driver. When I lost track of your schedule, he would lead me right to you."

"Jake?" Lillian's heart fell.

"Yes," Bentley said, "he was so protective of you." He sneered. "I think he felt sorry for you. He wouldn't let anyone else drive you except him."

"I requested him," Lillian said.

Bentley seemed not to hear her. "So I just attached myself to him. I hired him to work for me."

"He's your driver?" Lillian asked.

Bentley laughed. "Don't sound so disappointed."

He tipped the gas can and splashed the remaining gasoline around the house. Lillian watched as Kitty's antiques, art, and quilts were soaked.

"He didn't know my plans," Bentley said. "If he had, I'm sure he would have done something to stop me."

"So you—you killed my family?" Lillian had only meant to keep him talking. The rest had just slipped out.

He sneered, setting the gas can down with a clunk. "I didn't mean to kill Sheyenne and Lee, Mrs. Hastings." She cringed at the sound of their names on his lips. "I love children. I'm sorry about that." He retrieved the lighter, his bulging eyes fully transforming him into the psychopath had disguised so well.

"But rest assured, I did not act alone." He held the lighter out. "And rest assured, Mrs. Hastings, your husband deserved it."

Lillian wanted to cry out against the truth, but her mouth felt fastened shut.

He glanced at Geena. "And you were supposed to die too."

"I didn't," she seethed.

"Yeah," Bentley said, "well, let's see what we can do about that." He held the lighter in front of Geena. As he flicked it open and set the flame, the men charged through the door.

Bentley swiveled, holding the flame out toward them. "Don't," he said.

He stared hard at Truman. "That's my hat."

Truman reached up and pulled the hat from his head. "Do you want it back?"

Bentley looked at him. "On second look, it's not mine, but I do like yours better. Toss it here."

Truman tossed the hat and it landed at Bentley's feet.

Lillian saw the gasoline splatter as the hat landed, but Bentley was too wild-eyed to notice. He picked the hat up and placed it on his head, all the while holding the flame aloft.

As everyone watched, breath suspended, Bentley reached up with the hand that held the lighter, possibly just to straighten the hat, but nobody would ever be sure.

The hat burst into flames. Shock registered in waves across Bentley's face. He tore the hat off and tossed it away, but the house was already soaked, and the quilts hanging on one wall erupted.

Flames licked the walls and quickly stretched throughout the house.

Lillian screamed. Peter and Mario burst in and brought Bentley down. Truman and Blake ran toward Geena, but Lillian reached her first. The flames were licking up Geena's legs.

"There's no time!" Geena cried. "Just take the chair!"

"Take the chair!" cried Lillian.

Within seconds, everyone was out on the lawn. Bentley was yelling curses at Lillian and Geena as the officers, who had arrived a little too late, cuffed him. They shoved him into a police car that had been driven right over Kitty's lawn.

Lillian watched the flames grow, wishing a fire truck would arrive before the flames could take the entire house.

When they untied Geena's arms and legs from the chair, she clung to Lillian.

She pulled back and noticed Geena flinch. "Are you in pain?"

Geena nodded. "My legs."

Kitty appeared by their side. "An ambulance is on the way, Geena. We'll take care of you." She hugged each of them gingerly, tears in her eyes. "I'm glad you girls are okay. I was scared to death for a little while."

Lillian smiled sheepishly. "Sorry about your house, Kitty."

Kitty stepped back, obviously surprised. "What?" She shook her head disapprovingly. "It's just a house. What mattered to me were the people in it!"

Lillian made sure Geena was comfortable and stepped away to find Truman. He wasn't nearby, so she stumbled toward the house. There was one thing she wanted to see.

Someone plucked her back, but she wrenched herself from his grasp. She could hear sirens in the distance, and out of the corners of her eyes she saw rose vines withering, the thorns burning away, their blossoms seeming to melt and disappear instantly from the heat. She paused for a moment, overwhelmed as the growing flames began to engulf the house. When she had been inside, she'd feared that she and Geena would die in the flames, as their parents and brothers had. It was the second time, Lillian realized, that God had spared them from fire.

She moved toward the back door cautiously and peered in. The heat sent her stumbling back. Shading her eyes from the heat, she stared into the doorway. There was no sign of the painting. *Beauty and the Beast Within* had already burned. She felt an ache for its absence and also for the Rose House, but she felt strangely at peace as she realized neither of them truly mattered. It had always been what the Rose House stood for, its thorns and roses side by side, the same way Truman had seen a beast in her heart, but also beauty. Now Beauty had been saved, and the beast was finally gone.

Her shoulders and legs felt heavy as she moved away from the house to the coolness of the lawn far from the heat of the flames. She couldn't tell if the empty feeling in her chest was fear or freedom, as she stared back at the house.

Everything the painting had meant to her, the house itself, good and bad, swirled around in tufts of smoke that burned her nostrils.

As she returned to the front of the house, she saw Kitty and Blake standing off to the side. The two smiled happily at all the survivors, barely seeming to notice the roaring blaze of the Rose House.

Geena was perched on a stretcher arguing with the EMT, who tried to get her to lie down. Mario was beside her, which brought warmth to Lillian's heart. Geena deserved a new start. Maybe Mario would be part of that.

She glanced around and her eyes fell on Charles. He was trying to reassure his sister, but Kara just kept sobbing.

"Miss Lillian saved me. Now everything is okay." Lillian wondered if he understood the gravity of Kara's feelings. When he looked over and rewarded Lillian with the smile of a lifetime, she decided he did.

At another ambulance, Gracie sat smiling on her own gurney. Paige and Mark showered her with loving hugs. As she observed Paige's actions toward her daughter, pushing back Gracie's hair, constantly kissing her temple, Lillian rejoiced. She was glad she had never seen what Geena had seen under the sheet on Mosquito Road. She was glad there were no bloody sheets involved for Paige either.

Paige spotted Lillian and pointed her out to Gracie. Gracie reached out for Lillian.

Lillian saw each of her babies, their smiles only for her, their chubby toddler hands reaching. She walked toward the gurney and gently wrapped her arms around Gracie. She felt the softness of her cheek, the warmth of her body wrapped around her, and let herself imagine the feel of Sheyenne's and Lee's bodies.

And then she said Gracie's name out loud, breaking the spell.

"Gracie, I love you so much."

"I love you too, Auntie Lily."

"When did she start calling you that?" Truman asked.

Gracie pulled away and reached for Truman.

"While you were away," Lillian said. "Much changed while you were gone."

He winked. "I can't wait to hear about all of those things." He turned to Paige. "I know Mommy is wanting her time, but before you all ride off in the ambulance, somebody wants to say something to Gracie."

Lillian placed her arm around Paige as they watched Truman carry Gracie to Charles. They couldn't hear what Charles was whispering in Gracie's ear, but everyone heard Gracie's laughter. The crowd of people smiled and nodded in approval when Gracie leaned forward to kiss Charles. She paused to pat him gently on his cheek.

Their innocent display of friendship would have moved even the toughest observer, but when she saw tears gather in Truman's eyes, moisture gathered in her own. Even Charles and Gracie would have a new start.

After the excitement had died down, Truman and Lillian again walked arm in arm through the vines to the top of a hill that overlooked the vineyards so they could see the Rose House. As they watched, the house began to cave in upon itself. It would burn all the way to the ground.

"Here we are again," Truman said, pulling her close to his side.

Lillian's voice felt scratchy from breathing in smoke. "I never imagined the house would be gone," she said.

"Or the painting."

They stood watching the flames. The structure was now a charred heap with plumes of black smoke that marred the perfect sky above the sprawling vineyard.

"It's hard to see it burn," Truman said. Lillian noticed his face was drawn. His shoulders slumped with a burden she wished she could remove.

She leaned against him. "It's only a house. Even Kitty said so."

"But if I had never painted it, painted you, had never donated that painting—" His voice caught.

Lillian looked up at Truman. "You think it's your fault this happened?"

"It is," said Truman, deep sadness edging his voice. "None of this would have happened if I had minded my own business. My intrusion into your life has been an intrusion for the whole community. It's put the lives of those I care about in danger."

Lillian's hand went to her neck where she found the two charms she now wore on one chain: the cross and the lighthouse. One charm represented the past, the other a light to her future. Ironically, she didn't feel as sad about the house being gone as she would have expected.

She turned to Truman. How could she explain to him that it wasn't his fault? "We could blame ourselves all day and it won't change a thing." She looked at what was once the Rose House. "We could blame Geena. We could blame Robert. I've grown quite good at placing blame, Truman."

She watched his jaw work to fight back emotions she knew he must have carried for months.

"Ironically," she said, "I'm not as sad about losing the Rose House or the painting as you might think I am." She swept one arm out before them, gesturing toward the burning rubble.

"I feel free, Truman, as if that beast you saw when you painted me all those years ago burned with the Rose House. But," she sighed, "don't ever leave me again, Truman Clark. That I cannot handle."

He tried to laugh, but it only came out in a sort of raspy murmur. He cleared his throat. "Not a chance," and he pulled her head into his chest.

Her heart lifted with the promise of a new life. She had come close to death and survived. The burning, licking flames had devoured her fear and exposed the truth.

THE LENS ZOOMED IN ON Lillian in her long silk wedding dress, her curls reflecting golden highlights against the baby's-breath and pink miniature roses in her hair. Zooming slowly out, Truman's happy half smile joined Lillian's, along with Geena, also looking stunning in a knee-length black dress and pearls.

Little Gracie's smile beamed as she held an overflowing bouquet of roses to match the ones in Lillian's hair.

Paige, Mario, and Mark filled in the rest of the wedding party. Zooming out a little further, the lens captured Pastor holding a Bible in his hand. Beside him, Aunt Bren stood crying what looked just like happy tears.

The camera zoomed out further to reveal a gold-gilded frame that held Truman's latest masterpiece, a painting of the simple but elegant wedding between him and his bride held at Frances-DiCamillo.

Click.

The camera swept along the wall of paintings and paused in front of another. Truman and Lillian had been married in the gardens near where the Rose House once stood. After the wedding, Truman and Lillian had strolled over to the Rose House site for old times' sake.

In the place where the Rose House once stood was a small patch of turned-up earth surrounded by a white picket fence. In the center was a very young vine, a rose bramble, that by some miracle only Lillian and Kitty seemed to understand had emerged from the earth many months after the fire.

"Now, be careful, Charles. We need these photographs to be just perfect for the Web site, okay?" Geena said.

Click-click.

"Okay, Miss Geena. No problem."

Charles panned out to photograph the interior of the restaurant. *Click.* The dining area was very large, with a stone fireplace on one wall and french doors with a view into the wine cellar on the other side. It was the grand opening, so Charles was sure to include the tables with the guests of honor in his photos.

He zoomed in on Kitty and Blake, who seemed only too pleased to be in attendance. *Click.* They had grown to think of Lillian as a daughter and lavished as much attention on her as they did on their granddaughter, Lucy. It was a good arrangement for all of them since they had all known a similar loss in their pasts. Loved ones lost can never be replaced, but that space can be shared. At least that is how Kitty had explained it.

Kitty and Blake were joined at their table by Pastor and Aunt Bren, who didn't mind sharing Lillian with the other couple at all. If anything, Aunt Bren had said loudly, it made her feel better knowing Lillian had someone else to look out for her. *Click.*

Charles panned his camera over to Paige and her family. Gracie was laughing merrily. She waved in the direction of the camera. Charles was glad he and Gracie were such good friends. *Click.*

The lens scanned the room: Carlos, Louise, Jake, his sister, Kara, and her husband were all smiling as they sat together enjoying their meal. Kara turned to tie a bib onto her toddler son. *Click.*

Charles walked closer to the kitchen, zooming in on Geena. She had apologized to Charles for her silly accusations against him and he forgave her. He felt sorry for her when she left to spend several months in a rehab center. She had explained to him that she chose to go. The two had exchanged letters during her stay, and when she returned, he surprised her with a photo of her and Mario in a pretty oval frame. She had been so impressed with his ability that she asked him to take the pictures for the new Web site.

Mario nuzzled Geena's neck. She turned to playfully whack him with a towel. *Click.*

The double doors to the kitchen flew open and out walked Lillian, looking smart and chic in her crisp white chef's jacket and tall chef's hat. Chef George walked over and shook her hand. *Click.* Lillian had worked so hard on her dream. Truman did what he could to help out, and Chef George was her partner in the endeavor, but everyone knew the restaurant was wholly Lillian's vision. *Click-click.*

Charles stepped out the door and crossed to the other side of the street, where he turned to face the building. He wanted to get a full shot for the main page of the Web site.

Outside, the sun was just beginning to set and the streetlights were starting to cast light around the square. The restaurant, evocative of a Spanish villa on the corner of the La Rosaleda plaza, filled the lens. *Click.*

Above it hung a hand-painted sign, a piece of art in and of itself, with *The Rose* emblazoned across it. *Click.*

Truman had spent many hours on the sign and had presented it to Lillian with great ceremony weeks earlier. Charles had taken pictures of the occasion, and Laura, the reporter, had even put them in the newspaper with the heading "Local Artist's Muse to Open Restaurant." Lillian no longer minded when people teased her about being Truman's muse. It was true, after all. *Click-click.*

The lens zoomed out, then in on a window just to the left of the restaurant's sign. The well-lit room filled the lens. Truman was in his new studio standing in front of a large canvas. The view tightened to reveal the subject. It was of a scene that depicted Lillian sitting in a blue-painted rocking chair. In the portrait, Lillian held a sleeping infant. *Click.*

Painted in the scene's background was a bookshelf that held an assortment of furry zoo animals, a smiling doll with curly hair, and a copy of a children's book titled *The Rose House.* Truman's brush reached slowly toward the canvas to stroke the baby's cheek. *Click.*

Truman looked down and smiled. The camera followed his gaze to a blue cradle elaborately painted with tiny red roses and vines. Truman set down his brush and reached out to rock the cradle that held his infant daughter, nestled in a pink blanket except for one tiny fist that she was busy sucking on. Above the baby's head, painted in cursive along the cradle's top, was her name: *Rose.*

Click.

The camera zoomed out. One more shot of the restaurant. *Click.* It panned the streets, clicking along, capturing the square in the muted sepia tones of sunset.

The camera's lens swept in a circle, pulling out to capture the sunset across the vineyards beyond La Rosaleda.

Click.

Some things about La Rosaleda, like the sunsets, promised to never change, thanks to people like Truman and Lillian. They loved the land so much, they did what they could to keep La Rosaleda largely undeveloped except for the types of agriculture and industry that were vital, not to mention historic, to the area.

The vine-covered hills rolled gently away into the darkening trees, and in one long swoop, the camera landed back on The Rose, capturing the happy people inside.

Click.

They all knew Charles was darting around taking pictures of the opening, but so lost were they in their celebration that they rather forgot. And in a way, Charles was glad. He had found that once people knew they were being observed, it became more difficult to capture the truth of the moment on their faces in a photo. Truman had taught Charles to search for ways to show truth in his photographs.

Truman himself would likely never capture as great a truth in his future paintings as he had in *Beauty and the Beast Within,* but he had found a new, more reflective, truth to paint. His new paintings involved scenes that seemed rather domestic to some, but for those who grew to love his work, there was a secret to be found. They learned to look deeper to see if there was a secret image hidden somewhere in the brushstrokes of color that would reveal a deeper meaning, a kind of secret message for the admirer.

Click.

The camera's lens caught the joy on the face of each of Lillian's guests, pausing the moment where it seemed that their lives, and hers, were poised at the edge of a blank canvas just waiting to be painted with the rich shades and hues of a dazzling new scene.

Click.

The lens zoomed from window to window, capturing the happy people inside who, with a raise of their glasses and a clinking salute, celebrated more than the opening of a restaurant.

The camera zoomed in close and settled on Lillian. She reached up to touch the two pendants she always wore.

Click-click.

Nobody in La Rosaleda had ever seen her looking more at peace than she did that evening. The beast had gone, and in its place nestled nothing but beauty.

READERS GUIDE

1. When Lillian discovers her most private moment of grief has been captured on canvas by an anonymous artist, her journey to come to terms with the artist and the painting leads her to discover the true meaning behind the Rose House. What is the meaning behind the Rose House for Lillian? For Kitty? And for Truman? What, if anything, does the Rose House mean to Geena?

2. Have you ever had your own personal Rose House—a place or group of friends or family that brought about healing in your life? Share your experience.

3. What role does Aunt Bren play in this story? Describe someone who has played a similar role in your life.

4. Why does Lillian cling to the memory of her deceased husband even after she learns he wasn't everything she thought he was when he was alive? What does this say about the nature of love? Do you think Lillian ever stops being in love with Robert? Why? Is it truly possible to love two people in one's lifetime, or is there only one soul mate per person who makes everyone else pale in comparison? Explain.

5. Lillian vacillates between being head over heels in love with Truman and not trusting him. Why? Is it ever possible to be 100 percent certain that a person is the right one? What makes it so hard to know?

6. What drove Geena to essentially abandon Lillian after the acci-dent? Was there ever a time in the story that you thought

Geena was trying to harm Lillian? How does Geena's attitude toward her sister change throughout the novel? How do Lillian's feelings toward her sister change?

7.   When is it okay to draw a line between yourself and another family member, as Lillian did between herself and Geena? Do you think God always expects total forgiveness? What actions and events led to reconciliation between Geena and Lillian?

8.   The cross necklace that belonged to Lillian's daughter is very meaningful to Lillian. Why else is it significant to Lillian's journey?

9.   Lillian drew a line between herself and God after losing her children. Why do you think she did this? What events and encounters eventually began to close that gap?

10.   How much fault, if any, did Lillian bear when it came to her troubles with Geena? Do you think she did enough to make amends with Geena? What about Geena? Is it even possible for someone like Geena to make up for what they have done to others? Can we ever truly erase the harm we do to others? What makes two sisters, raised in the same family, take such different paths in life as Geena and Lillian did for many years?

11.   Truman seeks to show truth in his paintings, but truth isn't always what the viewer of the painting wants to see. How well do you think *Beauty and the Beast Within* mirrors Lillian's journey of grief and healing? How does Truman's depiction of her change over time? Why does Truman sometimes paint secret images in his paintings?

12.   Truman knows his own private loss. How does meeting Lillian help him find healing? How does the grief Truman and Lillian each know bring them together? Does it ever push them apart?

13. Truman leaves Lillian behind for a time to give her time and space. Do you think he did the right thing? Why or why not?

14. Charles is an artist too. What do you think he means in the end when he says that once people know they are being observed, it is more difficult to capture the truth of the moment on their faces? Why does Truman tell Charles to look for truth in his work?

15. What did the author mean by describing each character at the end as being poised at the edge of a blank canvas?

16. Imagine that God is the Master Artist who is purposely painting your life on a canvas. What do you think your portrait looks like now? Describe what you hope it will look like when the paint dries.

ACKNOWLEDGMENTS

Thank you to my readers. Bless you!

Thank you to my husband and biggest fan, Albert. I could not do this without your support and your ability to eat more pizza than any husband should have to endure. A big thanks also goes to the children we share who love the extra pizza, the lovely Hannah and the handsome duo Jake and Dawson, for the endless hours of entertainment at our own "Basement Improv Theater." Your comic relief got me through those long days when I didn't believe I could finish the manuscript.

Special acknowledgment goes to Cheri Kaufman. *Rose House* would never have been completed had you not been cheering me on every step of the way, bossing me around, and making me laugh. Your talent and expertise has kept me going. Thanks for pushing me out the door without my coat on time after time, even when I wanted to run back inside where it was safe and warm. And thank you, Lance, for supporting Cheri.

Thank you to my parents. I dedicated this book to them, so that says it all.

Thank you, Chaz Corzine and BHCC Management, for giving me the chance to become a published author. I shall never forget it.

Thank you with all my heart to Waterbrook Multnomah for having the best publishing team imaginable. I cannot name everyone who has helped in marketing, sales, and editorial lest I forget someone, but special thanks to Kelly Howard for another fabulous cover design and to Jon Woodhams for his amazing attention to detail and patience extraordinaire. Thank you to Shannon Marchese for diving in and to Jessica Barnes for her consistent hard work.

Special thanks goes to Jeanette Thomason for being the first editor in the world to notice my work. Our hearts always connected.

Thank you to my brother, Troy Gray, and to my "other sister" Laura. I love you both so much for always standing true. And to Taryn, I hope you like this one too.

Thank you to all of my family on both sides from cousins, to aunts and uncles, and grandparents. This book is about a very small family, but I have the biggest, best, extended family of all. You are too numerous to name, but I love that we stick together no matter how much or how little we see each other and no matter how high or low things get.

Thank you, Dardi Roy, another cheerleader, as if I need any more, but you are the captain. Thank you, Patti Lacy and Jeffrey Overstreet, for lending encouragement and wisdom during times that only other writers can understand. Thank you to my B&N Coffee Sisters and ACFW e-mail friends for pretty much the same thing.

Thank you to the Laramie County Library and its Foundation Board for their amazing welcome, and to the amazing community of Cheyenne, Wyoming, for unending support. Thank you to the folks of the Colcord, Oklahoma, area for not forgetting a former small-town cheerleader who always dreamed of being a writer. I'll be home for a visit soon!

Additional acknowledgment goes to my friends at MOPS, Tyson and Jeane Wynn, Katie Mosley, Nancy Forkner, Kim Giffin, Ronda Clark, Helen Ryan, Marcy Curran, Cindy Armstrong, Ashley Linde (because I neglected to thank her last time), friends of American Christian Fiction Writers, Rocky Mountain Fiction Writers, Janet Dixon, Rachel Kirsch, Ed Curtis, Linda Holland, and especially to my wonderful friends. I cannot name you all, but you know who you are. Thank you.

And every day, thank You, God, the master artist, for this gift. Though my canvas is not perfect, I hope it will only improve with time.

TINA ANN FORKNER writes fiction that challenges and inspires. She lives with her husband and their three bright children in Wyoming. Tina serves on the Laramie County Library Foundation Board of Directors and volunteers with her local Mothers of Preschoolers groups. Tina is the author of *Ruby Among Us* and *Rose House*.

Visit her online at www.tinaforkner.com.

THREE WOMEN with one story between them.
ONLY ONE remembers how it began.

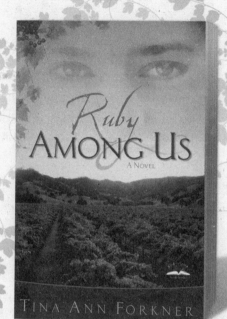

From the streets of San Francisco and
Sacramento to the lush vineyards of the
Sonoma Valley, Lucy DiCamillo follows the
thread of memory in search of a heritage that seems
long-buried with her mother, Ruby. What she finds is as
enigmatic and stirring as it is startling in this redemptive tale
about the power of faith and mother-daughter love.

www.tinaforkner.com
www.waterbrookmultnomah.com

Available in bookstores now.